Scales of My Heart

Kelly Morgan

Scarlet Nova Press

Contents

Content Warnings

This book contains explicit sexual content, sexual assault, and violence. Reader discretion is advised.

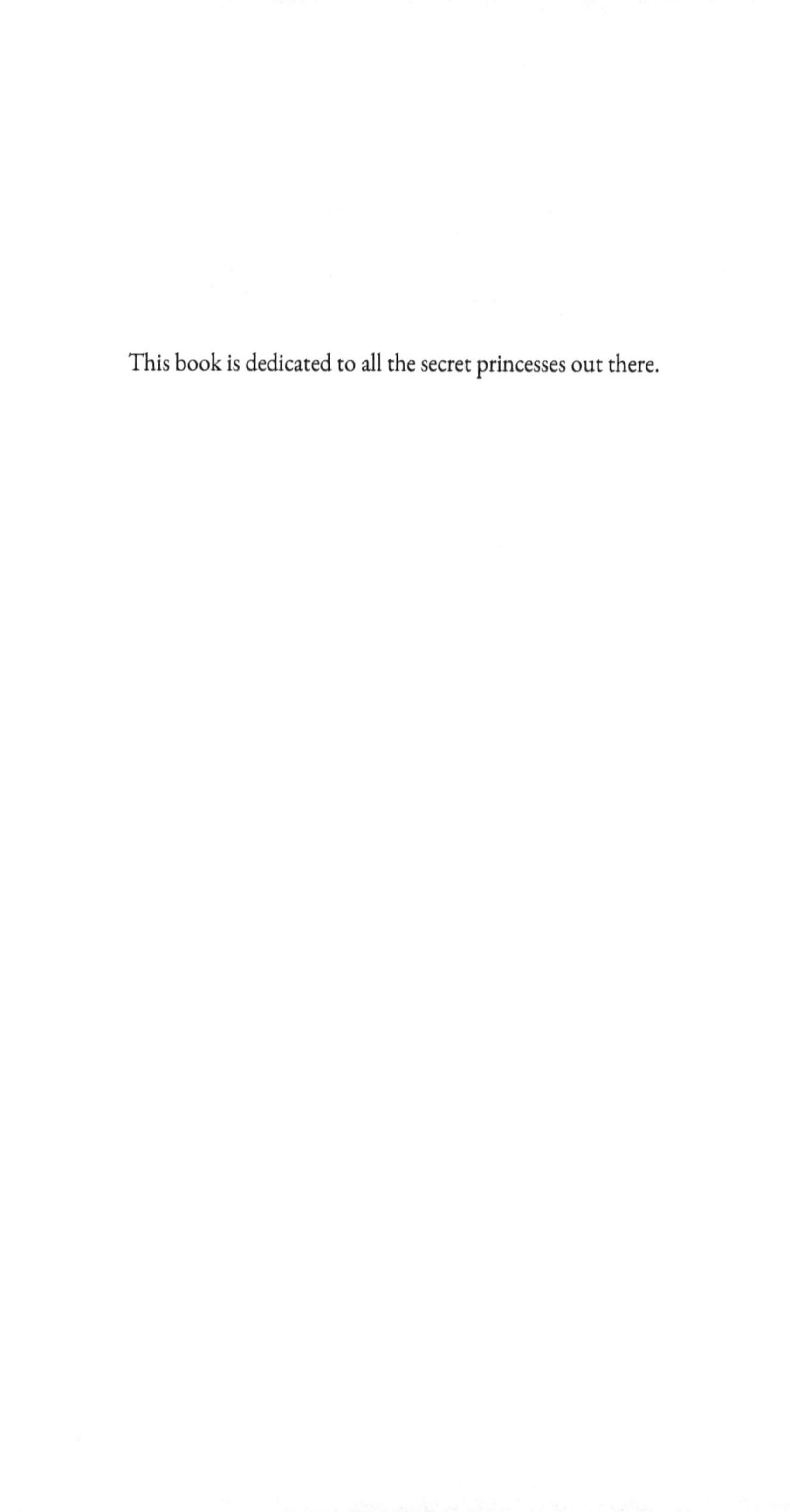

This book is dedicated to all the secret princesses out there.

Chapter 1
Stories ~ विरासत

"As she completed the trials required to test if a warrior had what it took to become ruler of the Nagas, she would look her foes in the eyes and tell them..."

My nani got into her best impression of a fighting stance. She acted as if she were pointing a weapon at an unknown opponent.

"I am Durga..." Her stance changed, embodying the warrior goddess.

"I am Kali..." She swiped her imaginary weapon through the air, acting as the goddess of time and destruction.

"I am Manasa..." She made a serpentine movement with her body, mimicking the goddess of snakes and the Nagas.

"I am their servant. I am their tool. I am their vessel." She stood with her hands on her hips, looking mighty and proud.

Oh Nani, I wish you could see me now.

My grandmother used to tell me stories of the Nagas. They were serpentine shapeshifters who were the guardians of treasures and sacred sites. They had power over water and could even control when it would rain. She told me many times of a fierce Nagini warrior who became the queen of Patala, the realm that the Nagas inhabited. As I drove back home to Almora for the weekend, all the memories of her stories flooded back into my mind.

My Nani's stories sealed the deal. I became an archaeologist with a specialty in Naga iconography and places of worship. The Naga capital city Bhogavati was my El Dorado, my Shangri-La, my Atlantis. My current project was an archaeo-logical site near Patal Bhuvaneshwar, an ancient limestone cave in Uttarakhand, India. Patal Bhuvaneshwar was already a place shrouded in mysticism. Legend has it that Lord Shiva, god of destruction, was enshrined within the cave.

Recently, my team made discoveries of historical Naga glyph carvings, and we were currently excavating the site to see if there were any hidden sites of worship or buried sacred sites within the mountains. The site was a two hour drive from Almora, so I stayed at the base camp during the week and came home on the weekends.

Home was a lot of things to me. It was getting to see my family after a long week. It was indulging in way too much Bal Mithai, the dense roasted khoya that left my fingers sticky and coated in those tiny sugar balls I could never stop picking at. And it was getting to use my vibrator without a camp full of scientists hearing me cum. The men would probably tell me I was doing it wrong.

Silly me. A silly woman not knowing how to pleasure herself.

Almora sat on a three mile horse saddle-shaped ridge between two rivers. Its crowded tiled roofs came into view and I breathed a sigh of relief. I was tired of driving and ready to rest and enjoy my weekend.

***

"You smell like sweat and dirt."

"At least I get paid to dig and sweat. You smell like rat piss. What's your excuse?"

My brother Vikram hugged me tight as I entered the house. I squeezed him back, making sure he felt how my muscles had defined themselves digging through rock and stone.

"Priya, meri bacchi!" No matter how many rocks tempered my athletic build, my mother could always hug me with the strength of a sumo wrestler.

"Oof, Hello Maa!" I almost couldn't speak because she squeezed the breath out of me.

My mother made room for my father. His embrace was slower, softer.

"Priya, how was the drive?"

"It was long. I think I'm going to go unpack in my room and have a quick nap."

My father cupped the side of my face gently.

"Of course, that drive must be dreadful."

"But beautiful I bet?" My mother chimed in. Vikram gave my shoulder a pat and retreated to his room.

"Yes, stunning!" I picked my suitcase up off the floor where it had landed when the affectionate assault began and made my way to my room.

I opened the door and set my suitcase on the floor. My body fell on the bed and I lay there with my eyes closed, happy to be home. My bed was basic, but when you sleep in a tent during the weekdays, you don't realize how much you miss even a basic bed. I sat up and started going through one of the drawers in my dresser next to my bed. Behind my undergarments I found my vibrator.

There you are. I need some urgent attention, my special friend.

I got under the covers of my bed and slid my shorts and panties down my legs. My vibrator found its way to my clit and joy spread through my body. Within a few minutes, I was ready to release. As I climaxed, I put one of my bed pillows over my face and moaned loudly into it. When the tremors subsided, I lay there panting, my legs still spread and resting to either side of me. I put my vibrator back in its hiding spot and lay there staring at the ceiling.

I wonder if I'll ever find a place where I can be my true self sexually. Where women could be bold. Where I don't have to muffle myself with a pillow.

***

"Wef foun' sumfin innereshting." My mouth was packed with fudgey Bal Mithai.

"Chew your food, Priya." Maa's scolding eyes were upon me. Vikram snickered. I swallowed the chocolate fudge goodness and continued.

"We found something interesting. Glyphs and inscriptions. According to the inscription, there's a doorway to Naga-Loka somewhere within the cave. The crew will be blasting next week to see how expansive the cave system is."

"So you're off to join the Naga and leave us mortals behind?" Vikram chimed. Papa passed behind me gathering my empty dinner plate as he went to the kitchen to dispose of his own — leaving just the small plate with my treasured Bal Mithai. He kissed my head as he went.

"Priya Bhandari has been leaving us mortals behind since she could walk!" The whole table laughed. It was true. Ever since I was a girl I was always running off to explore, to discover, to be free. Jungle tree lines and mountain caves were my invitation. Uncharted territory was my party. I stared back at Maa and Vikram seriously now.

"If this site turns out to be an expansive cave system like Patal Bhuvaneshwar, the world of Naga archaeology will be shaken to its core. History could be changed forever." Maa and Vikram exchanged glances. I could tell Maa and Vikram were happy for me, but they just didn't understand how much this meant to me and to history. Mother's hand found mine.

"Whatever you find there, Priya, I hope it's what you're looking for. Do you remember the stories Nani used to tell you?"

"Of course! How could I forget? The tale of the Nagini warrior who became queen." Maa shook her head.

"Do you remember what else she told you?"

My head tilted sideways, trying to remember. Vikram rose to take his leave, he stopped by my chair and leaned down.

"She would always say that you were the incarnation of the Nagini warrior." If my brain hadn't been processing the memory of Nani's stories I would have snatched the Bal Mithai he stole from my plate back. A specific memory replayed in my mind.

"There, now you're truly a Nagini princess." I was seven, Nani had just placed green and gold jewels in my hair. Nagas wore jewels on their hoods in the same manner.

Clattering plates brought me back to the present. Papa always cleaned up the table and helped wash dishes after dinner. In most households, fathers were less likely to help with cleaning. I asked him about it one day. He told me it was his house and he would clean if he wanted to.

You're my hero, Papa.

My family had a tradition to gather on the balcony after dinner and read, talk, or just be in the moment with the family. Vikram was a stargazer. He stood on the balcony staring up at the heavens trying to spot specific stars and constellations. My mother's spot was off to the side and she was reading a book on unique dessert recipes. It's a good thing my job was physically demanding, otherwise my mother would have me overweight from the sweets she fed me. My father and I usually sat next to each other and chattered. We were the talkers of the family.

"If this site turns out to be as important as we think, I may not be coming back as often for a while. I hope that will be ok." Maa's face soured at the thought of me spending more time away. Papa's hand found mine and squeezed.

"My Beti asking for permission to be away? That's a first." I muffled a giggle with my free hand.

"You know, most children run away from the dark. You ran towards it. Caves, forests, anything that could swallow you whole — you wanted to see what was inside." He squeezed my hand. "That's your dharma, Priya. You dig where no one else bothers. A true pioneer. Just promise me you'll be careful." He kissed my hand and released it.

"Can I have Priya's room if she never returns?" Vikram looked back at me with a grin. A book hit him in the back. He looked back at Maa and she shrugged innocently but couldn't contain her laugh.

***

On Monday, I left at four in the morning for my two hour drive into the mountains. It was summertime and there weren't any clouds to block the view of the mountain peaks. It was beautiful. As soon as I arrived at base camp near the dig site, I went to my tent to catch a small nap. I was interrupted right as I put my suitcase down. There was a slap on the outside of my tent's entrance.

"Priya? That you?" It was Arun, our crew's geophysicist. He was responsible for using special imaging techniques to detect subsurface structures underneath dirt, stone, and other surface material.

"Hey Arun! What's up?" He popped his head through the tent entrance. His head appeared to be floating in mid-air.

"The weekend crew found something. I've got new images. You're going to die when you see this."

My fingers tingled at the thought of fresh images. Arun's energy was contagious.

"Awesome, I'll be there in two." His floating head disappeared. I put on some deodorant and changed from my casual shoes to thicker boots.

I met Arun and the others in the imaging trailer. It was a mobile imaging lab of sorts. Arun had ground-penetrating radar images on a large screen.

"Priya, Priya, we've struck gold this time!" The imaging showed a sprawling network of caverns beneath the surface.

"Oh Arun, are those what I think they are? Are those tunnels?"

"Yes. I think so. They look man-made, too, not natural."

My heart leapt. The others who were looking gasped.

"When can we go in?"

"The excavation crew is opening the entrance now. It's located here." Arun pointed to the radar image. "It should be ready for exploration within the hour."

I literally jumped for joy, high-fiving Arun and hugging the other colleagues around me.

"I'll go find Sunil and tell him to be ready." I was halfway out of the trailer when Arun's hand grabbed my shoulder, stopping me.

"Hey, real quick, there's a mining operation a few kilometers from here. They are blasting, so watch out. We've been coordinating with them so we can anticipate when blasts are going to happen, but you know how things are sometimes."

I nodded and went to find Sunil. I had hired Sunil straight out of university. My boss wouldn't allow me to hire someone more experienced. He said it would cost too much. As I ran with fresh energy of new discovery to go find Sunil, my boot caught a section of rugged terrain and I found myself on the ground. The spot I landed had a pile of semi-fresh mule dung which now covered my shirt.

Well shit.

I returned to my tent to change into a fresh shirt. I removed my shirt and sighed in dismay. The dung had gone through to my sports bra as well. I had just removed the sports bra when I heard the flaps of my tent open. I turned around to find Sunil standing there.

He stared at my breasts in the microsecond they were out free before my arm went across them and I turned around. Sunil didn't even attempt to turn the other way. Arun was one of the few men at the camp that bothered to knock before entering. The others didn't care.

"Sunil, what have I told you about knocking first?" I asked as I put on a fresh bra and shirt.

"Sorry." There was no apology in his words. By the sound of his voice, he was glad he had entered when he did.

"Did you need something? I was actually coming to find you about—"

"Pankaj is about two hours out. He said not to do anything without him." He interrupted me all the time, despite me being his supervisor. Pankaj was my boss, but I was supposed to have authority when he wasn't present. Supposed to.

"Well Sunil, I think we should do a preliminary walkthr—"

"He said to do nothing without him. Sorry."

Sunil left. An anger boiled inside of me. I wasn't going to just sit back while a major discovery sat open for exploration.

***

While everyone else sat on their asses waiting for Pankaj, my boots were already in the cave. A layer of dust hung in the air from the fresh excavation. I turned on the headlamp from my hardhat as the cave went away from the light of the entrance. I put on a dust mask as the particles in the air grew thicker.

Pankaj will just have to be angry with me. I've waited my entire life for this. I am a Nagini princess after all. I smirked at myself. A Nagini princess in a hardhat and dust mask. Nani would have loved this.

As I went deeper into the cave tunnel, man-made glyphs and carvings started to appear. They seemed to grow rampantly along the walls. I stared at them in wonder as I walked. I wanted so badly to trace my fingertips along them, but that might compromise these delicate carvings. I couldn't wait to have the photos of them to take my time with. I came upon a three-way junction in the cave tunnel. On one of the walls was a carving of a Nagini. Her tail had three golf ball-sized pearls on the end. I'd never seen a Naga tail depicted this way before. I gasped when I saw the Nagini's reptilian hood on the back of her head. It was decorated with green and gold jewels.

The jewels on her hood look like...

I found myself stroking my own hair unconsciously. The Nagini had a sword pointed at a Naga warrior on the ground in front of her. I could hear her in my mind.

I am your queen. Kneel.

Could Nani have heard ancient stories of this same Nagini depicted here? I continued my exploration. At the three-way junction I took the path to the left. I saw carvings of Nagas and Naginis face to face. The images depicted some sort of dance they were doing while looking into each other's eyes. Another image depicted a meditating Naga with the realm of Bhu Loka above his head — the mortal realm, Earth's plane of existence. As my gaze swung from wall to wall, I saw the tunnel's end. There was a hole about ten feet across at the end of the tunnel. I looked down the tunnel and even with my headlamp, I only saw endless blackness.

Looks like I'll have to go fetch some rope and climbing gear. Sunil would probably protest, but I'm pretty sure I'm faster than him.

My father's voice echoed in my mind as I stared into the pitch black of the hole.

You dig where no one else bothers.

My own lips said the words as they played out in my head.

Okay, let's be a true pioneer. Let's dig. Let's make history.

I turned to make my way back from where I had come, but the ground shook beneath me.

Is that...blasting?

Another tremor rocked the ground. I lost my footing and fell towards the hole in the earth. As I fell I saw a boulder get knocked loose from the shaking and cover the hole I fell into. Blackness swallowed me. I didn't even scream.

Chapter 2
Descent ~ जागृति

My eyes opened to a grassy grove lit by an iridescent glow. I groaned and tried to rise, but the pain of my contoured body hit me all at once. I was lying on my side with my leg bent at an angle that made my breath stop. I grabbed it with both hands and screamed as I wrenched it back into place. The pain was blinding, like a white flash behind my eyes that tasted like metal. My leg didn't feel broken, but it throbbed with a deep, angry heat that told me it wasn't okay, either.

"Hello?" I yelled into the grassy grove. I winched as a pain shot through my leg again.

The iridescent glow was coming from hundreds of jewels embedded in the ground. There was no sun here, nor was there a sky for it to be in. My hard hat was missing from my head. It must have fallen off on my descent. I took my phone out of my pack. The screen was cracked all over and it wouldn't turn on.

Well, I guess I wanted to be a true explorer.

A sweet scent filled the air when a mysterious wind blew. It was the grassy stalks next to me. The grass nuzzled my face as it bent in the wind. I found myself leaning into the cherry and lavender fragrance. I stood and felt my leg limp in pain from the fall.

How far had I fallen? How had I not died?

I walked as fast as my injured leg would allow. The illuminated grove I was in gave way to a lake. The lake's water shined more brilliantly than it should have. As I got closer, I saw why. It wasn't a lake of water. It was a lake of crystals.

Crystalline bodies of water. Groves illuminated by jewels. It's not possible, is it?

These were characteristics of Naga-Loka, the realm where the Nagas dwelled. I was in Patala, the netherworld.

"You don't belong here." The voice came from behind me.

"Arre baap re!" My heart nearly shot out of my chest.

A feminine, raspy voice behind me cut through the air. I spun around to see a tall, feminine shape wrapped in a black cloak.

"I fell because of the blasting actually. Can you call for help? I'm with the archaeology team examining this site." I walked closer to the cloaked woman. The glow from the jewels in the ground revealed her face beneath the cloak now. It was covered in white and silver scales. I stopped walking.

"I know not what you speak of, human."

It's not possible. This has to be a dream.

I gulped, words stolen from my throat.

"I have a camp not far from here. You can rest if you'd like."

She started to walk away. My mind was excitedly following her already, but my legs didn't share my mind's enthusiasm. The woman turned back at me.

"Are you coming?"

"Yes," was all I could mutter.

As we walked my eyes explored the landscape. In the distance, rolling hills glowed like scattered embers — the same jewels that littered the grove, but spread across the land like fallen stars. The treeline of a forest stood between the grove I was in and the hills in the distance.

If this is a dream, I never want to wake up.

A flock of jeweled, glowing birds flew above us as we walked. I could hear them and others singing as we went along. My academic brain could no longer deny it: I was in Naga-Loka. The actual Naga-Loka.

***

I followed the mysterious reptilian woman for about ten minutes until we made it to a crude, make-shift camp. There was a fire pit, one tent, and some leather bags lying around. My eyes were glued to the woman's face each time her hood shifted enough for me to see.

"Would you like something to eat?" I averted my stare.

"Yes, that would be lovely. Thank you."

The woman entered her tent. I heard the sound of her rummaging through her belongings. The pain in my leg hit me hard now that I had calmed down and the adrenaline was wearing off. I rubbed it, trying to soothe the painful jolts.

The woman returned and handed me a bowl of fruit and mushrooms soaked in a very citrus smelling liquid. I was hesitant at first, but upon putting some in my mouth, I couldn't get enough of it. Fruit juice fell down my face like a waterfall. This wasn't fruit I had eaten before. Each bite seemed to produce exponentially more juice.

"What's your name, human?" She removed her cloak. Instead of hair, she had a snake-like hood of scales that flowed downward in the same manner that hair would. Red and purple glowing jewels adorned her hood. She didn't have legs either. Below the waist was a serpentine body of coils, ending in a tail with three pearl-like globes on the end; the same pearls I saw in the cave glyph.

"Priya Bhandari." The food in my mouth kept my jaw from hanging low as I looked over her body. Some parts of her had just white or silver scales, and other parts had a mix. She was stunningly beautiful. She could have seduced me if she wanted to. Her scales were pristinely young. Her purple eyes held ages of wisdom.

"I am Nishala. I welcome you, Priya." She caught me staring at her body. "Would you like to touch me?"

I swallowed a piece of fruit prematurely.

"Excuse me?"

She moved closer.

"You've never seen one of my kind up close, have you?"

"No, I've only seen carvings on walls."

She moved directly in front of me, taking the bowl of fruit and mushrooms and setting it aside.

"You may touch me." Her words made my heart quiver.

Without hesitation my hand went forward. My fingers ran down her hood and caressed her cheek. My fingers danced down her neck and swiped slowly across her chest. The scales of each part of her felt different. The ones on her hood, face, and neck were smooth as polished gemstones. The ones on her chest were jagged, but not sharp. She inched closer as my hands went lower, carefully moving my injured leg aside to be between my knees.

A real Nagini. Sitting here in front of me. Letting me touch her. This is a literal dream come true.

My hand continued exploring down her belly. I held my breath. She was slim, but her abs were toned like an athlete. My fingers flowed down her waistline and stroked the serpentine body all the way to her tail. I felt her heavy breath on my hair as I continued my examination. I was breathing deeper as well.

She lifted her tail to my eye level. My hands wrapped around the three pearl-like globes. They were white with a green sheen to them. Her own hand was planted firmly on my thigh. Her fingers gripped my upper thigh as if she was about to pull me closer. My hips moved forward with unconscious anticipation.

"What are these for—"

The sound of slithering across grass and earth stopped me. I released Nishala's tail as I saw seven silhouettes emerge from around her camp.

"Who is this outsider, Nishala?"

A deep voice pierced the darkness between us and the silhouettes. They slithered closer. Seven Naga came into view, each of their hoods glowing with the same jewels Nishala's hood was adorned with. The one who was speaking was front and center. He was pointing at me. His scales were a mix of mostly green with speckles and small patches of sapphire. He was enormous, probably seven or eight feet tall. He had a small scar; slash mark across his left eye.

"A visitor to our realm. She was only passing through. She wasn't aware I am an exile."

An exile? Exile for what?

The Naga looked my way, studying me up and down. He was superbly handsome. The scowl on his face was less so.

"A human entering Naga-Loka is something the King will know about." He pointed at me again.

"You will be brought before his highness."

Laying on a pile of leather packs in Nishala's camp was a sword. I instinctively grabbed it and held it pointing at the Naga man.

"I'm not going anywhere." All seven of the Naga laughed. Men always laughed when women said no.

"We only want you to have an audience with our King, but if you choose violence then so be it."

He drew his own sword. He slithered toward me twice as fast as a human could have crossed the distance. I swung my sword haphazardly at him, and he parried my swing. Metal clanged. My hand was hurt from impact. He struck with the strength of a yak.

"I'll be taken nowhere without my permission!" I swung again. His sword met mine with such force that it was knocked from my grip and sent to the ground. He sheathed his sword. The other six Naga snickered.

"Then I'm asking your permission. Will you come and meet his highness, King Vasuki?"

"Strange way of asking for perm—" My words exploded from my mouth before my brain could process the name he just spoke.

King Vasuki. The King Vasuki? The divine snake depicted around Lord Shiva's neck?

"I will see your King Vasuki."

The Naga warrior's face turned to confusion when I changed my words.

"Well, it's settled then. Come with us, we will see his majesty at once."

I caught Nishala in my peripheral vision. Her fists were clenched at her sides. She gripped my shoulder.

"Are you sure you want to go with them?" She whispered in my ear. "I could down at least two of them before they swarm us."

The offer was appealing, but if I wanted answers, I'd need to see the King.

"I'm sure. Thanks for everything, Nishala. I'll be back to thank you properly."

Her hand took mine and gripped it one more time before I went. She smiled at me as I turned to face the Naga warrior party.

Let's do this. Let's go meet the King.

***

I walked with the Naga warriors through the grassy grove and into the forest I'd seen before. Bioluminescent frogs pulsed amber and blue from the underbrush. Their croaking sounded almost like music. After a while, the Naga who had humiliated me at sword fighting spoke.

"What's your name?"

"I have an audience with your King, not you, warrior."

"That's true. I'm surely below a King in station."

Was that sarcasm, or a joke?

"How did you know I was at Nishala's camp?"

"Something changed in the realm. We all felt it. The King was curious as to what entered our realm."

King Vasuki, curious about me? Good. Let him be curious.

As the trees began to dwindle in number, we found ourselves climbing the hills I'd seen in the distance from Nishala's camp. My injured leg ensured the trek up the hillside was difficult. The Naga warrior with the scar over his eye was in front of me and held out a hand.

"Here, I'll pull you up, the climb can't be easy with that le—"

"I'm doing just fine, thank you."

The other Naga laughed at him being scolded. Good, allow me to humiliate you for a change.

Once we were on the hilltop, I saw a brightness in the background. It was a city. Its buildings were made of thousands of pinpoints of glowing light. Some of the larger buildings were made of gold.

Bhogavati.

"Bhogavati..." I thought at the same time as I spoke. I was breathless and full of questions at the same time.

"So you know where you are?" The Naga warrior with the scar on his eye again. He sure was insistent I talk to him.

"I definitely know where I am."

Walking for another minute or two I heard running water. A river came into view. Only a twenty foot piece of it was visible. It looked to be coming from an underground source, and then disappearing underground again. I gasped when one of the Naga jumped in and swam into the current, disappearing beneath the dirt. The others followed until it was just me and the Naga with the scar on his eye. He held out a hand.

"You'll want to hold on tight for this, human. It may be unpleasant at first, but it's over quickly."

I could swim alright, but not great. I took his hand. His grip was strong, but not in a harsh way. He gripped my hand with tenderness instead of hostility that he showed me earlier. He pulled me to his chest and my arms instinctively wrapped around his neck. I was just starting to process how he was more than a foot taller than me when the cold water hit me. He jumped into the river with me attached to his chest like a barnacle. My arms tightened around his neck and my body relaxed against his before my brain could object.

Please don't let me drown in a mythical netherworldly river. Please. Please.

I felt enveloped in ice other than the warmth from the Naga I was clinging to. His tail flicked in the water and we traveled magnitudes faster than running. It felt like I was in a speed boat. We surfaced about a minute later. I immediately let go of the Naga man and began wringing the water from my hair. The water simply slid off the Naga men, not soaking them at all. The Naga that ferried me here produced a blanket from a leather pack on his hip and threw it over me.

"Thank you. For letting me hang onto you and for the blanket." He showed me the first smile I'd seen from him since we met.

As I dried myself, I realized we were on a bridge made of marble stone. In front of us were the gates to the city. The marble bridge and the gates themselves had a unique pattern of swirled carving all over them. I'd never seen any architecture like it, and I look at old architecture for a living. The Naga with the scar gestured me forward.

"After you." He bowed at the end of his gesture.

I dried off as much as I could and returned the blanket. At the gates, the other Naga warriors spoke to the guards. They looked at me several times before opening the gates for us. We continued down the streets of Bhogavati. The streets were made of tiled marble slabs. All of the Naga in the streets stopped and stared at me.

I'm in a place where I'm the alien. I'm the creature.

Chapter 3
Decree ~ तैयारी

As we walked through the city and to the palace in the center, my head swiveled in all directions analyzing the jewel-studded buildings. Each jewel produced its own glow. The glow was so bright that street lamps weren't needed, and so there were none. Each Naga and Nagini who stared at me had their faces lit up by the glow of the jewels on the buildings. Each Naga face had a symmetry and bone structure that made every supermodel on Earth look unfinished.

"We're here to give this outsider an audience with the King."

We arrived at the palace. Time had escaped me as I was studying the city.

"The King is expecting you. A chamber has been prepared for the outsider."

Oh great. They're sticking me in a chamber. I'll have my own dungeon.

The Naga group closed in on me, putting me in the middle of them as we entered the palace and they escorted me down its ornate halls. The Naga with the scar on his face stood beside me, ensuring the others didn't squish me. Paintings covered every corridor for their entire length. There were many with themes of rain, rivers, lakes, and other bodies of water. A good majority showed mountains of sacred treasure and Naga guarding them.

"I'll take her from here." The scarred Naga dispersed the others.

Now that it was just us, I couldn't stop stealing glances. His purple eyes were ridiculous. No one's eyes should be that color. His chest was a sculpture of green and sapphire scales stretched over muscle that made my brain forget I was supposed to be angry at him.

Bas, Priya, bas!

I looked away before he caught me staring. I looked back almost immediately.

"The King shouldn't be long. You can stay here until then." He opened the door and my eyes widened before I could protest. The chamber was lavish. It had a large canopy bed and a polished wooden dresser. The other furniture in the room shared the same quality of a master artisan.

"I'll come get you when his highness is ready for you." I didn't even speak as I walked slowly inside, amazed by the quality of the chamber. I didn't even register the door shutting and the outside lock bolting. I sat on the bed, laying back on it and taking a breath. This was the first time I'd felt safe in hours. My leg winced in pain as I laid back.

I don't know how much time passed when I heard a knock at the door. I heard the door unbolt and a voice on the other end.

"Are you decent, human?"

I sat up and ran my fingers through my hair, styling it as best I could without a brush. If I was to meet a King I wanted to not look ragged.

"I am." I called out when I was satisfied.

The scarred Naga opened the door and gestured to the corridor.

"It's time. King Vasuki awaits."

I stood and marched into the corridor. Two other Naga guards stood on either side of me. They each reached out to grab my arms. The scarred Naga stopped them.

"I've got her." He didn't try to grab me like the guards did, he simply stood shoulder-to-shoulder with me. It was more arm-to-shoulder, given his height.

The Naga warrior escorted me through the endless corridors, and finally to a grand set of double doors made of polished, dark wood. He forced the doors open and the sound died. Every sound. Hundreds of Naga faces stared back at me. There may have been thousands. My eyes couldn't analyze fast enough. My breathing was irregular. The expansive throne room was made of glossed marble, with the intricate swirled carved patterns I saw on the bridge outside the city. Cold seeped up through the floor and into the soles of my boots. There was a ground level and a balcony level for the audience. I felt as though I'd entered a grand theater, and I was the star actress. Guards on each side of me stopped me as I reached the end of the walkway, just before the steps that rose to the throne chair.

I've got so many questions. I hope I brought my journal so I can take notes. Also, I hope this isn't where they declare me a witch and execute me.

Drums thundered from the balcony and a procession of guards entered from the far end of the room. A Naga with gold scales and a silver crown entered behind them and took the throne without ceremony. This was King Vasuki. Every Naga I'd seen so far was stunning, but Vasuki didn't look like them. He looked like time. His scales were gold but worn, like temple walls that had been beautiful for so long they'd become something more. His eyes carried the weight of the cosmos in them, not fierce, but patient, like they'd been waiting for something and had all the time in the world to wait.

"What is your name, outsider?" His voice was calmer than I expected. There was a warmth to it that didn't match the weight behind his eyes.

"Priya Bhandari." My voice was proud when I spoke my family's name.

"So Priya of the Bhandari Kula, you're the outsider who entered our world."

"Yes. I came upon this world by accident. A blast of dynami—"

Would they know what dynamite is?

"The ground shook while I was examining a cave and I fell into a chasm. When I awoke, I was here."

"And what were you doing in this cave?"

"I'm a...historian of sorts. I look for secrets of the past. If there's anyway I can be sent back to my world that would be the best outcome here."

The King's eyes lowered.

"I'm afraid that's not possible, human. A Naga can travel outside of this world, but I've never heard of a human doing so."

My heart dropped into my stomach. For a moment I wasn't in a throne room. I was on our balcony, Papa's hand in mine, Maa reading her recipe book, Vikram pointing at stars. Then the marble floor under my feet pulled me back.

"That being said, you're here now and with no way to return to your world, you have but two options: you can be an exile on the edges of Naga-Loka, or you can be part of our society."

Part of their society. The words felt unreal, heavy. I swallowed and steadied myself.

"I would be honored to be part of your society."

He said he's never heard of a human doing so, not that it was impossible.

Thousands of voices whispered. They were silenced by a simple gesture from King Vasuki.

"I do want you to be informed of the process to be part of our society. You would either need to be of Naga blood yourself, or be the consort of a Naga."

Does Nani telling me I was a Nagini princess count?

"Since you are a human, your only option would be to become a consort to a Naga in our kingdom. This is a big decision, so I'll give you the night to deci—"

"I will become a consort." I interrupted the King, King Vasuki.

I can't believe I just did that! To the guillotine I go then.

Thousands of whispers erupted again. The King showed more concern on his face than offense. Another flick of his wrist silenced the audience.

"I do want to make sure you understand what this would mean, Priya." He stood from his chair and slithered down the steps to face me.

"To become a consort there would need to be an immediate consummation ritual to seal the union." A fly's wings could be heard in the room, it was so quiet.

I don't know why I answered so quickly. My brain told me I was out of my mind. My heart told me I'd be a fool to pass up the opportunity to be part of a Naga society.

"I understand." The audience boomed with conversation. King Vasuki took my hands into his.

"Then it is settled. I will choose someone for you to union with."

King Vasuki released my hands and looked around the room.

"Sarvaan of Karkota Kula, you are not unioned. Priya of Bhandari Kula shall be be your consort."

The Karkota bloodline, known for diplomacy and trade. At least I'll have a reasonable Naga to serve.

I looked around anxiously. The man I was to spend my time with had been chosen in mere seconds. Everyone in the audience was looking around as well. Then I saw him slithering forward. It was the Naga warrior with the scar over his eye who escorted me from Nishala's camp. The Naga who had humiliated me and laughed at me.

King Vasuki addressed me one last time before disappearing behind a door in the back of the room.

"You will be my guest here in the palace tonight. In the morning you will be bathed, spiced, and prepared for the consummation ritual."

Sarvaan joined my side now. He smiled down at me.

"Well, hello again."

The only reason I didn't run then and there was because he was impossibly handsome. His purple eyes stirred something inside of me.

***

A clean towel and a freshly washed ceremonial robe awaited me when I returned to my chambers. The robe was a dark emerald color with gold thread lining the sleeve cuffs and lapels. I was instructed to get dressed, let the guards outside know I was ready, and then I would be escorted to the bathing chamber.

Green and gold. Good colors.

I thought back to the green and gold jewels in my hair as a girl. My shorts, shirt, and undergarments met the floor and I picked the robe up to give it a look. The stitching was perfect and it was silky smooth to the touch. I wrapped it around me and tied the sash. I walked over to the mirror and twirled around slowly. I wasn't a Nagini, but I sure looked like a princess.

The guards escorted me down several flights of stairs, each flight giving way to more warmth and moisture that contrasted the upper level's coolness. Steam kissed my face and neck as I descended. We ended up in front of a large metal door. A guard opened it and gestured me inside. The door closed behind me but didn't lock. The room was the size of a school gymnasium. It was filled with steamy mist and the center formed a large bathing pool. It looked like it could have several dozen people in it at once.

It's a bit much for just me, but I'll take it.

I removed my robe and placed it on a stone bench on the edge of the water. The bathing chamber witnessed as my nude form slowly walked into the pool. Upon my first toe touching the water, I was surprised to find that it was warm, almost hot. It felt like I had dipped into a natural hot spring. Given that we went several flights down to get here, I shouldn't have been surprised.

So if this world has underground springs like Earth does, are we under the actual Earth? Or did I stumble into an entirely separate dimension of existence?

Thoughts about how this world connected to Earth collided in my mind as I submerged myself in the pool. When I came up I ran my hands backwards through my hair, letting the water run down the back of my neck. It was then I noticed there was a basket on the edge of the pool, opposite from where I had entered the chamber. I swam over to investigate. When I peered inside, I saw a glass bottle filled with liquid, pouches filled with different colored powders, and dried flower petals.

Hey, they got me a gift basket. Nagas are thoughtful people.

I picked up the glass bottle and swirled the liquid. The liquid clung to the side of the bottle for a moment before flowing down again. I poured a drop onto my fingers and rubbed the liquid between them.

It's oil. Smells like ripe cherries warmed by the sun.

I picked up a tiny pinch of the powder next. I sniffed it. I caught sandalwood and saffron. The combination had a creamy, earthy, honey-like sweetness to it.

Oh that's nice. I'll have to take some back to my chambers.

I picked up some of the dried plant matter. Gulab ki patti. I stroked my face with them. They smelled faintly tea-like and felt like silk on my skin.

They are really spoiling me with this.

I looked around the room and noticed there were two other baskets around the pool.

Why would I need three baskets?

I heard a door open. I instinctively submerged so that only my neck and head were visible and swam to the middle of the pool to hide in the steam.

Well, nice knowing you, Priya. I guess they didn't want the stinky human in their kingdom after all.

Three silhouettes appeared behind the steamy mist that hung in the air. They were feminine, graceful, and moving as if they were dancing. As they approached the edge of the pool, the silhouettes revealed themselves to be irresistibly glamorous Nagini women. Each of them had sweetness all over their faces, with hints of playfulness. They locked their eyes on me when I came into their view. They took off their own ceremonial looking robes and descended into the pool, as nude as I was. I watched as each Nagini swam to a basket and brought it with them as they swam towards me. Each of them set their baskets on the water's surface and the baskets floated.

Okay, when King Vasuki said I would be bathed, he meant I would be bathed by others.

I felt the flick of a forked tongue on my ear from behind.

"You can relax. We're going to take good care of you." Before I could respond, I felt oiled hands on my back.

They started to rub and massage. My body responded immediately. The scent of hot cherry juice marched into my nostrils, making me inhale deeply. Surprisingly, the scales on the Nagini's hands weren't rough, they were smooth, smoother than human skin. Another Nagini woman approached my front, sandwiching me between her and the one to my rear. She put the sandalwood and saffron powder in her hand, then kissed the powder with her lips.

Well this is interesting. How's she going to apply—

She kissed my shoulder, then my collarbone. She kissed the lower part of my neck, then the middle. She left imprints of her lips from my shoulder to the top of my neck made of sandalwood and saffron spices. It was like a trail of discarded clothes leading to a bedroom in a romance story. My body shuddered. As she kissed me, I felt the scales of her breasts brush against mine. Her scales raked my nipples, sending shivers through me.

I...think I like this...I think this is great...

Under me in the water, I felt a scaled serpentine body swimming around. The third Nagini woman had swam under me and was starting to scrub and massage my feet. Her tail swam between my legs, giving me chills even in the warm water. The three globe-like pearls on the end of her tail squeezed through my legs. She flicked the end of her tail so the pearls rubbed back and forth between my thighs. The globes came closer to my labia until finally the pearls rolled on them softly with each flick.

That's a nice...unique feeling...

The Nagini below me really started to put some work into massaging my feet. I've never had a foot massage before, and it was breathtaking. She moved to my calves, then my thighs. After treating my legs like royalty, she rubbed and caressed my butt. The way she was positioned, her face was between my legs. Bubbles escaped her mouth and ran between my legs. These Nagini women would have seen my pussy glistening with juices if I hadn't been in water.

My heart is pounding like I'm running a marathon. Oh wow.

The Nagini who was rubbing my back reached around and ran oiled fingers over my breasts. The Nagini kissing my skin with spices was now kissing the other side. She kissed the top of each breast, then where my neck and chest met, then my chin. My eyes grew heavy with relaxation and closed. I wasn't expecting the kiss on the lips. Her lips smacked on mine loud enough to be heard over the splashing of the pool water. Her tongue tasted of tea and honey. The sandalwood left a slight cooling sensation in my mouth.

Oh shit...I'm gonna...I'm gonna...

Everything suddenly stopped. My eyes slowly opened and all three Nagini were in front of me. The middle one spoke.

"You have been properly bathed and are ready for your consummation ritual. Manasa be with you."

With that they all swam to the edge of the pool and exited as quickly as they had entered.

I wish I had brought my vibrator.

Chapter 4
Ritual ~ संगम

I'm sure that what Nani had in mind when she said I was a Nagini princess was far different from my current situation. I was waiting in a bedchamber of a Naga palace to be fucked by a Naga warrior and be integrated into their society. I kept fidgeting with my hair and robe as I sat on the bed waiting for Sarvaan. I kept changing my pose, seeing which one felt the sexiest. I caught the smell of myself as I moved restlessly. I smelled sexy. Really sexy.

Why do I care how the Naga I'm to serve sees me posed?

It was because of his dreamy face. Strong and determined, full of confidence.

If only I could have met Sarvaan at karaoke, or a dating app. I would swipe right for tail pearls.

I forced myself to think happy thoughts. Each sound outside the door was making me anxious. I remembered Sarvaan being by my side so I wouldn't be crowded by guards and warriors as I was escorted around. I remembered the sly grin when he stood next to me after King Vasuki gave me away to him.

You know what? This is my moment. I shouldn't be trying to impress him, he should be trying to impress me.

Filled with temporary courage I stood off of the bed and shed my robe to the floor. Then I sat down cross legged and waited. I didn't have to wait for long. After a few minutes there was a knock at the door.

"Priya, it's Sarvaan."

"You may enter." I felt powerful commanding someone to enter rather than scolding them for not knocking.

Sarvaan opened the door slowly and stepped inside. He didn't slither; he had shapeshifted to a human form.

"Hello Priya, it's nice to see yo—"

"Do you mean to insult me?" His face dropped.

"I'm not sure what you mean? How have I offended?"

"I willingly agree to be a consort, to a consummation ritual with someone I barely know, and you offend me by presenting yourself as a human."

His head cocked to the side.

"I'm not a naive virgin girl. I'll have you as a Naga or I won't have you at all."

"Very well. My apologies." He smirked and his body morphed within seconds to his Naga form. I haven't noticed before, but his eyes were wonderful to look into directly. His pupils were a deep purple. After he was in his true form I uncrossed my legs, opening them as I sat on the edge of the bed. There was visible wetness between my legs from the bathing earlier.

Come and get it, Sarvaan. Crave me. Yearn for me.

He slithered forward. A pouch with a vertical opening just under his waistline opened producing his dick and scrotum. Both were a pale white color. His scrotum looked similar to a human scrotum, but it looked to have five testicles inside instead of two. His penis was about seven inches in length. At the base it was four inches wide and it tapered as it went on until it was only an inch wide at the tip. It looked prehensile. It swayed and curled in a way a human penis could not. Sarvaan was looming over me now. His face came down to meet mine. I put my hand against his chest and pushed him backwards.

"Kissing is for intimacy. This is a ritual." I stood and turned around. I slowly bent over, using my hands to lean on the bed in a standing doggy style position.

"Whatever is best for you, Priya. I will cherish this moment."

I felt his hands grip my hips. They were strong, but gentle at the same time. He effortlessly pulled my hips backward and I felt his cock enter me. The texture was like having a giant tongue inside me. With each thrust his tapered girth went further in me. The one inch portion made my eyes flutter. The two inch portion had me pushing back on each thrust, wanting more. The three inch portion made me spread my legs further apart to accommodate the girth. When the four inch base went in, I let out a loud groan that could have been confused for pain. Sarvaan stopped, leaning down placing a hand on my back, caressing my spine slowly.

"Are you alright, Priya?"

I'm more than alright.

I thrust my hips forward and his dick fell out of me. I turned to face him and sat on the bed, spreading my legs once more. Sarvaan took the clue and slithered on top of me. His heavily muscled warrior body felt safe. He entered me again. His eyes never left mine. Each thrust started with a tongue sensation and ended with that four inch base pounding the sense out of me. Sarvaan leaned down tonguing my neck and ears, I heard him sniff my hair and skin. He thought I smelled sexy too.

I want more. I need more.

At the end of one of his thrusts, I wrapped my legs around his serpentine waist and flipped us to where I was on top of him. His body was huge. I was sitting on a massive, scaled throne. I started working my hips back and forth, and side to side, trying to see what worked with Naga anatomy. I finally found the correct motion and started working it. My legs trembled each time I brought myself down on the base of his cock. My leg reminded me it was injured as I moved, but pleasure overruled it. I felt his hands reach up and cup my breasts. His hands were large enough to cover my c-cups entirely. His hands blanketed my tits in warmth.

"You're so beautiful, Priya." I felt the hot breath of his moans.

"So are you." Escaped from my quivering lips.

My hands rested on his scaled chest. My fingers gripped and traced his stone-hard muscles underneath. I remembered how the Nagini women's scales and coils of their serpentine body felt against me.

"Wrap your coils around me. Play with my breasts and ass."

"Are you sure that's what you wan—" One of my hands landed on his balls with a wet slap. My juices were all over them by this point. I started working his testicles between my fingers, massaging them. His dick spasmed inside me. My spine arched.

"I won't ask you again, Sarvaan."

"As you wish, Priya." He moaned through me working his cock with my hips.

I gave his scrotum a light squeeze, then a slightly more firm squeeze. He got the idea. He wrapped the coils of his body around me. One coil was around my tits and the other was around my ass cheeks. Each coil had a mind of its own, slithering over my body, the scales tenderly raking my skin. I wanted to explode so badly, but my mind remembered something else from earlier.

The tail pearls. This will be interesting.

"Your tail pearls, fuck my ass with them." I saw the confusion in his face but I was close and didn't have time to explain. I placed my hand on his chest and sensually slid it to his neck. My pussy was starting to spasm. My fingers gave his neck a squeeze.

"Not..." My legs started to shudder and squeeze.

"A..." With each movement of my hips I exhaled a mouthful lustful breath.

"Request!" I felt his tail pearl rest on my puckered asshole, then it slid inside and Sarvaan began to alternate thrusting his dick into me with thrusting the pearl in me. My pussy clenched hard as I let out a feral roar of success. I heard Sarvaan moan loudly, my pussy must have been squeezing the life out of his cock. In this case I squeezed his load out of him. I felt his dick flick in rapid succession and spray warmth inside me.

Oh yes, that was...wow, yes...

I fell forward, using my arm to stop short of Sarvaan's face. I was so close, I felt his heavy panting on my face and I'm sure he felt mine. I was breathing harder than I ever have before. My mouth suddenly collided with his, the sound of teeth clacking and lip smacking filled the air. Sarvaan moaned and panted into my mouth.

"Oh, Priya..."

No...wait...yes...

He tried to raise his hand and touch my face. My hand met his and pushed it into the bedsheets. When his other hand attempted the same thing I pinned it to the bed as well. The kiss felt so good I lost track of time. I felt his dick reharden and relengthen inside of me. He must have liked it too. I pulled back and looked at his absurdly handsome face. He smiled at me.

Why does my heart skip a beat every time I look at you?

What I actually said to Sarvaan was very much less romantic.

"I'd like you to leave while I get dressed."

His smile faded into confusion and then to a semblance of understanding.

"Of course, take as much time as you'd like. I'll be waiting in the ballroom when you're ready to go."

He rose from the bed and dressed himself quickly before slithering to the door. I started to dress as well when it struck me.

"Wait." He stopped just as he was about to close the door and reemerged inside the doorway. "Go where?" I asked half alarmed and half curious.

"To our home."

***

The Nagas provided me with some dresses, gowns, and robes that fit in a bit better than the clothes I came here in. After getting dressed, Sarvaan and I were escorted out of the palace. As we walked, I kept thinking about Sarvaan's words.

Our home. He said our home. I got fucked by a Naga and became a home owner.

It was beginning to be clear to me that although I was the Naga expert in my world, I was a novice here. I was eager to learn, being a part of these rituals and this culture excited my heart and my mind. As we continued to the palace entrance, Sarvaan took my hand into his. My hand was so small compared to his, but he was delicate and encased my fingers with his. When the palace doors opened, I noticed a crowd outside. There were fifty Nagas at least.

I hope this isn't a torch and pitchfork kinda crowd.

They began to cheer. Sarvaan scooped me up into his arms and they cheered even more.

Well, color me surprised.

"Who are all these people?" He nuzzled my face to be able to whisper. His breath in my ear gave me chills.

"These are Naga from my kula. They are my family, my bloodline."

I saw his tail reach up to my left ankle and place a golden anklet around it. Gold, delicate, bearing the symbol of Karkota Kula, the same symbol from his attire when we first met. I watched the way it caught the ambient light.

How pretty...

The crowd started to chant. They were chanting indistinguishable syllables, possibly some sort of cultural slang.

"They are expecting us to kiss, they are here to celebrate our union with us. Are you okay with that?"

I wrapped my arms around his neck and gave him a passionate kiss. The crowd erupted in cheers and clapping. I stayed wrapped around his neck longer than I expected myself to. When we pulled away, there was a moment that I looked into his eyes and everything around us disappeared. It was just us on the palace steps. No people, no noise, just us.

Come on heart, what's wrong with you? Why am I feeling this way?

Sarvaan lowered me gently to the ground and we walked through the crowd hand in hand. I was astounded at these rituals I'd never heard of as a Naga archaeology specialist. The bathing, the consummation, the kula celebrating the union. I'd heard of none of this, and here I was in the midst of it all. I was a Naga consort and felt like a university student at the same time.

As we made our way through the streets of Bhogavati, I began to notice things about the way Naga lived their lives. I saw Naga and Nagini singing and dancing in the streets. Sometimes they danced and sang to music played by musicians, other times they danced and sang to silence. We made a turn and the neighborhood changed. I noticed the scale coloration of the Naga in this part of the city were like Sarvaan's.

"This is my neighborhood. Karkota's part of Bhogavati."

"So each kula lives in their own part of the city?"

"Yes, we grow up together and make a community together."

I saw multiple Naga and Nagini along our walk who were partially or completely nude. No one seemed to mind. Sarvaan must have seen me staring.

"In our culture, our scales tell what kula we are from. We like to show and celebrate our heritage as much as possible. Clothing would hide our scales."

The Naga and Nagini we passed all stared at me. Most saw my anklet and smiled, or showed a semblance of pride. I was one of them now. I was of Karkota Kula. Another thing I noticed was that people seemed to make way for Sarvaan. After they looked at me, the eyes of onlookers shot to him immediately.

Who are you Sarvaan? Who are you really?

***

As I entered my new home I wasn't sure of what to expect. Was there a dungeon where the consort was kept? Did Sarvaan have other consorts? Every woman that laid eyes on him seemed to perk up with anxiousness. What I actually found inside was a home much like one on Earth. It had a food preparation area, food store, a den-like lounging area with incense and shelves of books, and multiple bedrooms. The main differences were that there was no electricity, natural lighting from the glowing jewels embedded in the walls, and the rooms were more spacious, with higher ceilings. This made sense, Nagas were longer and taller than humans.

"Do you mind if I sleep in my own room until I get used to all this?"

"Of course, take your time." I could see a hint of sadness as he accommodated me.

I just want to give him a hug when his face does that.

I put my clothes in the bedroom I claimed and slipped into one of the comfy gowns gifted to me. I found Sarvaan drinking an amber colored liquid from a flute-like glass in the den. A table was beside where he sat with a pitcher of the same liquid. I sat beside him on the elongated couch-like piece of furniture. He offered the glass my way.

"Oh, no thank you. So, hey, I wanted to ask you something."

He put the glass down and turned my way.

"What would you like to know?"

Damn look at those chest muscles. Focus, Priya, focus!

I reached out and stroked his chest before continuing with my inquiry.

"I noticed you had multiple bedrooms. Why have so many bedrooms if you don't have children or a wife?"

That chest had been heaving on me earlier. Strong. Safe. I could feel his heart beating for me.

"Nagas are a communal people. I have guests over frequently."

That chest was heaving on top of me. Fucking my brains out.

"Speaking of children, I didn't see any on our way here. I haven't seen any at all. Why is that?"

He had shot his load in me. Our worlds collided.

"Ah, yes. Well, there are nurseries around the city, usually in each kula's neighborhood. When Nagini fertilize their eggs they deposit the eggs in the nurseries. As they hatch, the young ones are raised in the nurseries by communal mothers and fathers who specialize in educating young Naga on essentials like history and culture."

"Wait, Nagini fertilize their own eggs?"

"Yes, after their Naga mate deposits them into their womb."

"Then what did I feel when you climaxed earlier?"

"An organic lubricant. It assists the eggs as they get pumped into the womb."

I imagined Sarvaan pumping me full of eggs. I really needed my brain to calm down so I reached for Sarvaan's glass flute and took a gulp. It tasted of honey and wildflowers. My gulp turned into finishing the entire flute. Sarvaan eyed me curiously and then a smile washed over his face as I finished the remainder.

"Oh, wow, that is really good. What is it?"

"Madhu, it's a honey-based mead. Do you like it?"

Oh wow, this stuff could be dangerous. I'd better not drink too much around him or this couch would be covered in cum by the end of the night. Wait, was it day or night? There's no sun in the sky so it can't have a day and night cycle like on Earth.

"Very much, but I'm afraid I'll get into trouble if I drink too much of that."

"Of course, you're probably tired and wanting to retire for the night."

"Oh that subject..." My hand took his, gripping his large, strong fingers.

Oh Sarvaan, what strong fingers you have. A shame they aren't in me. Okay, no more mead for me.

"Since there's no sun in the sky, how does the day and night cycle work? Or is there even such a thing? When do Naga sleep? Do Naga sleep?"

He laughed, wrapping his arm around my shoulders and pulling me closer. The mead made me lean into him and snuggle.

"It's true, there's no sun to show us when it's day and when it's night. But, the jewels that glow on our buildings glow at different intensities to create our own version of day and night. Right now, for example, the jewels glow dim to signal 'nighttime.'"

Telling the time of day with glowing jewels. Fascinating.

As I listened to Sarvaan, I found myself unconsciously tracing the scales of his hood. I leaned in and gave him a brief, sweet kiss on the lips. His fingers grazed my cheek. The mead made me lean into it.

"I noticed when we were walking that everyone seemed to stare at you. Are you known around your neighborhood?"

"Actually, yes. You've come into our realm with interesting timing. King Vasuki has been ruler for one hundred years now. When a ruler has been in power for one hundred years, the Trial of The Crown commences, and a new ruler is chosen."

"King Vasuki is known on Earth and has been for thousands of years, the time frame doesn't quite match. How is that?"

"King Vasuki is no ordinary Naga. Long before he ruled Naga-Loka, he was known as a companion of Lord Shiva. It is said that Shiva's presence bound him beyond the limits of time, allowing him to endure where others do not."

My eyes stared into his dreamy eyes as I listened. Everything else around me started to tune out.

"When a ruler's hundred years are complete, it is tradition to pass the crown. They say Vasuki will return to Shiva's side willingly, not because he is called, but because the bond between them is older than his rule. Most other Nagas live for around three hundred human years."

I lifted myself into Sarvaan's lap then reached and poured a flute of madhu from the pitcher on the table.

"You said it's been a hundred years now. So what is the Trial of The Crown and what does it entail?" I took a sip of the intoxicating honey mead.

"It's a trial by single combat. It's structured like a tournament. The combat isn't to the death. The goal is to make your opponent yield."

"Interesting. And what is your connection to this competition?" He took my hand and stole a sip of madhu from my flute.

"I'm a competitor." My eyes didn't blink. "I represent Karkota Kula in a bid for the throne."

"So you...want to be King then?" He stole my flute from me and finished what was left.

"I do. It would be an honor."

My brain malfunctioned. I was consort to a contender for the throne of Naga-Loka.

I laid my head on his chest, stroking his scales and muscles.

"I think you'd make a great King."

We ended up sharing two more flutes of Madhu. I fell asleep curled up in Sarvaan's lap using his chest as a pillow and his arms around me.

Oh, Priya. What are we gonna do, girl?

Chapter 5

Masks ~ मुलाक़ात

I woke up to a cozy warmth surrounding me. As my eyes fluttered open, I saw that I was lying on the couch with a blanket far too large for a human wrapped around me.

Falling asleep and waking up to the same lighting; that'll take some getting used to.

I ran my hands through my hair to tame it from its sleeping style. I sat up and stretched, inhaling deeply. A sweet, citrusy aroma filled my nose. I heard Sarvaan slithering around in the kitchen where the smell was coming from. He was wonderful. I really did like him. But, the closer my heart grew towards Sarvaan, the more this all felt permanent. If I let my heart choose Sarvaan, it felt like I was abandoning my family. Maa making chai in the morning. Papa pretending to read while actually watching cricket. Vikram sending me stupid memes at 2am.

The King said a Naga could travel outside of this world. I wonder, is there a way I can become a Naga?

Sarvaan set a plate full of sliced toasted bread spread with an assortment of jams and mushrooms. The bread had blue grains in it. I must have looked like a zombie sitting there staring into the void. The plate being set in front of me snapped me out of my trance.

"Thank you, what's this?" I picked up a piece of jam covered bread and took a bite. It tasted like the fruit Nishala had offered me at her camp.

Nishala...I wonder how she's doing.

"Gomluvira, a common breakfast dish in this realm. I picked a few different jams that a human probably wouldn't have tasted before to give you a tour of our sweets."

He sat beside me. I had eaten two slices already. I realized my diet for yesterday had consisted of only fruit, dick, and semen. Some jam had smeared on the corner of my mouth as I shoveled the bread in. Sarvaan offered me a napkin.

If I let myself be true to my feelings for Sarvaan, I would have a hot Naga King as my husband. Would that make me queen? Is this the future Nani saw for me? Come on, this can't be real.

The thought raced through my head like wild horses. There would surely have to be a way in this netherworld to become a Nagini. I'd be queen of a Naga kingdom, and since Naga were shapeshifters I could assume my human form when I visited my family. I could have everything: true love, a King for a husband, and my family.

"Priya? Are you ok?"

I'd been staring off again, my toast was sideways and jam had spilled on my lap.

"I'll go grab a wet towel." He slithered to the kitchen and was back in a few seconds.

"Sarvaan, have you ever heard of a way to transform someone into a Naga?" I asked cautiously as I cleaned the jam from my gown.

He looked at me sideways. A bit of pride flashed across his face.

"I haven't." My face dropped. "But the archivists of Shesha Kula might know. They are keepers of knowledge and ancient secrets. It is Shesha Kula where most of our scholars and priests are trained."

My face lit up. He leaned in and placed a brief, sweet kiss on my lips.

Your kisses make me not want to ever go back to my world, Sarvaan.

His hand caressed my face. "I hope you know that I don't think ill of you for not being a Naga."

"No, of course not. But me becoming a Nagini would make things a bit easier."

I didn't have the heart to tell him I was thinking of becoming Naga in order to leave this world.

His fingers played with my hair, slowly running through over and over.

"I know this situation can't be easy for you, Priya. I'll help you any way I can. How about tomorrow I introduce you to Shesha Kula and see what can be found? I'm sure we'll be exhausted from the ball later."

The...ball? I guess I'll need my glass slippers, Prince Charming.

"Do you remember the Trial of The Crown I told you I'm competing in?" I nodded. "There's a ball and ceremony today to announce the competitors and officially begin the trials."

This would be a once in a lifetime event, literally for me, to be able to attend the opening ceremony of a competition which determines the next ruler of this realm.

"Sounds interesting!" I stood up and took his hands, swaying them as if I were dancing. "Will there be dancing?"

"Dancing, food, the eight kulas mingling, you may even get to witness kula drama first hand."

"Do the kulas not get along?" I sat back down.

"We recognize that we are all Naga, but there's a degree of competition between the kulas that can get ugly sometimes." His arm went over my shoulders, wrapping me in warmth. "But don't worry, I'll protect you." He flexed his arm that wasn't over my shoulders. My hands instinctively reached out and caressed his muscles.

Holy fuck, his bicep is the size of my head!

***

Sarvaan informed me when the ball was imminent, so I went to my bedroom and started looking for something to wear. I rummaged through the clothes I was given before leaving the palace. There weren't many options, but I knew when I saw the dress that it was the one. It was a dark green lehenga choli with gold embroidery and a sweetheart neckline.

Green and gold again. If we keep meeting like this, I'm going to think you're stalking me.

I put it on then looked in a mirror nearby. I gasped, covering my mouth.

Everyone's head will be on a swivel if I wear this! I look so fucking pretty!

There was one more thing I wanted to do. When I was a girl and Nani would gather me for story time, she would weave my hair into a waterfall braid as she told her tales. Today I would honor her, not just in the dress colors, but with a waterfall braid on my head. When I was finished I checked for every angle to make sure it looked right. My hair fell in soft waves and gathered into the braid that swept across my head like dark silk. I teared up and pointed at the mirror.

"This is for you Nani. I'm going to turn heads tonight."

Within the clothes I was given there was some simple makeup and an assortment of accessories as well.

Good. I cried before I put my makeup on. Good job Priya.

I found a set of gold earrings depicting a swan and snake swirling around in a vortex. It was surely a reference to Manasa, the goddess of snakes. She sometimes has a swan near her to represent fertility. Tonight I would embody Manasa. I put on my makeup and earrings. When I was completely finished, I stared at the person in the mirror. Gone was Priya the rugged archaeologist, and in front of me sat a Nagini princess.

Let's do this, Priya. Let's bring it.

When I emerged from my bedroom, Sarvaan was waiting for me in the den. I walked in front of him. The lehenga was long and flowing and made it seem like I was floating rather than walking. He stood immediately and bowed, taking my hand and kissing it.

That's right. Bow before your queen.

"Priya, I've never seen anyone so stunning. If I searched Patala a million times over, I wouldn't find anyone so captivating."

I blushed and grinned from ear to ear. He looked gorgeous as well. He had on a warrior's leather armor and shoulder pads, making his already enormous shoulders even more enormous.

"Thank you, Sarvaan. You look dashing yourself." I ran my hands over his swollen chest and arms before putting my hand into his.

Mission complete. I'm embodying the goddess of fertility, and Sarvaan definitely wants to fuck me.

"Shall we?"

***

"Presenting Sarvaan and Priya of Karkota Kula."

As we entered the ballroom arm-in-arm, we were greeted by the master of ceremonies. He was a gold-scale Naga like King Vasuki. I blushed for a moment from the attention thrown our way at a moment's notice, but I quickly held my head high.

These people should be lucky to have me at their ball. I am Priya of Karkota Kula.

When the others ahead of us were announced, it got some reaction, but when Sarvaan and I were announced, we had *everyone's* attention. I saw hands on mouths, widened eyes, and hanging jaws. The gold embroidery reflected the light from the jewels in the room like I was a chandelier. Then I noticed something else. The Naga men looked at Sarvaan like they'd kill to be him. The Nagini women looked at him like they would jump on him if they could. Through the crowd I saw a Naga with swollen muscles like Sarvaan's piercing me with a stare. His scales were mostly black with some shades of gray thrown into the mix as well. The way he stared at me wasn't admiration, it was possessive venom.

"Everyone, this is Priya, my consort." I snapped my gaze away from the black-scaled Naga and found myself being introduced to a circle of Naga with varying scale colors. They all made a quick courtesy bow. A Naga with white and silver scales reached forward and took my hand delicately.

"It's a pleasure, Priya. I am Vikshan, Archaka of our temple to Lord Shiva. It's good to see you here. We welcome you."

A Nagini with iridescent, rainbow colored scales took my hand next. It was then I realized she was the only Naga there with that scale coloration.

"Drishani, Rishika of Bhogavati." She placed her hand on mine and for a moment I wasn't there anymore. There was blackness all around me. There were no walls, ceilings, or floors.

"Hello? Sarvaan? Are you there?"

"He's not here. But I am." A feminine voice behind me echoed into this nothingness. I spun around. Her scales were green and gold, a combination I hadn't seen so far. She was dressed in warrior's leather.

"Who are you? I feel like I know you."

"You do." She smiled.

"Your name is on the tip of my tongue. What did Nani call you?" My mind tried to tap into my memories as a girl.

"You're searching in the wrong place. My name is in your heart, not on your tongue."

In an instant the visuals and sounds of the ball crashed back into my eyes and ears. I was looking up at the ceiling. I had fainted, and Sarvaan had caught me. His hands stroked my hair gently.

"Priya! Priya, what happened?" I sat up and stood, looking around. Drishani was gone.

"Sorry, I guess I need something to eat." Sarvaan's concern softened when I stood on my own.

"I'll go get you some refreshments. Will you be alright by yourself?" I was about to answer when King Vasuki walked over to me and locked my arm in his.

"Go on Sarvaan, I'll keep your beloved company until you get her something nice." Sarvaan bowed fully, touching the ground almost when Vasuki walked over.

I dressed like a princess and get to keep the King company. How ironic.

"Thank you, your highness, you are a beacon of gratitude." The King smiled and shrugged.

"A King's duty is to their people. I am only doing my duty." Sarvaan bowed again and went off to the refreshment tables. King Vasuki walked me around slowly.

"It's nice to see you here, Priya. I was afraid your entry into our world would be too jarring."

"It has been a very strange but interesting couple of days. Everyone has been very affectionate and kind so far."

"That makes me glad." He gestured to my dress. "I love the colors of your dress. I once saw a Nagini warrior wear those same colors. Her name was Prathavi. She would later become Queen."

Prathavi...that was it! That's her name! The Nagini warrior who became queen that Nani told me about!

Sarvaan returned with some exotic smelling cheese bathed in herbs and some wine.

"Here you are, I think you'll like this. It's Naga-Loka cheese, aged in our caves here." He bowed once more to King Vasuki. I curtsied to the King as well.

"Well then, I'll do my best to channel my inner Prathavi tonight." I said jokingly to King Vasuki.

"Then her spirit will get you through the rest of the night and I'm no longer of need. I bid you farewell, Queen Prathavi." He raised his palm out to me with his elbow bent.

"Ayushman Bhava" He said into the silence of the ballroom. Everyone was staring.

"I am...honored by your blessing." I managed to choke out of my throat.

With that the King was gone. Sarvaan put his arm around me, drawing me close.

"He must see great things in you."

"He is certainly a strange one. But he's sweet, I like him." I ate some of the cheese and drank wine to chase it. The cheese tasted of garlic and butter. The wine was a bit more savory and bitter than the madhu from last night, but I liked it. It went well with the cheese which had a bit of a sweetness to it.

An orchestral set of horns sounded throughout the ballroom. I looked around, searching for the source. Sarvaan leaned in and kissed me sweetly. A lifetime passed in that kiss alone.

"That's the signal that they are ready for the competitors. Watch the stage; we're going to put on a ceremony for the crowd."

I looked toward the back of the ballroom, there was a stage I hadn't seen when I walked in. The jewels on the walls and floor softened slightly to more intimate lighting, signaling a show was about to begin. I walked toward the stage and my arm was grabbed from behind. I spun around with a playful smile expecting King Vasuki again, but instead I was face-to-face with the black-scaled Naga from earlier.

"Priya, is it? My name is Balnak, of Takshaka Kula. You look absolutely divine tonight, I must say." There was something in his tone. I'd heard it before when men wanted something from me. There was a fakeness to it, like a sweet jam covering rotten fruit. I tried to pull my arm from him, but his fingers pressed into my skin, holding me in place.

"Thank you. The ceremony is about to begin. Excuse me." I flexed my muscles and pulled harder this time. I felt his fingernails start to stab into my skin as his grip held. I glanced around. Everyone was facing the stage. No one was looking.

"Balnak, is it? I'm spoken for if you didn't hear the master of ceremonies earli—"

"Sarvaan is one of my opponents in the trial. If I best him in combat would you consider being my consort?"

My cheeks reddened. My teeth pressed together.

"I'll pass." I yanked my arm as hard as I could and barely escaped even his relaxed grip. I was glad to see his face shrink as I walked toward the stage, putting a crowd between us. King Vasuki took the stage just as everyone gathered. Everyone stopped talking.

"I've been your King for one hundred years now. It has been my honor to serve you. But the cycle turns, as it always does. My path now leads me back to Lord Shiva's side, and a new ruler of Naga-Loka must be chosen."

The curtain of the stage opened revealing ten Naga men on the stage. Sarvaan was one of them. When our eyes met we both smiled and shared another lifetime within a split second together.

You're getting harder to resist by the moment, Sarvaan.

Balnak was also on stage. I almost threw up in my mouth. The King continued, gesturing to the competitors.

"It's been an honor to be your king for the past century. It's an even greater honor to introduce the competitors in this century's *Trial of The Crown*. Someone in this very room will be your next ruler."

King Vasuki bowed to his feet toward the audience and to the competitors, and left the stage. The master of ceremonies slithered to the stage and started to introduce each competitor.

"Vrishal of Takshaka Kula. Dhravan of Vasuki Kula. Keshnak of Shesha Kula. Nethrak of Takshaka Kula. Kiirvan of Karkota Kula."

Each name and kula announced brought on various levels of cheers and clapping.

"Shirvan of Shesha Kula. Trivash of Vasuki Kula. Sarvaan of Karkota Kula. Balnak of Takshaka Kula. "

Sarvaan had the loudest roaring applause yet. The clapping drummed like thunder. Balnak had an equally impressive applause and ovation.

What do they see in that slimy man?

After the introductions, the competitors did a graceful dance, pressing their elbows and tails together and swirling about. They moved with purpose and serenity, fully in the moment. When the dance was done the competitors bowed and dispersed from the stage. I met Sarvaan as he walked down the steps to join the crowd. Everyone who passed by him put their palm to his, took his hand, or bowed. The Nagini women blushed when he walked by them.

Careful, ladies. He's mine.

When we met, his arms went around me, lifting me two feet off the floor to meet his eyes with mine.

"How was I?" He asked nervously.

"It was quite a spectacular dance. I didn't know you danced. We'll have to dance together sometime."

"Nothing would please me more." He let me down, my feet touched the floor. We locked arms and went to mingle some more. My good time was interrupted by one last piercing stare from Balnak across the room. He raised a glass of wine at me.

Stare at someone else, you vile man.

***

"So how long did it take to learn the dance you did on stage?" Sarvaan and I were walking back home after the ceremony had ended. The glowing jewels indicated it was close to nighttime.

"About seven months. It's quite intricate."

"I noticed. I liked it." I looked down smiling. "I met one of the other competitors before the performance. Balnak."

"*Oh*, how did that go?"

"Well I've determined his ears don't work very well. He tried to flirt with me and when I told him I was spoken for, he didn't listen."

"Yes, his fighting skills are among the best in the kingdom, but his manners are among the worst." A strong, warm arm draped over my shoulder. "I'll set him straight in the arena."

When we got home, we spent the remaining waking hours sharing a few flutes of madhu. I brought back some of the Naga-Loka cheese and it was delicious with the honey mead.

"I think I'm going to retire." He stroked the side of my face. My heart wanted to go to bed with him. My brain told me I'd never see my world again. The madhu told my heart and brain they were both crazy, and that I should straddle Sarvaan's face and feel that forked tongue.

"Ok, thank you for a wonderful night." My mouth searched his for treasure, our honey mead breath mixing and swirling together.

"Good night Priya, dream well." He rose and slithered to his bedroom.

What am I going to do? Why can't I have this amazing man and have my world back too? Wait. He said he'd take me to see someone from Shesha Kula tomorrow. Maybe they can tell me if there's a way to become Nagini, then I could have my muscled Naga King husband and see my family again.

I drank the last gulp of madhu in my flute and set it down.

Hold on. Maybe I wouldn't have to wait until tomorrow. Nishala's scales were white and silver. Nishala's is a Shesha Naga. If this is a dream, I'm going to be in control of how it plays out.

I stood, teetering a bit from the alcohol, and snuck out the front door.

Chapter 6
Current ~ गहराई

As I approached the guards at the gates of Bhogavati, I kept trying to come up with some excuse to leave.

I need some air from the hills. I'm going stargazing. Wait, there aren't any stars. Maybe I'll just tell them I'm out for a stroll.

As I neared the guards, my mouth opened to try one of my excuses. As I was about to utter the word first, I saw them glance at me with recognition.

"Nice time for a meditation walk. May you find your peace." And just like that, the gates were opened for me.

"Yes, it's a splendid time for a meditation walk. Peace be with you." Luckily I didn't slip up and say something foolish. They didn't suspect that I was leaving to go see an exile. I still stumbled slightly from the madhu in my system, but I played it off by stopping and acting like I was taking in the sights. I looked at the hills in the distance. They looked further away than they did before. The sound of running water flowed into my ears.

Oh right, the river we traveled through. It could save me hours of travel time.

I walked down to the river from the bridge I was on. I stood before the wild current, gazing into the rushing water nervously

I am a Nagini princess. I am a Nagini princess. I can do this.

I jumped into the water. I was wrong. My body was immediately thrown about like a wet noodle. Water flooded my eyes, ears, and nose. The sting of cold water pierced my chest.

No, not like this. Please, not like this.

Each time I tried to wrestle back control from the river, it pinned me down harder. I felt myself getting faint. I started seeing faces flash before my mind. I saw Papa, Maa, and Vikram. I saw Sarvaan's wonderful face.

It's a dream. It's a dream!

My brain was malfunctioning from not breathing. I saw Balnak next, his twisted mouth opened and his tongue flicked at mine. I felt an acidic wetness on my face. Luckily, his face disappeared. I saw King Vasuki's face next. His face was full of wisdom

"Tell me what to do!" I screamed through bubbles.

"I could tell you what to do. But, would you do it?"

I don't have time for philosophy at the moment!

The King's face faded and Nishala's took his place. She looked at me the way she did the first time we met.

Please. I need you. Make me Nagini so my two wonderful worlds can collide!

The next face I saw I barely recognized. It was Drishani, the Nagini from the ball whose touch made me black out.

You, who are you? Why did you make me see Prathavi?

Drishani moved forward and kissed me. Water filled my mouth as it opened for hers.

"It's not time to go yet." She whispered impossibly through the water.

Well yeah! I'm trying to live, not die!

Her face disappeared and blackness crept around the edges of my vision.

No. I'm more than this. There's more for me to do.

I was on the verge of consciousness when a voice tickled the inside of my mind.

"See where you want to go, and be there."

I saw Nishala's camp. Her face. Her body. Her scales. The next thing I knew I was laying on my back, staring up at the forest trees. I coughed up a torrent of water and just laid there, wet and cold on the ground.

Where did that voice come from?

I recognized where I was. Nishala's camp was just through the trees.

***

I saw the firelight from Nishala's camp as I approached. She heard as I stumbled, shivering through the long grass of the grove. Seeing me shiver and stumble she raced inside her tent and produced a blanket. She met me and wrapped the blanket over me.

"Priya! What happened to you?" She walked beside me until I got to a place I could sit around the fire.

"I tried to use the river without fully understanding it." I coughed some more water from my lungs.

"Are you out of your mind? Only Naga can use the rivers." Her hands caressed my hair and face, helping to dry me off with the blanket. She stared at the lehenga choli I'd worn to the ball. "This is beautiful. I sense there's a story to be told?"

"Yes, apparently there was a ceremony today to honor the competitors in the Trial of The Crown. It was quite an experience."

"You've had a lifetime of adventure in just a couple of days, it sounds like."

"I have, yes..." My lehenga was soaked so I pulled it down from my body to dry it with the blanket. The madhu was still in my system and told me not to mind that I was fully nude at the moment.

"I got to meet the King. He's an interesting one."

Nishala stopped talking as soon as my lehenga came off. She was watching the firelight dance across my face and breasts. I watched it dance in her eyes and across her scales. When she helped to dry me off she had positioned herself between my legs as we were the last time I was with her. My hand stroked her face.

She's so. Fucking Beautiful. I hope I'm as beautiful as her when I'm a Nagini, if I get to become one.

"Nishala, you're really pretty." She grinned, stroking my face in return.

"Did you come all the way back here and nearly drown to tell me that?" She moved closer. Her breasts pressed against mine.

"Actually no, I came to ask you some—"

The kiss was soft. The only sound around us was the fire crackling in the wind. Her lips moved over mine lovingly, slowly, ending in a soft smack. I wrapped my legs around her and pressed her against me hard. My breasts, stomach, and legs felt her smooth scales hug them. Her fork tongue twisted and flicked against mine. She pulled back and hummed into my mouth.

This is surely a dream, right? I'm not really in a subterranean netherworld. Dreams have no rules to abide by.

"Mmmm, your tongue tastes like madhu. Bring me some next time."

Her hand pushed me to lie back on the log I was sitting on. Her hands reached up and caressed my tits, grabbing my nipples softly as her face went between my legs. A wave of hot breath licked my clitoris. I was instantly wet, the aroma filled the air around us. I lifted my hips in anticipation of her mouth exploring me. Then nothing happened. I sat up. Nishala had backed up, her expression distorted into pain. Her eyes were on the golden anklet I had been given by Sarvaan.

"Priya, are you unioned?"

"The King said I could either be exiled or be a consort. There are worse things to be than a consort, right?"

I didn't think before I spoke. The madhu was fighting my sense. Nishala tossed my lehenga at me, it fell in my lap.

"You should get dressed...and leave."

I slipped my choli over my head and stepped into the lehenga. The cold, damp cloth shocked my skin. It wasn't warm like she had been moments ago.

"Wait, Nishala, I didn't mean—"

Nishala picked up the same sword I had when Sarvaan first showed up. It was pointed at me this time.

"Leave! I no longer wish to know you." Her eyes turned toxic. I backed away slowly. Tears formed in my eyes. I turned and didn't look back.

No. No, no no. Dammit! I guess this isn't a dream. Dreams don't end like this.

***

When I arrived back home. I just stood in the den, shivering and seething with anger towards myself. My brain hurt from trying to process everything. My clitoris throbbed between my legs. My skin yearned for warmth. I went to my bedroom to lay down and try to sleep off the horrible events that had unfolded. My lehenga hit the floor and I hit the bed.

Don't worry. Sarvaan said he'd take you to see Naga from Shesha Kula tomorrow. It's all going to be fine.

My mind tried to calm me down. But my fogged brain only caught one word: Sarvaan.

Sarvaan would be warm. I got out of bed and walked nude to his bedroom. I watched him for a moment while he slept.

You're fucking hot, Sarvaan. Wow. Those swollen muscles. Those large hands.

I climbed in bed and tucked myself against him under the sheets. He stirred for a moment.

"Priya..."

My mouth was on his before he could speak anymore words. My kiss was hungry for his. I climbed on his chest, straddling him.

"Sarvaan...I need your mouth on me..."

I was straddling his face now. My engorged clit was an inch from his mouth. Without hesitating, he plunged his tongue into the creases of my legs, kissing, biting, and teasing my skin. My hand reached behind me and massaged the pouch containing his cock and testicles until they revealed themselves. I gripped his cock and slid my hand up and down, caressing his balls on the way down.

"Yesssss...." I hissed as if I were already a Nagini. My other hand grabbed his head and pressed his face between my legs. I felt his forked tongue go into a frenzy on my clit. The tips of the forked portion pricked my clit and labia in a way that made my hips buck forward.

"Fuck...oh shit..." I felt Sarvaan's lubrication fluids leaking from his dick. I gathered them and used them to make my hands slick and stroke him faster. I bathed his balls in his own fluids on each trip down. I felt the warmth of Sarvaan's mouth expand over my entire pussy lips and clit. His mouth had widened beyond what a human could and covered all of me between my legs. He alternated sticking his long tongue into my pussy, writhing it around, then swirled around my clit.

"Oh yeah...Yes...Yes!"

I felt one of his large fingers enter me as his tongue danced on my clit and thighs. His fingers were almost as big around as a human dick. I moved my hips up and down on his finger. I kept pulling his face between my legs as he worked his tongue magic on me.

"Sarvaan...I'm there...give it to me!" Time stopped. Nothing made a sound. My eyes rolled into the back of my head. My spine bent as far as it would go. A howl of ecstasy pierced the silence. My body was shaking and tears filled my eyes. All of the events of the day had exploded in my brain all at the same time as I exploded on Sarvaan's face. I sat on Sarvaan's chest trembling like a leaf in a typhoon. His hands stroked my back and sides.

"I'm here Priya...I'm here...you're ok."

Oh, you wonderful fucking man. I'm glad you're not a dream.

I got off the bed and kneeled beside his waist. My hands returned around his cock and I stroked with full force.

"Cum for me Sarvaan. It's your turn."

"Priya, Agh!"

His cock started to spasm. I leaned forward and gulped it into my mouth, sucking as hard as I could. A burst of warm, thick, oil-like fluid filled my mouth. When my mouth was full his cum spilled out of the corners of my mouth all over my tits. I pressed my breasts together and rammed his cock between my tits. It was a rush feeling the warmth flow down my nipples and belly. The river of cum slid down my clit and pussy lips. I would have mounted and fucked him if I wasn't so tired. I sucked on the tip of his cock softly as Sarvaan rode out his orgasm. Each time I sucked his body quivered from sensitivity. I removed my mouth and climbed back in bed beside him.

"That was amazing, Priya." I kissed him. His fluids on my mouth mixed with my fluids that were on his mouth. I snuggled to his chest, listening to his heartbeat. It was racing at first, then it calmed down.

"You deserve it, Sarvaan. You're a good man."

And I want to be with you. I want to have a life with you. I want to love you. I'm glad you're not a dream.

Chapter 7
Prayer ~ भाई

For the second day in a row I woke up on the couch wrapped in a cocoon of blankets. I hoped that I wasn't doomed to repeat yesterday's chain of awful events. There were some great moments, but the bad ones scarred my mind.

Balnak's fingers cutting into my arm. Sneaking away from Sarvaan like a thief. Nishala's face cutting into me more than the sword she pointed at me ever could. What a shit day.

"Hello, beautiful." My heart fluttered like a hummingbird was trapped inside me.

Sarvaan put another tray of breakfast on the table in front of the couch. This time there were green berries connected in a string of ten or twelve, and large fist-sized mushrooms filled with cheese.

"Sarvaan, you're so pleasant to wake up to." I noticed he was wearing a ceremonial looking cloak today as I took a bite of cheese stuffed mushroom.

"Gah, I'm only making you the good stuff to make you love me." I choked on a mushroom. We both chuckled.

Sarvaan, you've already got me hooked.

"What's with the cloak? Special occasion?" I reached out and touched the fabric. It was rigid to the touch. He sat beside me, coiling his tail about my waist lightly and caressing me with his tail pearls.

"Yes, there's a practice we Naga do here called astral meditation. We meditate and bond with the triloka..." I knew what he was going to say before his words came out. I enjoyed the deep hum of his voice in the morning, so I let him continue.

Triloka, the universe of three realms.

"That's the three realms of the cosmos…"

Svarga, the celestial realm.

"There's svarga, celestial abode of the devas…"

Bhuloka, the mortal realm.

"Bhuloka, realm of the mortals, where you're from…"

Patala, the nether realm.

"And Patala, where we are now." He glanced down, as if he was embarrassed. "I feel silly, you're a historian in your world. You probably know all of this."

"I do, in fact, but I like hearing you speak. Astral meditation is new to me though. How does it work?" His fingers played with my hair, twirling it around, letting it fall, and repeating the process. It felt heavenly.

"Well there's a special grove in Bhogavati that has a connection to the three realms. The trees there have roots that go so deep into the ground that they reach every realm. We meditate under their leaves and the trees help amplify our minds and spirits to connect with others across the realms. Sometimes we connect with those seeking enlightenment, sometimes with those already enlightened, and sometimes those praying for others."

So it's like a projection of consciousness. I wonder if I could somehow connect with my family.

"Could I come along? I'd like to experience it with you." I hugged his arm. It was so thick he probably could lift my whole body with just one of his arms.

"Of course, I hoped that you would." His face lightened with happiness.

"Excellent, let me dress and I'll be ready." I stood. I felt a pop on my ass when I went to go to my bedroom. I looked back to see Sarvaan shaking his tail pearls at me as if they were a rattle. He smiled innocently.

Naughty, Naughty. I love it.

After I slipped into a matching ceremonial cloak, Sarvaan took me to the astral grove. As we neared the grove, I felt the noise of the city streets die down.

It was as if there was a dome of silence around the grove to create an atmosphere ideal for concentration.

"Are there any rules I should be aware of?" My arm wrapped around his as we walked.

"No loud noises. Keep talking to a whisper. The goal is to connect with the realms, everything happens internally."

"Sounds simple enough. Do you think me being a human will change anything?"

"I'm not sure, you're the first human to set foot here."

The weight of that statement squashed my brain.

I amthe very first human to be here.

We rounded a corner and I stopped. In front of us was a grove of about fifteen parijat trees. Their trunks were thick enough to drive a car through. They sported roots that buried into the ground at a completely downward angle. The trees carpeted the area with white flower petals. A heavy jasmine aroma filled my lungs with sweet, floral air.

"It's beautiful." I sighed out the fragranced air from my lungs.

"Not as beautiful as you are, but yes, a sight to see." I melted into a puddle of Priya.

"Oh you. You're the beautiful one." Sarvaan pretended to flip his reptilian hood on the back of his head as a woman would flip her hair seductively.

I like goofball Sarvaan. I need more of this.

"Come, here's a secluded place for us." He took my hand and led me to the third tree into the grove. This tree had no one else under it. There were almost a hundred other Naga dispersed between the entire area. They sat in quiet contemplation. Serenity covered their faces.

"So I just...calm my mind and meditate?"

"That's all to it, yes." Sarvaan picked a comfortable position to curl his tail in and closed his eyes. He placed his hands on his gorgeous swollen chest muscles.

I think I won't grab my tits while I do this.

I sat, folding my legs, letting my knees rest on the thick, petal covered carpet of the ground. At first I didn't feel anything.

Come on, universe, what do you have for me? Who needs me?

The sounds and smells of the grove disappeared. I tried to open my eyes but I couldn't.

"Om Namah Shivaya...Mahadev..." a young man's voice filled my head.

Wait, I've heard that voice before...

"My sister Priya is missing..."

No. It can't be. It's Vikram. Vikram! I'm not missing, bhai! *I fell into Patala!*

"Please protect her from evil if she is in danger..."

Vikram! Can you hear me? I'm not in danger! I love you brother! Tell Papa and Maa that I love them!

When I came back to consciousness my hand was clamped over my mouth and my eyes were swollen with tears. My hyperventilation made Sarvaan open his eyes. He immediately saw I was in distress and picked me up, leading me out of the grove and around the corner. As soon as we were out of the grove I collapsed to the ground on my hands and knees and wept loudly, choking out sobs.

"It was him! It was Vikram! He thinks I'm missing!" Sarvaan's arms were around me like a shield of warmth, protecting me from anything that would try to harm me.

"Hey, what are you talking about? What did you see?"

"I saw my brother..." Tears fell out of me like a waterfall. I could barely speak through the sobs. My chest hurt like a bowling ball had been thrown into it.

"He prayed. That I. Be protected. From evil. My family...my family..." I couldn't finish my thought, I jumped to the safety of Sarvaan's chest and put a large pool of tears on his cloak. He didn't say anything, he just held me and rubbed my back.

"My family thinks something horrible happened to me." I managed to put together a whole sentence through my tears now. Sarvaan wiped away my current layer of tears with his fingers.

"Well then, we'd best go talk with the Shesha archivists and see if they can help you speak to your family, or project yourself to them somehow to let them know you're alright."

I nodded my head through the sobs.

"I'd like that very much."

Don't worry Papa, Maa, Vikram. I'm going to find a way to let you know I'm okay.

***

As I walked with Sarvaan to visit the grand archives of Shesha Kula, my pace was noticeably slower. Sarvaan's hand on my back helped dull the pain that my emotions were experiencing. I stopped, taking Sarvaan's hand.

"Sarvaan. I hope you know that I don't regret being here, being with you. My heart just breaks knowing that my family and friends think something terrible happened to me." I kissed his palm and nuzzled it with my face.

"I understand. If I suddenly found myself in another realm and had no way back, I would not be happy either." He smiled. His fingers traced my face.

"Thanks for understanding." I gave his hand a squeeze before walking towards the Shesha Kula neighborhood of Bhogavati.

Suddenly the Naga scales changed from green and blue to white and silver. I noticed the Nagas of Shesha Kula were calmer than the Nagas from Sarvaan's neighborhood. Towards the back of the neighborhood I noticed the towers of a castle-like building starting to appear. It looked ancient compared to the buildings around it.

"The grand archives, it's where we're going. It's one of the oldest buildings in Bhogavati." Sarvaan must have seen me staring.

I wonder what sacred knowledge is buried in this place. Of all the knowledge in all the realms, I just needed one specific piece of it.

As we entered the grand archives, it was as if I'd traveled to yet another new realm. Statues of Saraswati, goddess of knowledge and wisdom, were in almost every corner of the place. They weren't gray, weathered stone statues, they were painted and pristine. The goddess rode on the back of a swan while playing a veena. Her white dress was mesmerizing. My hands touched one of the statues. My fingers danced across the goddess and her swan.

Om Aim Saraswatyai Namaha. I ask to find the knowledge I seek. Knowledge that will allow my heart to go to Sarvaan, and my family to know I am alive and well. Knowledge to bridge my two worlds together.

Sarvaan's hand found my shoulder.

"They're ready for you. This way, in the vault of knowledge." He pointed to a hallway off to the side and I followed.

The hallway led to a large area with high ceilings. It was full of bookshelves being attended to by the archivists there. A Nagini dressed in a silver robe met us as we entered.

"Ah, hello, Sarvaan. So this is your consort." She extended a hand to me. I took it and she gave my hand a gentle squeeze.

"My name is Keshira, It's a pleasure to meet you. Sarvaan tells me you have a request for knowledge that Shesha Kula may be able to help with?"

"The pleasure is all mine, Keshira. And yes, I was wondering if you've heard of any ways to turn someone into a Naga?"

The confused tilt and expression worried me. We were in a realm of untold mysticism, after all.

"I haven't heard of any such thing happening in our history. Apologies."

All of my hopes and dreams were destroyed by one sentence. I felt a lump growing in my throat.

"No problem. Thank you anyway." This was all I could manage to say. Keshira walked away and Sarvaan put his arm around me.

"Don't worry my dear. I'll keep investigating this and see if any of the other kulas have more information."

Sarvaan, you have a heart of gold.

I moved slowly as we exited the vault. Sarvaan rounded the corner into the hallway before I did. I felt my cloak being tugged on and turned around. It was another shesha archivist.

"Just because it hasn't happened before doesn't mean the answer doesn't exist." His voice was a whisper. My face lit up.

"An exile known as Nishala holds the knowledge you seek." My face dropped again and the archivist went back to his duties just as Sarvaan came back into the room.

"Priya? I thought I'd lost you."

"Sorry, I was looking around and lost track of time." Lying to him felt like knives on my tongue. I doubt he'd approve of me learning from an exile.

Great, the only person who can help me is angry at me. I wonder what she did to earn her exile? I've got to figure out how to fix things with her.

***

Sarvaan took me a lengthy way home, showing me the sights of Bhogavati to cheer me up. He showed me the various Naga cuisines as we strolled around Bhogavati. A memorable one was a flavored ice dessert made with rose syrup and that extra juicy fruit I tried when I first arrived. I left some syrup on my face after a particularly excited first bite and Sarvaan leaned down and kissed it from my face. He had some on his fingers and I brought his hand to my mouth to suck it off for him. His fingers probably stayed in my mouth longer than they should.

Sarvaan, you gorgeous Naga with your gorgeous face.

As we sat on stone benches enjoying the scenery of Bhogavati, I realized that I'd never seen any currency exchange since I arrived here.

"Sarvaan, why haven't I seen any payment exchanges for food or other goods?"

"We don't have currency here in Naga-Loka. Naga are the guardians of treasure, we have hoards of it in our vaults. Currency would be priceless here, which would defeat the purpose of a currency."

"So, everything is...free?"

"To a degree, yes. We are very communal as you've seen. We offer goods and services at no cost in currency, but each member of our kingdom is expected to contribute to the kingdom in some way."

A world free of capitalism. Interesting. The concept crippled my brain.

"The treasure you speak of, where do the Naga get it? What happens to it ultimately?"

"We gain treasure either through trade with other kingdoms, or from offerings given by mortals. We guard it in our vaults and use it to trade with other kingdoms that have more currency-oriented cultures. Most of the treasure goes towards completing the prayer cycle with offerings. You've already seen how we perform astral meditation. We hear the calls and prayers of people from across the realms. Once we hear a prayer or call to the gods, we make an offering in treasure to complete the cycle."

"Vikram prayed to Lord Shiva for my safety. Is there a way to complete the cycle for his prayer?"

"Absolutely. Write down his prayer and we'll drop it off at Lord Shiva's temple on the way home."

He produced a small piece of parchment from his cloak.

"Do you have something to write with?" His hand collected mine and placed it on the parchment.

"Let your soul do the writing. Reflect on what you heard."

I closed my eyes with my hand on the parchment and thought back to my astral meditation. I heard Vikram's voice again. Praying to protect me from evil. When I opened my eyes there were tears in them. Vikram's prayer was on the parchment. I held it to my chest and wept softly as Sarvaan's arm comforted me.

"What do you say we drop this off at the temple so its cycle can be fulfilled?"

"I'd like that," I said through my tears.

When we arrived at the temple to Lord Shiva, Sarvaan led me to an alcove within it where an offering bowl was placed. Incense and candles burned around it. There was already a pile of parchment in the bowl.

"So I just place it here?"

"Yes. A representative from the Bhogavati treasury will collect them, allocate an offering from the treasure vaults, and then have an archaka from the temple make the offering."

I placed the parchment on the stack in the bowl and stared at the tiny flames of the candles for a few minutes. Sarvaan stood behind me with his hands on my shoulders. My hand reached up to touch his.

Don't worry Vikram, your prayer will not go to waste.

***

When we arrived home, I went to my bedroom to lie down for a nap and process the day. Right as I sat down, Sarvaan entered my room.

"There's a natural hot spring in the basement. Why don't we soak and let the water cleanse your mind?"

Oh, we have a private hot tub. That will be lovely.

"That sounds grand. I'll be there in a moment."

He smiled and exited the doorway. I looked through the clothes I was given and didn't see anything resembling a swimsuit. Then a thought hit me.

Why would Naga have bikinis? They can control water. Water is their domain.

I decided to go nude and give Sarvaan a sight to see after the warmth and generosity he's shown me. I found my way to the basement and was met with a sheet of warm mist on my skin. When I reached the spring, Sarvaan was already soaking. He was nude as well. The water produced an eye-catching sheen on his emerald and sapphire chest scales. He was definitely happy to see me without clothes. I wasn't in the emotional state for sex, knowing that I had to find a way to get Nishala to forgive me in order for me to see my family again, but I was happy to give Sarvaan the sight of my bare body.

"Arre wah! This is warmer than I expected." I dipped my feet and then my body into the pool of hot water and leaned against the rock wall that made up the border around it. The pool was just right for two people.

"Yes, any hotter and it would cook us."

"Sarvaan, I want to thank you for being so kind and patient with me." My legs reached out and tangled into his serpentine coils.

"We are unioned, Priya. You never have to thank me for being kind or patient with you. I always will be."

I'd obviously had some misconceptions about being a consort since I arrived here. I swam into Sarvaan's lap, pressing my breasts to his chest scales. His large arms wrapped around me, encasing me entirely.

"What does being unioned mean, exactly?"

"It means we are devoted to each other. It means we lift each other up when we are down. Being unioned means being soul companions."

My heart stopped and beat faster at the same time. He was essentially my husband, and I his wife. I was married. My hand went to his face.

"I'm sorry if I haven't been acting like a soul companion for you. I didn't quite realize that's what being your consort meant. I didn't understand what any of this has meant." His hands rubbed and scratched my back and hips softly.

"I had a feeling that was the case. As I've told you, I understand this has been a shock for you. You've had to give up your world and learn a new one. I was willing to wait."

I leaned forward and kissed his lips. I kissed his chin and his chest. My mouth opened and found his open mouth. Our tongues danced like lovers under the stars. I felt his cock rise from its pouch and kiss my labia. Our mouths pushed closer into each other.

"You don't have to wait any longer." I said into his mouth.

I turned, putting my back on Sarvaan's chest, cuddling up to him to relax in the warmth of the water and his arms around me. I put his cock between my ass cheeks and rubbed them against him slowly. I felt his hands go to my hips, guiding my ass to grind on him. I took his arms and wrapped myself in them like a blanket.

"Tell me what's on your mind, Sarvaan. I want to know what your aspirations are, what you dream of." His arms tightened around me.

"Well, lately my mind has been on the trial. Ever since I became an adult I've always wanted to be a leader and inspire my people."

The thought of my husband being a King sent chills through me even through the hot water.

"Do you know the other competitors?"

"A few of them, yes."

"Will it be strange competing in combat with them?"

"Not really. It's all good fun and ritual. The fights aren't to the death, and there are rules against mutilation or torture."

"Good, I won't become Naga-Loka's first human widow then."

"I'll see to it that you don't. I would never let you be without me."

This man. Oh, this man.

After drying off from our soak in the hot spring, we sat tangled on the couch, talking as the light from the jewels softened to indicate sleep time.

"It's been a day. I'm so tired." My fingers traced Sarvaan's bulging shoulder muscles as we talked.

"I can retire and allow you to get some sleep." My arms clutched him, not letting him up.

"Stay with me." His body relaxed.

"Okay Priya, I'll stay." His hand played with my hair. It fell on his chest like a silk blanket.

"When does your first fight in the trial happen?"

"Two days from now."

"I'd like to go, and cheer you on."

"I'd have it no other way."

Sarvaan's fingers dragged through my hair, over my head, down my neck, and to my shoulders. Then he'd repeat the process. I started falling asleep. My face nuzzled his and landed on his chest.

I think I love you, Sarvaan...I think I love you.

Chapter 8
Ritual ~ बंधन

I woke up yet again wrapped in blankets on the couch. I started to feel like I was in a time loop, destined to repeat the same morning over and over. On the table in front of the couch there was incense and candles lit today. A rolled up parchment paper sat next to the setup. There was also a wine bottle.

I wonder what the occasion is?

Sarvaan slithered into the den from the kitchen, placing a bowl of breakfast on the table. This time the meal was some sort of snail shell filled with herbs and berries.

"Sarvaan, I don't think my human jaw will be able to eat those shells." He picked one up.

"Oh, they're not for eating, they just flavor the filling." He demonstrated by slurping the herbs and berries from the shell and placing the now empty shell on the plate. Images of him slurping between my legs brought a grin to my face.

"And what's all this?" I asked, sitting up and gesturing to the incense, candles, and wine.

"It's a ritual for newly unioned couples. We drink juulava wine and answer intimate questions."

Oh wow! A couple's drinking game. This will be fun.

"What's juulava?" Sarvaan went to the kitchen to fetch a couple of flute glasses and sat them on the table.

"A citrus fruit here in Naga-Loka. Extremely juicy." My mind thought back to the very first food I tried, at Nishala's camp. I wondered if it was the same fruit.

I'll show you juicy, soul companion.

"I do have to warn you, juulava wine is made stronger than other wines." He poured us each a flute and handed mine to me. We clinked glasses.

"To us." We said it at the same time. I drank from my flute with a smile on my face, never losing eye contact with Sarvaan.

My mouth filled with a burst of sweet and sour at the same time. As I swallowed, my throat was bathed in strong fumes from the alcohol.

Okay, now we're talking.

"Are you ready to begin the bonding ritual?" He grabbed the rolled up parchment.

"Yes, let's bond." A smile made its way to my face. Sarvaan unrolled the paper.

"What are your aspirations for our union?" His eyes locked onto mine.

"Being true to you. Holding you up as you hold me up. A complete and perfect union." I took another gulp of wine. "How about your aspirations for us?"

"I want you to feel like you belong. I want to protect you from anything that would do you harm. I'd like to have a union that makes me the best man I can be."

He handed me the parchment but my mind was replaying his answer in my head. I snapped back to the present moment and read the next question to myself first.

Oh, this will be a good one.

"What is your favorite body part on your companion that's below the neck? Oh, Sarvaan, this ritual wants us aroused!" We both blushed a bit and drank more.

"Yes the discussion from the bonding ritual can get sensual."

"I'm all for it. So what body part of mine below the neck gets you going?" I teased him. His eyes went to my mid-section.

"Your hips." His hand went to my hip.

"Why is that?" I inched closer with a curious grin.

"They're good for pulling, gripping, and touching. And they lead to your rear and legs." I slapped Sarvaan playfully on the chest. My hand hit with a warm, firm thud.

"Oh you! Sarvaan, you naughty thing. I like when you talk dirty to me." His hand gripped my hip.

"Your turn. What part of me do you favor?"

My eyes shot to his muscular chest. I slipped into his lap and rubbed my hands all over them. He let out a breath of excitement.

"Your chest. It's so strong and hot and large." His arms brought me in for a quick kiss before I slipped off of his lap back to the spot beside him. We took another drink of juulava wine.

"I'll keep it nice for you as I condition for the trial." He puffed his chest out at me. I was wet instantly. I handed him the parchment. He looked at the paper and set it down. His face relaxed from the playful expression he was wearing.

"What are you afraid of?"

"Oh, this ritual decided to get serious." I thought about it. I was afraid of so many things at the moment.

"I'm most afraid that I won't see my family ever again, that they'll think I fell down a hole and just died lonely and alone." I gulped. My chest felt heavy.

"I'm afraid I've found the perfect man and that there's no way I can have both worlds." I choked back a sob, Sarvaan's tail wrapped my waist and his tail pearls caressed my arm.

He warned me the wine was strong. I went from horny to crying.

"I have a similar fear." My interest piqued.

"Really?"

"I'm afraid you'll find a way back to your world and I'll have to lose you." My arms were around his neck and my ass was back in his lap. I kissed him hard.

"Let's make sure that doesn't happen, Sarvaan. Deal?"

"Yes, I agree." His hand touched my face. It was so large that it covered my head from my hair to my chin. His expression changed again. He was thinking.

"I have an idea. Take a walk with me. I'd like to show you something."

I'll go anywhere in the universe with you, husband.

***

Sarvaan's hands were wrapped around my head, creating a make-shift blind-fold. He told me he was taking me somewhere to surprise me. We must have walked about ten minutes with me stumbling around tipsy and in darkness.

"Almost there, just one more block." He giggled as we tried to walk as one. His breath in my ear ignited my libido.

"Okay, we're here. Ready?"

"Yes..."

His hands moved from my eyes and before me was a botanical garden of untold beauty. Exotic plants and flowers of all kinds made shapes and walkways that stretched into secret areas. The plants were decorated with the same glowing jewels found in all of Bhogavati. The jewels pulsed and flashed to create an intimate atmosphere.

"Let's go explore, shall we?" Sarvaan kissed my head. My hand went to his and I took in the beauty of the place.

As we walked and marveled at the beauty of this place, I hung on Sarvaan's arm like a jungle woman on a tree branch. There were painted and well cared for statues of deities in the garden as well. There was Shiva and his third eye, and Vasuki in serpent form around his neck. I saw Ganesha with his elephant head and broken tusk. And there was Manasa, with serpents forming a canopy over her head. I was in archaeological bliss.

"Was this a good surprise?" My hands tightened around Sarvaan's arm.

"It's extraordinary. Thank you."

After about an hour of wandering around, we found ourselves in a secluded circular shaped area of the garden with a stone pillar in the middle. I stopped next to the pillar and admired the red and yellow flowers in this area. Sarvaan stood behind me with his arms around me. His fingers were gripping my hips.

The juulava wine coursing through my veins told me to be naughty. I spun around and backed up slowly, motioning him to follow.

"Come here..."

A curious grin splashed across his face. My back hit the stone pillar and I turned so my ass was against Sarvaan's body.

"And just what is on your mind, Priya?" He asked innocently as my ass pushed and rubbed the spot where his genital pouch was. His dick was produced on cue.

"Take me. Now. Right here." I shed my clothes to the ground around my ankles.

"Here? Now?" He looked around more.

"Yes. Grab my hips and take me. My hips are your favorite body part, remember?" I rubbed his already hard cock between my ass cheeks, letting it slide over my asshole and labia.

"I remember well." He gripped my hips as I leaned against the stone pillar with my ass out toward him. He entered me without resistance due to my wetness, which had been building up. My pussy remembered and relished his wide base; I squealed each time the base slammed into me.

"Han, aise hi. Give me all of you." My hand shot between my legs and I played with my clit.

"Jaan...you feel so good."

You're so hot and you're mine and I love you Sarvaan.

As Sarvaan pounded me from behind and I played with myself I felt heat building in me.

"Aur...give me more! Fuck me like the warrior you are!" Sarvaan easily lifted my hips from the ground and fucked me hard as my legs flew around like flimsy grass in the wind. His scrotum made a wet slap against my labia with each thrust.

"I'll give it all to you..." He moaned.

"I'll take everything you can give. Don't you dare hold back." My words hissed back at him.

I felt the pressure exploding. Sarvaan sensed it and pushed my legs back on the ground as my body seized and shook. Sarvaan's arms wrapped me as I reveled. I took his hands and put them back on my hips and leaned against the pillar once more.

"We're not done yet. It's your turn, darling."

I rubbed my ass on his still hard cock. Sarvaan started back slow and worked his way to long, hard strokes.

"Ahh, fuck..." Sarvaan's moans rippled through me, the bass in his voice vibrating my legs.

I felt his tail swaying about on my leg. I brought it up to my ass as he pumped into me over and over.

"Put it in my ass again."

I felt a pearl enter my asshole.

"Haan...aur..." Sarvaan lifted me from the ground to get a better angle for double penetration.

Pop. Another pearl slid inside me.

"Yes! Aur andar..." I felt his tail tense as the final pearl was pushed into my ass. I'd never felt so full in my life.

Pop.

"Fuck! You drive me crazy, my whole body."

I heard footsteps around the corner. A Naga rounded the corner and saw Sarvaan wildly thrashing into me with his tail pearls in my ass. I felt him start to slow. I bucked my hips at his cock in protest. The Naga appreciated our privacy and left.

"I told you not to stop. Warriors don't stop. They keep fucking."

"Yes love, I won't stop."

That's better. You keep going until you fill me with your seed.

The image of the Naga looking at us in the act excited something in me. My nipples hardened. My hips shot back to meet Sarvaan's strong thrusts. Each thrust pumped on the tail pearls, sending shockwaves through my ass and pussy at the same time. I know he noticed. His pace and intensity picked up.

"I'm close..." He was on the edge.

"That's it Sarvaan. Fuck me. Fill me!"

I shot my hips backwards as hard as I could. Each of his thrusts slammed his four inch base into me. I let out an audible scream of pleasure each time the base squeezed through.

"Fuck me...like you mean it..."

I felt his cock start to pulse.

"Fill me with cum...I'm your dirty consort..."

It writhed inside of me, slapping my inner walls.

"Fuck me like you love me!"

A hot explosion filled me with his seed. I felt it run down my leg and splash on the ground.

Bingo. I found the magic words. I guess he does love me.

I put my clothes back on in time for my legs to stop working. They ached from standing and getting pounded from behind. We both collapsed on a bench nearby and held each other. We panted in each other's face, exchanging slow kisses.

"I have to admit, that was a first, Priya...making love in public."

"It was for me, too." I sucked softly on his lips as I pulled away from a kiss. "I loved it."

I love it, and I loved you...and I love you.

Chapter 9

Bargain ~ निर्वासन

Sarvaan spent the rest of the day showing me more of Bhogavati. By the time we got home the jewels in the streets had dimmed, and we were ready for bed. This evening it had grown colder than the last few nights. Sarvaan noticed my visible shivers.

"There's extra blankets in your room's closet if you need them."

"I know where you are if I get too cold." I leaned up and he bent his head to kiss me. It was a slow kiss with a single *smack* at the end of it.

"Yes, yes you do. Sleep well, Priya."

He left for his bedroom and I turned to go to mine. I felt a slap on my ass. I spun around and saw no one. Sarvaan's head peeked around the corner with a mischievous grin. I laid there staring at the ceiling for a few moments, fidgeting with my fingers.

Alright, time to win over Nishala and see what she knows about Naga transformation.

I made my way to the kitchen and retrieved a bottle of madhu. This would be my peace offering. Now that I knew what my union to Sarvaan meant, I'd need other means to convince Nishala to share her secrets with me. I waited a few minutes to sneak out until I heard Sarvaan's breathing calm so that I knew he was sleeping. As I made my way to the city gates, I felt a hand grab my ass and squeeze again. I stopped dead in my tracks.

Oh no, Sarvaan heard me, he's going to ask where in the world I'm going with a bottle of madhu. I don't know what to say.

When I turned around, my situation worsened considerably. It wasn't Sarvaan behind me: it was Balnak.

"Well nowwww...where are we off to tonight?" There was a rattling rasp to his syllables.

"Uff! Balnak what do you think you're doing? I told you I'm spoken for, you can't touch me like that."

His tail shot out like a spear and wrapped my legs and my waist in his coils. He slowly pulled me towards him. I tried to remove his coils but he was easily ten times stronger than me.

"Balnak you bastard! Get off me!" I started hitting his tail with my fists.

His coils tightened around my legs, squeezing them together. I couldn't move them at all. Then I felt his tail pearls stroking my ass.

"Oh don't worry, I'll get off. You could too if you were more open minded."

Shitting fuck...I'm about to be raped and the only person who can save me doesn't know I snuck out.

Balnak had me face to face now. With one yank he pulled my robe up revealing my nude lower body.

"Balnak, if you don't unhand me...I'll be the one to put you down like the uncivilized beast you are." I felt his cock come out of the genital pouch and stiffen against my leg. His hands squeezed my bare ass cheeks.

"Has anyone told you that you have a foul mouth? Let's wash it out shall we?" His forked tongue flicked out of his mouth and slapped my lips.

As I prepared myself to have to bite off a penis, a group of Naga slithered on to the block me and Balnak were on. They were talking and laughing loudly. This made Balnak drop his concentration and release his coils around my legs. I ran faster than I ever had before. When I got to the city gates, the guards were alarmed. One of them approached me.

"Priya Karkota, you are fiercely winded!" Concern was in his voice.

I looked back, but Balnak was nowhere to be found.

"No no, I'm fine, just getting my nightly exercise."

I really have to start coming up with better lies.

***

On my way to Nishala's camp, I traded the sweet air of Bhogavati, always with a smokey incense fragrance hanging in the streets, for the earthy and floral scents of the hills, forest, and grassy groves of the Naga-Loka wilderness. I had noticed the chill in the air before I left, but as I traversed the terrain between the city and Nishala's camp I noticed it even more with no walls to protect me.

It was especially cold after I used the river to transport me quickly from one side of the hills to the other. After exiting the river I was in the forest again. I coughed water from my lungs.

I hope I get the hang of river travel and don't drown myself.

I wrung the water from my hair, then took off my robe and did the same to it. There was something freeing about being completely nude and wet in the forest. The jewels in the trees were dimmed to dusk level of brightness, casting patches of soft, intimate light on my skin. I put my robe back on after getting as much water out as I could. I looked up to the sky.

Oh wow, the stars are pretty...

I realized Naga-Loka was in Patala, which is a subterranean set of realms. Those weren't stars above me, they were the same jewels found around this realm, embedded in a cavernous ceiling. After taking a moment to admire the starry cavern ceiling, I headed for Nishala's camp. When I exited the treeline I saw the fire going in front of her tent in the distance.

I hope she doesn't impale me with her sword before I have a chance to apologize.

As I waded through the tall grass, I saw Nishala cooking something in a large pot over the fire. She rose, alert and swift like a fighter, as I came into sight.

"I remember telling you that I didn't want to see you again." After confirming I was not a threatening presence, she sat back down on the log she used as a bench.

"Yeah, well you also told me to bring you some madhu. I just wanted to be thorough." I sat the bottle of mead down next to her.

"I suppose our dealings are finished then. You may leave." Her eyes didn't move from the fire.

I took a deep breath.

"Look, Nishala, I apologize for the other night—"

"I said you may leave!" She rose again, towering over me like all the Nagas here did.

"No! Now dammit you're going to hear me out!" I stomped my foot and flailed my hands. She looked surprised and intrigued.

"I was almost raped coming here tonight by a warrior that my husband is competing in the Trial of The Crown against. My family thinks something terrible has happened to me, and I have no way to communicate with them. My world has literally been taken away from me!" My voice broke as tears gushed out of my eyes. I covered my mouth and cried into it.

All Nishala could do was stand there, her face and eyes softened, but she couldn't find words.

"I didn't know what the meaning of being unioned was in this world until recently. I'm sorry for leading you on." My hand reached out and touched hers, squeezing it.

"I need your help if I'm to ever see my family again, or my world." Her eyes furrowed with confusion.

"Priya, I'm truly sorry for what's happened to you, but how in Patala am I supposed to help you get back to Earth?"

I stepped closer.

"I've been to the grand archives. An archivist there told me that you know of a way to transform someone into a Naga."

Nishala grinned, taking her hand back and slithering in circles around me.

"Priya, I'm so proud of you. You've only been in Naga-Loka a few days and you've done so much research."

"I'm a resourceful woman. I'm a scientist in my world. Knowledge is power." Nishala stopped circling me.

"Fine, I'll tell you how to become a Nagini, but I have a condition."

"Name it!" I stepped toward her.

"Let me teach you warrior combat, then I want you to enter the Trial of The Crown."

Um...what? Did she just say that?

"Wait...um...why?"

"Do you care? Ultimately you want the knowledge I possess. This is the cost of my knowledge."

"Nishala, Naga warriors are much stronger than me, weigh four times as much as me, and stand at least two feet taller than me."

"So you doubt my abilities as a teacher then?"

"Of course not. Fine. I'll do it."

A grin crawled across her lips. It was a grin I'd seen as a scientist plenty of times in my life. It was a grin that signaled the start of an exciting experiment.

"Excellent. Next time you visit, your training begins."

I keep digging myself deeper and deeper in this place.

She produced a dagger from a sheath around her waist and handed it to me.

"What's this for?" I played with it in my hand, to get a feel for it.

"For stabbing men who choose to hear *yes* when you say *no*."

***

When I returned home and was in the safety of my bedroom I shed my damp robe to the floor and climbed into bed wrapping myself in blankets. I lay there, thinking about the events of the day. The bonding ritual. The garden sex. How much it excited me to get caught getting pounded into ecstasy. My growing love for Sarvaan. My heart fluttered thinking back to Sarvaan's description of our union.

Being unioned means being soul companions.

I cringed as my mind revisited my encounter with Balnak. Anxiety filled me as I recounted Nishala's condition. Excitement replaced the anxiety because she didn't say no. She didn't say she couldn't. There was a way forward. I shivered as the colder than usual air pierced my blankets and my nude form underneath. I thought of piling blankets on top of me, but my body wanted Sarvaan's warmth. I got out of my bed and walked down the hall to the master bedroom. I opened the door quietly, staring at Sarvaan under the dim glow of the jewels in the walls.

You beautiful man.

He was lying on his side, so I got into bed under the sheets with him and laid on my side facing him. I snuggled to his chest which made him stir out of sleep and into a half-woken state.

"Priya?"

I kissed his lips and ran my hands over his chest scales.

"Yes darling, I'm here."

His hands realized I was nude. They started roaming over my back, my ass, and my legs.

Yes. I'm yours. Your wife. Your soul companion.

His breathing increased as his hands explored me. Torrents of hot breath washed over my face and chest. I could tell he wanted more. It was time I let him.

"Do with me what you wish." His mouth was on mine in an instant. His long, forked tongue played with mine.

His hand grabbed my tits. He was being a bit soft with them. My hand went to his and showed him he could squeeze harder and play with my nipples. I let out a moan into his mouth. It was muffled by his tongue. I kissed back hard, sucking on his tongue. It felt good in my mouth and I wanted more. I used my lips and sucked more of his tongue in my mouth. I took his hand and moved it between my legs. I grabbed one of his fingers and shoved it into my pussy.

"Sarvaan..." My sigh of pleasure filled his mouth as we kissed into each other passionately.

His fingers were the size of an average human dick. I pushed and pulled his hand, fucking myself with his dick-sized finger. He pulled his head back and started kissing and sucking on my neck, shoulders, and chest. I felt immense, warm pressure on my skin where his lips moved.

That's right. Mark me as yours. I am yours.

"Sarvaan, I give all of myself to you." My hips rocked into his hand each time I brought it towards me to fuck his finger.

"If you give yourself, then I will take." His tongue flicked on my ears sending chills and shockwaves through me at the same time.

All of me is yours for the taking, my love.

Because he was so much taller than me and his limbs were longer than a human's, he kissed, licked, and sucked down my chest without having to take his finger out of me. With one flick of his other hand I was rolled to my back and his head shot between my legs. I felt his warm, wet forked tongue treating my clit like royalty. His tongue was large enough that it could easily bathe the entire area between my legs in a couple flicks.

"More...more," I moaned into the air as his tongue made love to my clit and I fucked his finger. Then Sarvaan put a second finger at my pussy's entrance.

Oh Sarvaan, I approve.

"Your body is radiating..." I felt hot breath on my clit when he spoke. My hips bucked at his second finger, trying to put it in me.

"You know you're the one that makes my body hot. Now stop talking and get that other finger in me." He did as commanded. It felt like I was being fucked by two dicks now.

"Oh! Yes! Good warrior, doing as you're told." I noticed his cock was hard and waving in the air. I grabbed it and started working it up and down. When his tongue hit a spot on my clit that I liked I gave it a squeeze for encouragement. The first time I did this, he was surprised and flicked my clit extra hard. I squeezed more and he got the idea. The extra hard flicking made my body convulse with pleasure.

"You like that?" He held back until my hips moved up, commanding his tongue to flick me.

"I do...I do...stop teasing me..." My hand on his cock went to his balls. I played with all five testicles one by one, then ran my fingers over all of them again before returning my grip to his shaft. It was wet from pre-cum. My body was overheating like a nuclear reactor. I needed him in me now, his fingers were pure bliss but nothing compared to his cock. I needed to feel his body on me.

"Sarvaan...I need you in me...come fuck your wife." His body moved faster than I'd ever seen before. He was on top of me, his chest's heavy breathing pressing warmth into my tits.

The tip of his cock pressed into my pussy, then slid in effortlessly because of my wetness. I spread my legs extra wide to get all of him in me. His mouth resumed its mission: kissing me as he slid into me. When the four inch base squeezed its way between my labia I let out a gasp into his mouth of pure pleasure. His hand caressed my hair from front to back as he gave me slow, long strokes of that godly dick of his. At the end of each thrust when the base went in I expelled another gasp of appreciation into his mouth as we kissed slow and hard.

"Sarvaan, I...I..." I whimpered, somewhere between orgasm and falling madly in love with him.

"What is it my dear? What is it?"

"I want you...I need you...I—" My pussy clenched hard around him inside me. "Oh, fuck! Sarvaan!" My fingers dug into the scales on his back as hard as I could. My insides were spasming. Sarvaan noticed how tight I was as I rode my orgasm and picked up the pace fucking my extra tight pussy harder.

"Dammit yes...fuck. My. Tight. Pussy!" His cock went wild writhing inside of me and I felt his hot fluid fill me then overflow out of me running down my legs and ass.

I continued to kiss him. I kissed him like I needed him. I kissed him like I loved him. I kissed him like we were a fairy tale and we were meant to be. As our rhythm slowed and our climaxes faded, I found myself still kissing him. Tears started to fill my eyes. He pulled away noticing the tears and rolled over to his side pulling me to him, holding me close.

"Priya, you're wonderful. I'm so glad you're in my life."

"I'd have it...no other...way." My words came between small, high pitched sobs. The tears were happy tears.

"I feel like since you've been with me, my life has clarity. It has meaning now. I don't just live my life with my own aspirations or actions in mind." His large, warm hands roamed over my back, massaging my exhausted muscles.

"And you've changed my entire world, Sarvaan. Even if I was here forever I'd be glad it was with you."

We laid there for several minutes, just breathing into each other. Sarvaan's breath drew slower and slower. Mine did as well.

"I love you Sarvaan. I truly love you." Sleep was claiming me. I looked to Sarvaan's face to see his reaction to my confession, but he was asleep already.

I just smiled and lay my head on him. My legs and his serpent body were coiled around each other, tangled in a mess of love and lust. I fell asleep in Sarvaan's bed. In *our* bed.

Chapter 10

Stone ~ रक्त

Warm, wet lips kissed my cheek. Then my head. My eyes slowly opened to find Sarvaan leaning over me. His fingers played with my hair as I stretched.

"My handsome warrior." I leaned up to kiss him.

"My stunning queen." He placed his hand on my back to keep me in his face to kiss more.

He lay down next to me, my mouth still locked to his. The sound of our smacking lips filled the room. My clit started to throb and I found myself humping against his body, grinding my engorged clit on him. He pulled away from our kiss.

"We'd better not. Last night was amazing and I don't want to be too sore for my match today."

My clit pouted as my mind raced, remembering his first match of the trial was today. I playfully brought my fist to his cheek.

"You better win so I can give you your prize." I stretched again, making sure to bring my chest up, perking my breasts toward him. As I sighed a cooing exhale from the stretch my hand caressed from my neck, between my breasts, and under the sheets. He placed a quick kiss on my right nipple, making it harden from attention.

"I've already got you. What other prize would I need?" Another kiss to my forehead and he rose from bed.

You do have me, Sarvaan. That's for sure.

After we both had dressed and eaten, we left and headed for the arena. The trial took place in a large arena on the opposite end of the city.

"Do you think I'll be able to get good seats? I'm the shortest person in this realm currently." I stood on my toes and my head didn't even reach Sarvaan's neck.

"Of course, consorts of the competitors have a special area in which to sit. It's the best view in the arena." He laughed and wrapped one arm around me, picking me up to where our heads were at the same height. He didn't even grunt when he picked me up. It looked as effortless as a human picking up a small dog or cat. Everyone looked our way as we walked, Sarvaan holding me high with just an arm.

Oh wow, his forearm is thicker than my leg!

"I love the view, Sarvaan, but I'd rather not have all the attention on me."

As we passed groups of Naga in the streets, I noticed they weren't looking at me, they were looking at Sarvaan.

"Apologies." He chuckled.

He put me down and I looked behind us. People were indeed looking at Sarvaan, not me. I couldn't blame them. He was dressed in warrior's leather armor with Karkota Kula regalia draped over his shoulders. Banners of green and blue flowed into the air as he walked.

Yep, he's mine. All mine.

"Are you nervous about today?"

"Absolutely not. I've been looking forward to this. There's peace in the realms at the moment so there are no wars to fight, nothing to defend Bhogavati from. I get restless when I have nothing to do."

So that's why you've been fucking me so good. All that built up energy. Duly noted.

"Do you know your opponent well? Have you practiced with them before?"

"Dhravan of Vasuki Kula is my opponent today. I've only met him at the ball the other day. I'm sure of my victory today."

Cocky warrior aren't you?

***

Loud horns and trumpets greeted my ears as I walked arm-in-arm into the arena with Sarvaan. The arena was as large as a football stadium, square-shaped, with tiered seating rising around the ground floor where the fighting area was. The fighting area was dirt, with three stone pillars in a line directly in the center. Each pillar was about twenty feet from the next.

I wonder what those are used for? For the competitors to dance around and get cover from their opponents' attacks maybe?

As we entered into the view of the audience, the sea of green and blue scales in the seats began to cheer and slap their tail pearls on the floor in a rhythmic beat. Sarvaan's chest puffed out and his walk changed to a swagger-like strut.

Well look at you, my peacock.

He was in his element. His primal side was beginning to burst from beneath his scales. It was really hot. I wished we had a few moments so he could stuff me with his aggressive energy.

"Sarvaan, they really love you!"

I really love you Sarvaan.

"Karkota Kula at its finest." He declared with a large smile on his face.

You at your finest my dear.

Sarvaan escorted me to a raised platform on the ground level that had the closest view of the fighting area. I felt his fist close around my choli and pull me to his face for a kiss. My hands went around his face and I returned the favor.

"I love you, Priya." He pulled away with his chest heaving, ready for the combat to start.

He loves me. I love him. We can be happy.

"Sarvaan, I—" The words almost became real when trumpets roared across the arena. Sarvaan looked away, spotting King Vasuki walking to the middle of the arena.

"That's my cue. Cheer for me." He released me and I inhaled to fill my lungs to their maximum.

"I LOVE YOU Sarvaan!" The thunderous cheers of the crowd after seeing the King in the arena slapped my words from the air. I wiped a single tear from my eye as King Vasuki gestured for silence. I spotted Sarvaan against one of the three pillars in the fighting area. His opponent was against a pillar on the opposite side.

"It's been a wonderful hundred years. Now it is time for the Trial of The Crown once more." He spoke into a cone shaped shell. It amplified his voice to reach the entire arena like a megaphone.

As the crowd went absolutely wild with cheers, I noticed more Naga started to file into the seating area I was in and sit around me. Their scales were green and blue. These were Sarvaan's people. *My* people.

"It is now my pleasure to introduce the competitors for the first match of the trial. Warriors, positions."

Sarvaan and his opponent Dhravan both wrapped their tails and body coils around their respective pillar and hoisted their bodies into the air. I cocked my head to the side.

What in the world? I guess I've been on the receiving end of Sarvaan's lower body strength, I shouldn't be surprised.

One of the Naga seated by me noticed my confusion.

"During combat they have to stay attached to a pillar, and the first warrior to yield or touch the ground loses the match." His hand pressed on my shoulder. Other hands from other Naga around me pressed on my shoulders in suit. They all started murmuring some sort of chant.

I remembered Nani's chant. The one she told me Prathavi recited as she dispatched her foe.

Durga. Kali. Manasa. If you're listening, let Sarvaan be your servant. Let him be your tool.

"Today's match will be between Sarvaan of Karkota Kula ..." The crowd erupted again. The Naga around me shook me excitedly. I screamed into the air along with them.

"And Dhravan of Vasuki Kula..." More cheers. I noticed them coming from around me. I looked across the arena and spotted another platform with Vasuki Nagas in it.

That must be Dhravan's consort and his people.

"I hereby decree that the Trial of The Crown has begun. Warriors, you may commence at the sound of the horns." The crowd cheered again.

Sarvaan and Dhravan's bodies tensed, holding themselves at least ten feet above the ground, wrapping around the stone pillars. They each produced a sword and shield. The horns sounded. These four hundred pound warriors moved as quickly and gracefully as ballet dancers. They both unwrapped from their current pillar and leapt to the center pillar, wrapping around it and swinging their swords wildly. There were twenty feet between each pillar and they crossed it like a child jumping over a puddle. The arena was filled with sharp metal clangs and grunting of these monstrous men. Seeing Sarvaan performing such feats of strength and aggression made my pussy groan. I pressed my thighs together to stifle its call.

Whoa, is it getting hot or is it just Sarvaan?

Sarvaan parried a strike from Dhravan and shoved him. Dhravan almost fell to the ground but leapt back to his starting pillar. Sarvaan unwrapped from the center pillar and charged the pillar Dhravan was on. Seconds later they were back at it, exchanging blows. Sarvaan parried and caught more strikes on his shield that Dhravan did. Sarvaan was like a machine, his coils tightened around the pillar to hold him up and he flooded constant aggression at Dhravan with no stop in sight. I couldn't look away. I kept catching my breath. Sarvaan was first to draw blood. He slashed Dhravan's arm sending blood and scales flying to the ground. Dhravan mounted a counter strike, angered by the drawing of his blood, catching Sarvaan's body that was wrapped around the pillar.

Oh no!

I'm sure I overreacted. These warriors were only losing a few scales and some drops of blood. It felt like they were losing arms to me. Sarvaan hissed and used his shield to try to bash Dhravan's body, weakening it. Dhravan screamed with each strike of Sarvaan's shield. He looked to have had enough and struck out at Sarvaan, lowering his guard. Sarvaan slashed Dhravan's sword arm, sending the warrior's weapon to the ground. Without his sword, Dhravan retreated to hide behind the pillar and lash out with his shield, but after a few seconds of Sarvaan's relentless strikes, Dhravan unwrapped himself and let his body fall to the dirt below. The match was over.

He won. HE WON!

Cheers, screams, chants, and kissing filled the air in the arena. Sarvaan and Dhravan embraced in respect. The Nagas sitting near me rose and gestured me towards Sarvaan.

"Go on, you're allowed on the field now."

My face lit up and I ran off of the platform and into the dirt in the fighting area towards Sarvaan. I jumped and he caught me, bringing me to his face for a kiss. The crowd chuckled and cheered from this show of affection.

"I knew you could do it, I knew you could do it!" I felt a hand on my butt. Sarvaan lifted me into the air above his head now. He was showing me off like I was the prize instead of the win he'd fought for.

The crowd cheered and chanted harder now, the slapping of their tail pearls on the ground making a melody once more. My face reddened from all of the attention. I was happy for Sarvaan, but my feet touching the ground was a relief. Dhravan's consort and his people walked to us.

"Sarvaan fought valiantly today. Congratulations." Dhravan's consort and I shared a look of mutual respect, Sarvaan bowed before them.

"As did Dhravan. I'm glad he chose to take it easy on me." Sarvaan said while in his bow. Dhravan's consort and people walked off and left me and Sarvaan staring at each other.

The noise of the arena ceased. The sweat and adrenaline seemed to fade. In this moment it was just me and my love. I leaned in close, gesturing for him to give me his ear.

"I never knew you could do that with your body. I guess I have to make you work harder in bed now." I sucked his ear softly, and I felt a smile form on his face.

***

Outside the arena, Sarvaan and I greeted the exiting patrons. He told me it was a custom for the winner to be congratulated and thank everyone for coming. Most of the patrons congratulated me as well, hugging me and touching palms to mine as they left.

I mean, I like the attention, but I didn't really do anything.

King Vasuki was next in line. Sarvaan bowed to the ground and I curtsied.

"Riveting match, Sarvaan. You've definitely honed your skills since I last saw you practice. You fight like you have something to fight for now." Sarvaan's arm draped over my shoulder.

"Some*one* to fight for now."

"That is so delightful. Priya, what did you think of the match?"

"Well I've never seen combat like it before. Even if I had a tail I wouldn't be able to balance on those pillars the way Sarvaan did."

"I think you'll find yourself more capable than you think."

It's like he can see through me. See my desire to become Nagini.

His head snapped toward Sarvaan.

"Sarvaan, may I borrow you away from the crowd for a moment? There's just a few stragglers remaining."

"Of course, your majesty. I have all the time in the world for you."

King Vasuki's head faced me now.

"Don't worry, I'll have him back just in time."

"I find no offense with this, go ahead your highness." I giggled and walked out of the exitway and leaned against a wall. The excitement and social stimulation was starting to drain me. I needed to be home with Sarvaan. I needed intimacy. After a minute or two, I felt a hand on my thigh.

Naughty man.

"Here Sarvaan? Really—" The hand cupped between my legs and squeezed. It was Balnak.

Fool me twice.

I jumped back, slapping his hand away. My hand went to my side. The dagger Nishala had given me was strapped to my upper thigh.

"Who the fuck do you think you're grabbing, Balnak?"

"Hello again, Priya. I was hoping you were thinking about me over here all by yourself."

He advanced toward me putting his hands on my shoulders. I was about to give him a taste of my dagger when a roar shook the stone walls behind him. Green scaled hands wrapped around Balnak and tore him to the ground. Sarvaan. He and Balnak were on the ground fighting like grizzly bears during the rut. Scales and blood flew in all directions.

"Kameene!" Sarvaan roared like a freight train. He threw Balnak against a stone wall, sending cracks through it.

"I'll dismember you with my bare hands!" He was punching wildly with his fists and biting with his fangs. Their bodies and tails were like stray firehoses spraying in the air. I stepped back so I wouldn't get hit. Within a minute guards ripped Sarvaan and Balnak from each other's grasp.

"Break it up! Competitors are not permitted to fight outside of the trial matches!"

It took five Naga guards to calm Sarvaan. Balnak laughed through a series of hisses.

"Why are you delaying the inevitable, Sarvaan? Karkota Kula is no place for Priya. She deserves to be unioned to a real warrior."

"I'll show you a real warrior when I rip your arms from your body."

"You know where to find me if you want to settle this before the trial." Balnak grinned, shrugged off the guards holding him, and slithered into the shadows.

The guards holding Sarvaan let him go as soon as Balnak left. Sarvaan was immediately enveloping me in his arms. His hands checked every part of me from my head to my toes.

"Are you alright? Did he hurt you?"

"Not physically. I'm okay now that you're here. Let's go home."

In my mind I saw a hundred different and horrible ways for Balnak to die.

Chapter 11

Vengeance ~ नशा

"I just wish I could have him tied up in a room alone with a bunch of weapons at my disposal. I'd slit his throat. I'd cut his balls off. I'd feed them to him! Not all in that order of course."

I was tipsy and going further down the rabbit hole of juulava wine as the minutes passed. Sarvaan made dinner and we had eaten on the roof, admiring the starry jewels on the cavern ceiling above us. He thought dinner and drinks might be an avenue to let me emotionally process the day and vent simultaneously. Dinner had been over for an hour, the drinking was still going. My hair was a mess and I was waving my arms around like a mad woman.

"And don't forget to chop off his tail." Sarvaan added and held out a hand as I was about to stumble."

"Yes. Yes! I'd chop his tail off in the mix as well." I fell into Sarvaan's lap. He held me upright with just a finger.

Showoff. You hot, sexy showoff.

"Make me a deal." I grabbed his face.

"Anything, name it." I kissed him.

"Train me to be a warrior. Train me to slit throats and chop off tails."

"And the testicle removal? Shall I teach that as well?"

"No." I stood and twirled around like a dancer. "I think I can handle that."

Sarvaan just watched me, making sure I didn't fall off of the roof or to the stone floor below. I stood there for a moment, breathing heavily. The floral, spiced Bhogavati air filled my lungs.

"My Nani told me I was a Nagini princess. She told me stories of a Nagini warrior who made her foes kneel and call her queen."

"You're my Nagini queen."

Sarvaan, I could squish your stupid handsome face.

"Were her stories just stories? It can't be a coincidence she told me those stories and I ended up here."

Sarvaan slithered over to me, and held me in a slow dancing pose. We started to move. We danced to imaginary music.

"Is that why you made a career out of Naga history?" He dipped me as we danced. On the way up my world spun for a few seconds.

"Yes. It was. When she died I didn't have her to tell me stories anymore, so I went searching for more."

"Don't worry, I'm sure if we ask more Shesha archivists we'll find answers for you. I'm sure of it."

Oh Sarvaan. I already found my answer. I just can't tell you it's from an exile who wants me to compete against you in the trial.

"Thank you for supporting this cause."

"We are unioned. Your causes are mine as well."

He's too damn good to me. I don't fucking deserve it.

"I've told you why I took to history, how did you become a warrior?"

"There was a war about fifty years ago, when I was just a juvenile. I saw many good Naga perish. I wanted to stand for something and do something to honor the Naga we lost."

"So with no wars going on, I bet you've been looking forward to the Trial of The Crown?"

"That's right. Since it only happens every hundred years, I was grateful it would be happening in my lifetime while I'm in my prime. Peaceful times are good for the kingdom, but for warriors who train only to defend and to wage war, it's a cruel peace."

"If the trial wasn't happening and I hadn't come along, what would you be doing?" I laid my head on Sarvaan's chest. I listened to his heart thunder like a car engine in his chest.

"Probably doing drills, getting in practice sparring. Finding ways to stay sharp. There's always someone in the community who needs something heavy lifted."

My mind had been caught up in the events of the day. I had forgotten Sarvaan's declaration of love, and my own back at him. My words were drowned out by the cheering crowd. I removed my head from his chest and my eyes shot up to his.

"I love you Sarvaan. I tried to tell you when you told me earlier but...there was too much noise." His tail wrapped around me softly and brought me up to be face to face. My eyes were gushing with tears. I'd been holding it in all day. He was about to say something, but my hands slammed onto his chest as I tried to get my point across. I bet it just felt like a pebble landing on his thick muscles.

"I'm yours, Sarvaan. And you're mine. You're mine and you've been mine since I first met you. I love you...I love you so much."

I wiped my tears away with the backs of my hands.

I won't let Balnak spoil my mood. I should be flying high right now. Nishala has agreed to share her knowledge on how to turn me into a Nagini. I have this wonderful husband who loves me and will do anything for me and treats me better than I've ever been treated in my life. He's probably going to be the fucking King. I'll actually get to see my family again and have the love of my life. I've won. The only thing in my way is time.

Sarvaan held me against him with one of his arms now and unwrapped his tail from me. I could feel his muscles tensing with aggressive energy still. He held me just tight enough. Anymore pressure and he'd crush me easily.

"I'd ravage entire realms for you, Priya. I'll never hurt you so you'll never leave. There's nowhere you could go where I wouldn't follow."

My mouth was on his in an instant. I found tongue and pulled it out from hiding, demanding it go wild in my mouth. I pulled back and glared into Sarvaan's eyes.

"I command you to ravage *my* realms."

***

"Sit. I want to give you your prize for winning today."

Sarvaan sat on our bed as I told him to. I stroked his genital pouch until his cock and balls came out.

"And what would you have done if I had lost?"

I answered by kneeling in front of him and taking his cock into my mouth. Sarvaan's lower body jittered with anxious energy as I slurped his dick into my mouth over and over. His hand found the back of my head and guided me to the rhythm he wanted. His fingers ran through my hair caressing me with each stroke. His waist bucked forward, making his cock hit the back of my throat. I almost gagged but held it together.

"Here, let me try something." I pulled back, curious as to what he had in mind. He grabbed my hips, turned me upside down and started licking my clit and labia. I was now face to face with his cock again. I took it in my mouth and the room filled with licking, flicking, and smacking sounds. His forked tongue was able to touch my clit and my pussy at the same time and my legs were squirming and tensing.

"Haan...that's perfect...oh yes..." I pulled back to gasp for air and moan loudly as Sarvaan's tongue showed me how inadequate human tongues were.

His was easily nine inches fully extended and forked into two ends at the tip. To show my appreciation, I dove back onto his dick and relaxed my throat to take more of him into my mouth. Sarvaan held me in this position with one hand. His other hand grabbed my legs and spread them further apart. His entire tongue slid into my pussy now.

My toes curled and my knees tensed as his tongue traveled deeper into me than even his cock had. I was breathing hard, exhaling into his balls. I was so far down on his cock. I couldn't fit the four inch base into my mouth, but I was able to relax my throat more and suck more of him into me, closing my lips tight on him and pushing my neck down. I had all of his length in my throat that anatomy would allow.

"Cum for me, my Nagini queen. Cum for me. I want it all over my face." I felt his lip movement and breath on my pussy lips.

His tongue was doing wonders inside of me. Because of its length it was able to lick my cervix softly. It poked into my cervix and penetrated. It wasn't forceful or rough. It was tender. My eyes widened and my heart was racing.

He started playing with my clit while his tongue was in me and I couldn't handle it anymore. I came so hard I screamed. His cock was in my throat so the scream turned into a piercing hum that vibrated his cock and his balls. This, in turn, sent Sarvaan over the edge and I felt his cum start to squirt into me.

"Priya, I can't wait any longer..." He moaned like a primal beast into the now hot air of the room.

You don't have to hold anything back. Give it all to me, my love.

Each pulse of his cock squirted an entire human sized load down my throat. I swallowed hard each time, making sure he could feel my throat clenching him. His body jolted each time I swallowed because of the sensitivity. As I swallowed gulp after gulp of his load, a warm cozy feeling filled my belly. It swelled softly the more I drank. It felt nice. Satisfying. Comfortable. When his pulses of ecstacy ceased, Sarvaan laid back on the bed and I removed him from my throat, gasping for air and laying sprawled out on his chest.

"That was...fucking hot..." I rotated to lay my head next to his.

"You're such a wonderful woman, Priya."

"You have no idea, husband. You have no idea."

***

The hot spring water felt great against my overworked body. Sarvaan and I had migrated into the hot spring in the basement to relax and sober up a bit. Through the steamy mist my hands were holding one of his hands. Both of my hands could fit into his and still have room leftover.

"Your nani's stories, where do you think she heard them?" Sarvaan's giant hand closed around mine.

"She once told me that her bloodline traced back to the Naga tribes of India." Sarvaan's head tilted down and he gave me a bewildered look.

"Your nani had Naga blood in her?"

"Different Naga, a human variety. They held a deep connection to nature. Their art was full of color. They loved to sing and dance."

"Well then, I guess you really are a Naga princess one way or another." His arms wrapped and squeezed me. My own hands held onto his log-like forearms.

"In her mind I think they were one and the same. She viewed herself as the bridge between the two." My hands held Sarvaan's arms against my breasts.

"Maybe she was." His tail slowly wrapped my legs, undulating to massage my muscles.

I reached out with a finger and traced shapes in the steam above the water.

"Unfortunately, she forgot to tell me where the bridge was."

"Perhaps we'll find your bridge yet. Speaking of which, did you still want me to train you in combat?"

My body wiggled with excitement against his.

"Of course. Why did that remind you of combat training?"

"On the edge of Naga-Loka there is a crystal lake with a stone bridge over it. There are several holes in the bridge. It hasn't been used or repaired in quite some time. It will be perfect for some balance training."

"Planning to throw me off a bridge, are you?" I bit his forearm around my chest playfully.

"I'd never let any harm come to you." Sarvaan's body slid down into the water, covering all but his head, keeping me where I was so I wouldn't get dunked in.

"It's a date then."

"Fantastic. There's a cave with no jewels in it, so it is completely dark. I'd like to show it to you as well and do some sensory training."

"Sensory training?"

"We'll fight in the dark. It will train you to use more than just your eyes."

"You just want to get me alone in the dark..." I kissed his arm.

"Damn, you've discovered my master plan."

A giggle shook my breasts and made the water slosh around near my body.

"You won't be too tired after today?"

"You mean the trial match or sex?"

"Both!" I slapped his arm scoldingly.

"I've trained my body to perform even under immense physical strain. It's been my life for decades. It will take much more than today's *workouts* to tire me."

Ladies, I found the perfect man.

Chapter 12

Bridge ~ हथियार

"**R**eady?"

"Yes, I think so."

"Okay, here we go."

"Wait, give me one more moment."

Traveling through the Naga-Loka river system had gotten easier for me, but it still gave me the sensation of being on a roller coaster while wearing a helmet full of water. Sarvaan had me in his arms. He was patient with me to only dive in once I was ready. Breath filled my lungs one more time. I gave him the nod. He leapt into the river and a swirling vortex of blue and white swirled in my vision. At about thirty seconds, I braced for the exit. It never came. This trip was longer than my usual ones to Nishala's camp.

The bridge must be even farther away than I thought.

The exit came about a minute into the trip. Sarvaan put my feet on the ground and I coughed and gasped for air. His hands rubbed my back and I oriented myself

"Just breathe. We're here now."

"That felt like a longer trip than the last time you took me in the river."

"I'm surprised you remember that. And yes, we're further on the edge of Naga-Loka."

Around me was beauty in the form of raw primordial nature. We were in a grove of purple flowers and medium yellow grass. In the background stood a mountain lined with trees. Glowing jewels adorned the mountain and the ground for a gently illuminated backdrop straight from legend.

"The bridge I told you about is this way." My hand instinctively took Sarvaan's and he led me through the grass and flowers.

The flowers smelled of jasmine and milk. The grass's fragrance filled my nose with hints of clove and ghee. The combination made my mouth water. Sarvaan led me through a forest of towering trees with broad leaves and golden bark. They smelled of copper and loban. My wonder was interrupted by Sarvaan picking me up, bringing me to his face, and kissing me. A laughed escaped me as I was lifted.

"I'm so lucky you're mine and I'm yours, Priya."

"I'm the lucky one. I got a strong Naga warrior out of it. All you have is a short, weak, human woman who has to hold her breath to travel through water."

"That doesn't describe my soul companion at all. She's strong and fierce. She's a princess destined to be queen." We kissed again. A sigh of contentment blew into Sarvaan's mouth as we kissed. Golden leaves reflected spackles of light like a chandelier around us. I pulled away with a mischievous grin.

"You're right. I am pretty amazing."

***

When we came upon the stone bridge, my breath caught. It was massive, and it could easily hold hundreds of vehicles if it were on Earth. It was ancient looking. The stone was weathered and chipped. As Sarvaan mentioned, it was full of holes. Far below the bridge was a lake of crystals. It did not connect anything together. It was simply there. Why it was there escaped me.

Was this a remnant of the goddess Parvati's work? Something she left unfinished, or was it put here on purpose to be admired?

I inhaled sharply, remembering to breathe. Sarvaan extended his hand to me. I took it as I mindlessly stared.

"You're going to want to hang on. There's no easy way for a human to get to the top." My arms wrapped Sarvaan's neck and tightened. I knew I could hold as tight as possible and his massive muscles wouldn't feel a thing.

Sarvaan slithered to one of the pillars of the bridge and leapt. He began to climb the pillar as he did the pillars in the fighting arena. He would leap, wrap his tail around the base, clench the stone with his hands, unwrap his tail, and repeat.

Is every method of transportation in Naga-Loka designed to feel like a theme park ride to humans? I'm starting to think so.

One last leap and we were at the top. Sarvaan set my feet down on the stone surface of the bridge now. I bent over with my hands on my knees, thankful I wasn't flying through the air anymore.

"Here, you'll need this." Sarvaan produced a sword and handed it to me. Somehow it was the right size for a human.

"How did you find a weapon of the right size for me?"

"Juveniles train in combat at an early age."

"A child's weapon, how fitting." Sarvaan took the sword back, unsheathed it, and sliced downward at his forearm. I gasped as scales fell to the ground.

"A blade is a blade." He handed it back to me with a smirk. He didn't once look down at the small line of blood running down his arm.

Point taken.

"So where do we start first?" I asked, examining the blade.

"With trust."

"Come again?"

"There's a giant hole in the bridge behind you." My head turned. He was right, it was large enough for my entire body to fall through. "I want you to jump into it."

My eyes widened.

"Trying to get rid of your bride already?"

"Priya, I love you more than anything. If you die, I'd die too. Jump backwards into the hole."

I love this man. I trust him. If he lets me die I will haunt him for the rest of his life though.

I took a deep breath, summoned my courage, and leapt backwards. My feet weren't a foot off the ground when Sarvaan's tail wrapped around my waist, easily holding me midair. His body had moved as fast as lightning. If I would have blinked I would have missed it.

We trained for about an hour. Sarvaan showed me the correct way to hold and swing a blade. He showed me when to slice and when to stab. All of this while surrounded by holes in the bridge. When I asked how a warrior could assess a battlefield quickly and mind their surroundings, I couldn't tell if his answer was a joke or not.

"It's simple. Just picture yourself not dying."

"Don't worry, Sarvaan, I'm in a constant state of picturing myself not dying."

"Every warrior thinks that. You have to picture yourself in the moment you're afraid of. But instead of dying, you're alive."

Being on the bridge brought a flash of Nani back into my mind.

"I am the bridge between the Naga tribe and the Naga of Patala." Her finger pressed my nose playfully. It made me giggle. "And you are the river underneath."

"What do you mean, Nani?"

"A bridge connects, but it does not move. A river flows. It *moves.*"

Had Nani known something I didn't? Had she seen something in me?

Even though my mind was wandering, I sidestepped a hole in the bridge to dodge Sarvaan's sword swing. The look on his face was just as surprised as mine was.

"Very good. Let's go again." Sarvaan sent more strikes my way.

...you are the river...

I bent my body at an angle, bending like a river, to avoid the strikes. My feet flowed around the holes in the bridge. I imagined myself doing it, and I did as I pictured. I saw myself alive. Even though Sarvaan was only moving at half speed for my sake, I was proud of my progress.

"I think you've earned a lunch break." He put his sword into its sheath.

"I think I've earned ten lunch breaks." My hands were on my knees. I was panting furiously.

***

Sarvaan and I hiked up the mountain I'd seen in the distance when we first exited the river. He chose an area with a large rock that could be used as a table and small rocks around it so I could sit. Sarvaan coiled his body inward on itself and sat that way.

Must be nice to be able to be your own chair.

Sarvaan retrieved a leather pouch from his tunic and put it on the large rock. He opened the pouch and its contents were visible. Inside were various fruits, fungi, and cheese. There were also balls of what looked like fudge with sugar crystals covering them.

"Wah! These look like my favorite dessert on Earth, Bal Mithai." The ball of fudge was in my mouth in a split second. It tasted very similar to Bal Mithai. It was less roasted milk solid and more fruit. The sugar crystals felt of the same crunch the tiny balls of sugar did for Bal Mithai.

"Well look at that. I wonder how a confection from the mortal realm ended up here?"

Maybe the same way I did, who knows?

"Sarvaan...I'fe notifed...dere's no meaf down here."

Sarvaan stuffed his own mouth with goodies.

"Whaf did you shay, my loff?"

We both laughed so hard our stomachs hurt.

"Not dainty, I know. I was asking why Naga don't seem to eat meat?"

"Well, there is wildlife here in Naga-Loka, but there's not enough of it to sustain the population. Fruit, vegetables, and fungi are more plentiful and easier to cultivate."

"What about the cheese? What milk is it made from? I haven't seen any mammals in this realm."

"Your observation is sound. We import milk from other realms to make our cheese."

"That's so interesting. I'd love to learn more about how Bhogavati trades and conducts business with other realms."

"I could get you involved in the community?"

"I'd like that."

I crawled into Sarvaan's lap and reminded him how crazy I was for his tongue. Our mouths were sweet and earthy from our lunch. It made me kiss him more ferociously.

After lunch Sarvaan and I hiked up the mountain and to a dark cave he wanted to show me. The change in lighting shook me for a moment. I'd been accustomed to jewels glowing everywhere since I arrived. Pure darkness was strangely welcome. I felt Sarvaan hand me my sword.

"Are you sure about this Sarvaan? What if I stab myself? What if I impale your eye?"

"Well I'd have another scar over my eye then. I trust you. Trust yourself."

Do I trust myself with a sword in the dark? I'd have to stick a pin in that for the time being.

"Ok, I'm going to attack. Use your senses to anticipate."

I put my hand on the cave wall to stabilize myself. My fingers touched something I recognized. It was a glyph, carved in the stone.

Listen for his breath, his muscles contracting, his scales clicking.

Huh? Who is that?

I heard Sarvaan slither, I heard his breath exhale. I felt the air move as his sword came at me. I didn't parry or dodge. My hand shot forward and caught the blade.

That's impossible.

Are you divine? Who are you to say what is possible and what is not.

"Priya? Did you just catch my sword?"

"Um...yeah?"

Sarvaan's glowing jewels on his hood illuminated. I'd never seen true fear in his eyes until now. Not even when he was in combat in the arena. His eyes were wide, looking at my hand which was holding his sword's blade. Sarvaan put away his sword and examined my hand.

"You just caught a sword. My sword. You have no wounds."

"I guess I just caught it at the right angle—"

Sarvaan's hood jewels provided light to show what I felt on the cave's wall. It was the image of a Nagini in warrior's armor, thrusting a sword at a Naga warrior.

"Priya, something is going on here. This is all wrong—" My fingers grabbed his chin and turned it to the carving on the wall. He looked it up and down, looked back to my face, and saw the wonder in my eyes.

"Do you recognize this?"

"Yes. This is the Nagini warrior my nani told me of. Her name was Prathavi."

"Prathavi is the Nagini queen your were told of as a child?" His voice was slightly high pitched.

"Yeah...that's her."

"You continue to puzzle me."

"Why's that?"

"Prathavi's tale is thousands of years old. Mostly lost to time. Hardly anyone remembers all of it."

"Do you?"

"I remember pieces. She led Bhogavati when the Rakshasa kingdom of Lanka invaded during her reign as queen."

So Nagas and Rakshasas have clashed before, not just in stories.

A wave of energy draining exhaustion washed over my body suddenly.

"Could we start making our way back? I think I've had enough for one day."

"Of course, darling." The jewels in his hood stopped emitting light.

Sarvaan hugged me from behind and kissed my neck. I smiled in the darkness.

"Is this part of the training, too?" I turned my head and kissed him as he pecked my neck.

"Of course, you have to learn how to fend off your horny husband."

"What if I'd rather be fucked by my horny husband?"

"Even better."

***

When we got back to the river where we'd come from initially, we decided to spend a little more time here. The grassy grove by the river was stunning. We laid our heads by each other, with our bodies going opposite of one another, and stared into the jeweled cavern ceiling above. My hands were raised over my head and caressing Sarvaan's scales. Suddenly his head raised, then his body. I raised mine to look at him.

"Sarvaan, what is it?"

"I'd like to try something."

Last time he said that I was flipped upside down and my pussy was thoroughly searched by his long tongue. I'm intrigued.

"Okay, what would you like to try?" His face had urgency in it rather than lust this time. He rose all the way, extending his hand to me.

"I want to try and take you to the mortal realm, to your realm." He pulled me to my feet.

"You can do that?"

"It's never been done before, but I'd like to try."

"How?"

"The river. Naga can use it to traverse wherever they go. This one goes to your realm as well as Bhogavati."

My face lit up like a thousand lights at once.

"Ok, let's do it!"

"How long can you hold your breath?"

"I don't know, probably a couple of minutes?"

He led me to the edge of the river and hoisted me to his chest.

Oh, we're doing this NOW.

"Ready?"

Now or never I guess. Here I come Papa, Maa, Vikram.

Sarvaan slithered into the river holding me tight. For the first thirty seconds it was more of the same underwater rollercoaster I'd become used to.

One minute into the trip I started to feel my chest hurt. Just a bit longer and I could take a breath.

A minute and a half.

My head felt fuzzy.

Two minutes.

I saw the faces of my family. Whether they were real I wasn't sure. I saw my brother, weeping because his prayer came true. I saw my Papa wrestling me away from the crushing embrace of Maa.

Two and a half minutes. I think. Or was it three?

The roller coaster ceased. The river roaring in my ears faded.

Where do you think you're going? No one can run from who they really are.

I'll go where I want to go.

You are where you want to go. Stop fighting it.

Blackness. There was no sound and no thoughts.

"Pr..."

Huh?

"Priy..."

Sarvaan. He's talking to me.

"Priya..."

Were we there? Did we make it?

"Priya!"

When my eyes opened I was being held in a sitting position by Sarvaan's arms. His face flooded with relief when my eyes opened. He didn't even flinch when I coughed river water on him.

"Are we there? Where are we?"

Looking around I saw the grassy grove we departed from.

No. It couldn't have been for nothing. It felt like an eternity. Why were we back here?

"I turned back. The trip was taking longer than I anticipated. You went unconscious and I had to breathe into your mouth for you."

He brought me to lay on his body softly.

"I'm so sorry Priya. I tried."

My arms pulled over his shoulders and embraced his warmth.

"Don't worry, Sarvaan. I'm right where I want to be."

Chapter 13

Rain ~ समर्पण

My eyes slowly opened at the sound of movement throughout the house. I reached for Sarvaan but he wasn't in bed. The glowing light of the jewels was still soft, looking to be a few hours before 'morning' would begin. My body sat up with a stretch and a yawn. Sarvaan slithered past the doorway and noticed I was awake.

"Priya, apologies if I woke you."

"Why are you up so early, Sarvaan?" My fingers wiped my eyes.

"How would you like to witness the Naga rain ritual?"

So they do control rain.

"I'd love that."

He sat next to me, caressing my face.

"Excellent. The community will be glad to have you."

"Does it always take place at this time?" I made a playful frown at him.

"Yes. It is a minor inconvenience. But, the early hour will be worth your while." He planted a kiss on my neck and left the room. It was so quick and I was still sleepy that I didn't have the energy to kiss back.

When I'm a Nagini and I can slither as fast as you can, you better watch out, Sarvaan.

I grinned at the possibilities. As I stood and was figuring out what to wear, Sarvaan entered again. He was holding a very fancy garb that looked like a cross between a robe and a dress. Every inch of the fabric had symbols of rain, lakes, and rivers on it.

"Here, there's a special attire for this ritual."

He went to leave, turned around, and smacked my ass cheek with his hand, giving it a squeeze at the end. A joyful squeal escaped my lips and I shot him a warm look.

"You're so wonderful, Priya. Did you know that?"

"Yes I'm pretty amazing aren't I?" I struck a confident pose with my hands on my hips. Sarvaan stole a kiss before leaving the room again. I held up the ritual attire.

Okay, let's go make it rain.

Sarvaan looked amazing in his ritual attire. All of the embroidery flexed and stretched under his massive muscles. The light and deep blue colors of the symbols brought out his eyes.

"So what does this rain ritual entail?" My hand found his.

"Well, there's music and singing, and there's a very specific dance that goes along with it. During the dance, we collect water from the river into jugs. Then, everyone hands their jug to someone else to deposit into a fountain. The ritual is complete when water bursts from the fountain in an arcing stream."

"Sounds like this ritual demands quite the choreography."

"Don't worry, we can teach you the movements."

"The ritual doesn't break if I mess up right?"

"No no, nothing will break if you mess up." Small, deep chuckles escaped Sarvaan, they sent tiny vibrations through my body. It was comforting.

After about thirty minutes of walking, or in my case Sarvaan carrying me while he slithered twice as fast as I could walk, a pavillion came into view with a crowd of about fifty or sixty Naga gathered around it. Sarvaan set me on my feet and we walked hand-in-hand into the crowd. He led me to a stone table with several clay jugs on it, taking one for himself and handing me one. For Sarvaan, the jug could be held with one hand. Mine covered my entire chest.

I hope I'm as graceful as I think I am. If I spill this thing on me this ritual becomes a wet t-shirt contest really quick.

A Nagini woman approached us. She was stunningly beautiful, with a face that anyone could get lost in. Her scales were green and blue.

"You must be our newest member of our kingdom. Welcome, I am Vikshana." She turned to Sarvaan. "She's wonderfully pretty, Sarvaan."

"That she is." He puffed his chest muscles out. It was hot that he was proud to have me as his wife. Vikshana's eyes wandered all over me. I could feel her undressing me in her mind. The extra attention made my breathe harder. My breasts heaved against the ritual regalia. My eyes only looked away from Vikshana when an archaka approached the crowd.

"Jai Indra. Welcome, all. It is good to see so many gathered. The mortal realm thirsts, let us quench it together."

The archaka's holy robe had a thunderbolt symbol on it, and a white elephant's head.

Indra, rider of the clouds, lord of Svarga.

"Let us invoke Indra on this day." The archaka put his hands above his head as high as they could go. Then, he pressed his fingers together straight and firm.

I noticed everyone in the crowd doing as the archaka did. I mimicked this motion as well. Next, the archaka tucked his thumb tight against his palm. Everyone did this as well, followed by me.

"Om Indraya Namah..." As the archaka chanted, everyone joined in after he finished.

"Lord of the thunderbolt, rider of Airavata, breaker of drought, we are your servants beneath the earth..." I repeated it along with the group this time. The archaka made an 'X' with his tail. The group did this as well. I followed suit by crossing my legs to make a similar shape.

"Let our bodies carry your blessing. Let our dance bring your waters to those who thirst. We move so that the rains may fall." He straightened his tail, spinning in a one-hundred eighty degree angle, now facing the opposite way as he began. He brought his hands straight out from his chest this time.

The crowd and I mimicked this movement. Out of the corner of my eye I caught Sarvaan looking my way. He was smiling, proud. Everyone held this pose for a few seconds and then put their hands down and stood normally. A group of Naga went to one corner of the pavillion where instruments were setup. There were bansuris, shankhas, and sitars. When they played a slow, sensual melody filled the air. The Naga in the crowd hummed along with the music softly.

"Would you like me to show you the dance?" Vikshana was by my side. Sarvaan nodded, nudging me to take her up on her offer.

"Yes, that would be lovely, thank you." The crowd put their jugs on the ground and started to dance slowly to the music.

The men and women did a different dance. The men's dance looked more primal and angry. They made movements that looked like they were attacking the sky, trying to rip it open to produce the rain. The women's dance was more sensual, as if they were trying to entice the rain straight from the clouds. Vikshana stood behind me. I felt her warm scales press against me.

"Move like I do." Her hands gripped my hips firmly and she moved me.

A fragrance drifted from her that my nostrils became addicted to.

Tuberose. It smells so nice.

Her fragrance was rich, creamy, and floral. It filled my nose and lingered like mist in my mind. My hands touched and caressed hers as she moved me through the dance. Because Vikshana was over a foot taller than me, I felt her breasts on the back of my shoulders. Her scent made me want her touch even more. Her face moved to my neck. The humming she did with music was soothing on my skin.

"You move nicely, Priya." Her hands washed over my breasts and neck when the dance demanded we spin around.

Vikshana didn't spin, though; she continued facing me. I felt her tail pearls brush against my ass. My thighs trembled. She looked like she was about to say something, but the dance was over and the crowd clapped in the air. My eyes found Sarvaan, clapping while smiling at me and Vikshana.

Did he...like her touching me?

"See you around, Priya, and welcome again." Vikshana grabbed her jug on the ground and slithered away.

Sarvaan found his way over to me.

"Ready to bring the rains?" He held his jug up to his bulging chest.

"Yes...let's do it." Vikshana's tuberose perfume started to release its hold on me.

I hope Sarvaan was ok with how we were touching. It felt...great. With how Vikshana acted, and the bathing I received before my consummation to Sarvaan, I wonder if this is a cultural thing?

Sarvaan led me to the river. The pavilion was situated with the river on one side, and a fountain in the shape of a large, white elephant on the opposite side.

"So now we'll fill our jugs, and pass it to someone else. When you receive a new jug, pour it into the fountain."

Sounds simple enough. Let the raining begin.

When the crowd thinned at the river, Sarvaan and I filled our jugs.

"Can we exchange jugs with each other?"

"No, it needs to be with someone outside of your household. This symbolizes unity."

I looked around for someone who hadn't swapped jugs. I saw a Nagini woman standing by herself looking around. I strolled over and offered her my jug. She gave me a look I hadn't seen since I arrived in Bhogavati. The look was something between dismissal and disgust.

"Trot along, human pet. Our ritual is sacred and doesn't need you corrupting it."

I almost dropped my jug from surprise.

Kutiya, speak to me that way again and I'll corrupt your face.

A hand on my shoulder stopped me from saying it out loud. It was Vikshana. She offered me her jug.

"We meet again." She smiled as we exchanged jugs. As she slithered away she whispered into my ear. "Some Naga aren't as accepting as others. Don't take it to heart."

I exhaled my frustration and concentrated on carrying this giant jug of water to the fountain. Because I had to walk slowly with mine given its size, I was the last one to pour my water into the fountain. Sarvaan put his hand on the bottom of my jug and helped me get it into the fountain. As the last bit of my water was poured, a spraying stream of water erupted from the fountain through the elephant head's trunk. The crowd cheered.

"See, the rain just needed to be coaxed by the most beautiful woman in the kingdom." I blushed at Sarvaan's compliment as the crowd cheered and clapped at the water spraying from the fountain.

They all turned to face me and directed their cheers and claps my way as well. I felt Sarvaan's breath on my neck as he whispered in my ear.

"They love you, Priya!"

His encouraging words were soured by the thought of the Nagini woman's hurtful words from earlier.

I hope there's not too many in the kingdom who hate me.

***

As Sarvaan and I walked home I was more quiet than usual. I hated that there were people in this kingdom who hated my very being here. I was just trying to participate in their rituals, to show commitment in integrating into the community.

"You're quiet, my love." His hand brushed my hair backwards, giving me a small shiver of contentment. I loved when he stroked my hair.

"When it was time to exchange water jugs, someone said something hateful to me. They indicated I, as a human, wasn't welcome."

Sarvaan stopped. He leaned down to me and put his arms around me. My pouting calmed in response to his touch.

"I'm sorry. It's no excuse, but you are the first human to ever live here and be a part of the kingdom. It'll take time, but I believe everyone will love you."

"I hope so." He kissed me, making me smile more.

"Don't you think if a brute like me fell in love with you, then the rest of the Naga will follow suit?" We continued our stroll home.

When we turned onto the street our home was on, we noticed King Vasuki and his royal guard were standing outside our door.

"Your majesty at my door? Why has glory smiled upon me today?" Sarvaan shouted as we walked closer.

When we stood before the King and his guards, Sarvaan bowed to the ground and I curtsied low.

"Would you two accompany me? I have something I'd like to show you."

I hope this isn't about me sneaking to Nishala's camp.

"I'd follow you anywhere, your highness." King Vasuki and his guard started to move, Sarvaan lifted me to his chest so we could follow at their pace.

"Apologies if you were waiting long. We were attending the rain ritual."

"Oh no worries at all. The rain is important, I am but a servant to my people who wears a crown." I couldn't tell if he was joking or not. Vasuki was an odd one.

"Priya, how was your first experience with our rain ceremony?"

"It was amazing! I learned the dance and I loved the music that filled the air."

"That's good to hear. I'm glad your time with us has been a memorable one."

Is he...insinuating that my time here is about to end?

I started to sweat into my robe. My fingers tightened around Sarvaan's. If he was a human his hand would be mangled from my grip.

Eventually the King led us to our destination. We all now stood before Lord Shiva's temple.

Not what I was expecting.

My sweat dried and I loosened my grip on Sarvaan's fingers. Vasuki made a flicking gesture of his wrist and his guard stayed put on the steps leading into the temple's entrance. He walked up to me and offered me his arm. I took it and the King walked me into the temple with Sarvaan in tow.

"King Vasuki, if I may ask, what are we doing here?"

"You wrote down a prayer that you heard from your brother in the mortal realm. I thought you might like to complete the prayer's journey yourself."

Oh...OH!

I felt my emotions building in my throat. My eyes glazed over with tears.

"This is wonderful, usually only treasury members and temple caretakers are allowed to participate in completing prayer cycles." Sarvaan's words squeezed a tear from my eyes that ran down my cheek.

The King led me to an altar full of treasure on it and around it. The altar had a small statue of Lord Shiva upon it. Vasuki opened my palm and placed something cold in it. I opened my hand to find a small golden amulet.

"Your brother Vikram prayed to Lord Shiva to protect you from evil. I, as King of Naga-Loka, witness the completion of this prayer. You may place the offering."

My hand shook as if I was in freezing water as I reached forward placing the amulet on the altar. The King leaned into my ear.

"I'll ask Lord Shiva to give Vikram clarity that you are not in danger." And then he slithered away.

I collapsed into Sarvaan's chest, weeping and staring at the altar. His hands rubbed up and down my back, and through my hair.

It's done, Vikram. It's done. Tell Papa and Maa I'm safe.

Chapter 14

Gift ~ आज्ञा

When Sarvaan and I got back home from visiting the temple, my body ached to lie down. I'd been up since my equivalent of two in the morning. I'd danced, carried a heavy jug around, walked all over Bhogavati, and been emotionally wrecked from completing my brother's prayer. I shed my ceremonial regalia and fell into bed, rolling up in the sheets. Sarvaan joined me and coiled his body around me, softly rubbing my muscles with his.

"Do you think the King will address Shiva on behalf of my brother?"

"I do. His majesty is an honest king."

I inhaled deeply, pressing my breasts against Sarvaan's scales.

"I'm worried that Bhogavati won't accept me fully."

"They will."

"But what if they don't? What if when you become king—"

"IF I become king."

"WHEN you become king…" I rolled on top of Sarvaan's chest. When he inhaled I felt his chest muscles and scales press against my labia and clit.

"What if they hate me and won't accept me as their queen?"

"You'll be queen, you could command them to love you." He sat up, kissing me, his tongue flicking around my mouth as I laughed at his joke. I pulled away and held both sides of his impossibly handsome face.

"And if they don't listen?"

"Well you could always practice giving me commands. That way when you command the kingdom you'll have practice under your belt."

"Ok then, your queen commands that you kiss her." He gave my lips a single kiss with a popping *smack* at the end.

"Is that the quality of kiss your queen is to expect through our union?" He grinned and gave me the tongue I craved, and the lip sucking that made my blood run hot.

Sarvaan tilted my head to the side and he kissed and sucked on the area between my neck and shoulder. My head instinctively nuzzled his, and I cooed soft moans into his ear. Within seconds I felt his erection poking my ass. I scooted back, using my hips to slide him into me.

"Oh my queen...you were ready for me." His tongue flicked my neck and behind my ears giving me an ecstatic shiver.

"I'm always ready for you."

Because of how Sarvaan's body was shaped, I could ride him while he held me and sat up against me. His dinner plate-sized hands roamed and massaged my body as I bounced on his dick. I'd gotten used to the four inch base now. I was able to rear up and slam down on him as hard as I could without it hurting. I felt his cock curl in on itself and writhe in me.

We'll be able to be even more feral and primal when I'm a Nagini Sarvaan. You just wait.

Then a vision flashed in my mind. Me as a Nagini, our coils tangling, two primal shapes fighting for dominance. He would be able to give me his eggs.

His eggs...He has eggs.

I stopped bouncing and pulled his face to look at mine.

"Your eggs." My breasts heaved with my breathing, glistening from the sheen of sweat on them.

"What about them?" When he exhaled from panting it, was voluminous enough to blow over my entire body.

"Give them to me..." His eyes widened. I felt his dick pulse within me.

"Are you sure?"

"Yes, you make my world and unmake it at the same time."

"Priya, I must warn you, they're quite lar—"

I silenced him with my tongue dancing on his.

"Give. Them. To. Me. Your queen commands it."

Sarvaan flipped me onto my back as easily as a grown man tossing a small twig. His chest was pressed onto me in an instant and his forked tongue flicked both of my nipples at the same time. He started thrusting slow, long, hard thrusts, like he was trying to get his cock stuck in me. The tip of him tickled my cervix. His mouth found mine before I could register any pain.

"I want all of you Sarvaan. I want every part of you. I love you." I pulled back from his mouth and kissed the scales on his neck. They were smooth and tasted of salt and flowers. He leaned into it and I kissed his hood. I felt his cock twitch when I did that.

"Then I'll give you every part of me. You've made my world brighter and more lovely in every way, Priya."

His cock began to do something it never had before. The base swelled wider than its usual four inches. He brought his body back and then thrust forward. The first egg slipped into me, pushed through by his cock's pumping action. It was the size of a baseball. Pleasure and slight pain ripped through my body. Pleasure won. My back arched.

Oh yes...

The second egg made me catch my breath. My mouth found Sarvaan's chest and bit his muscles in a fit of feral lust.

"AGH!" His deep, primal moans rippled through my body as I squirmed, accepting his eggs.

Feels...so...good...

A third egg now was pumped into me.

Oh shit...oh shit...how many are there?

A fourth and a fifth followed.

"There's more...do you want them...all?" Each egg demanded a long stroke of a thrust. A groan escaped Sarvaan's lips each time, as if the process of pumping each egg was giving him a small orgasm.

Fill me Sarvaan, fill me...

"Don't stop...put them all in me..."

The sixth and seventh slid into me at the same time, widening me beyond even what Sarvaan's four inch base had before.

"OH! Fuck yes! Fuck yes!" High pitched screeches erupted from my lungs. I came. My pussy quivered on his cock, beckoning more of him to fill me.

"I can't...stop..." My pussy's quivering made him pump harder.

Fuck yes! Don't stop! Fuck yes!

My mind and mouth screeched at the same time. The eighth, ninth, and tenth were pumped into me at last, feeling like a string of globes filled with hot water.

Holy shit, holy shit! There's literally no more room inside me.

My entire body convulsed as my pussy held all ten of Sarvaan's eggs, with each thrust he pounded them against my cervix. My legs squeezed him so hard I was afraid I was going to break his dick in half. I could only pant into Sarvaan's mouth as I came a second time. My body writhed as if I were possessed by demons.

"I love you Sarvaan...I love you..."

"You're my queen and I'll love you until the end of time, Priya."

I slammed my tongue into his mouth and stroked his hood with my hands. I was still riding the tremors of two orgasms.

"Oh fuck...oh shit...FUCK!"

I felt my pussy clench hard. Sarvaan's cock slipped out of me. I felt a river of his fluid leak out of me along with five of his eggs due to the pressure. Each egg blasted a wave of pleasure from my chest to my toes.

"Oh...OH!...shit...yes...YES!" Each egg made my legs tense and my hips buck upwards.

I laid there with my breasts moving up and down into the air, covered in sweat, with my legs still spread. Shivers overtook me and Sarvaan curled up beside me and wrapped my body with his.

"Ah...oh...dammit...that was..." My mind wasn't able to think. The most it was able to do was babble in circles.

Sarvaan's hands brushed through my hair and caressed my neck.

"You're amazing Priya. You make my life feel complete."

"I feel them...I feel them in me...they're part of me. You're...part of me."

I murmured and babbled against Sarvaan's chest. His hands petting me and his breathing lulled me to sleep. The last thing I remember is running my hand down my abdomen and feeling the eggs that were still inside of me.

Holy fucking shit. I couldn't wait to experience that with a Nagini body.

***

Sarvaan was spooning me when I awoke the next day. His log-sized arms were wrapped around my chest and his serpentine body was wrapped around the rest of me. Only my shoulders and above were visible. My hand reached down to touch my abdomen. The eggs seemed to have been absorbed by my body. There was just a stickiness between my legs and on my labia, serving as the only reminder of last night.

Obviously I'm not Nagini, so my body wouldn't have been able to accept the eggs. It will one day, though.

Sarvaan stirred and kissed the back of my neck. Goosebumps appeared on my neck and shoulders making me snuggle into him closer.

"How are you feeling my dear?"

"Fucking fantastic, my soul companion. How about you."

"Incredible actually. Would you like some breakfast?"

"I don't know if I should, I did have ten eggs last night." I spun in his arms and we laughed together, smiling and remembering last night. "I am quite hungry though."

"I think I'll make us something special today." He rose from the bed and took me with him, pressing my nude body to his chest. I sucked his tongue and he wrapped mine in return.

When he released me I fell softly, bouncing into the warm spot in the sheets where he was. I inhaled slowly and deeply to take in his scent he left behind. Himalayan pink salt and sun-baked temple stone stained with incense. I rolled into the sheets, putting them between my legs and letting them cascade down my breasts and belly, remembering last night.

When I was dressed I entered the den and sat on the couch. As I walked past the kitchen I smelled bread baking. A few moments later, Sarvaan entered with a plate of what looked like fried bread with a pink syrup topping.

"And what is this?"

"My own dish. Bread infused with cherry oil and steamed over a boiling pot. Today is my second match of the trial, the sugar will give me energy." Sarvaan was certainly more energetic today, but I knew why. Each time his eyes caught mine I saw us tangled together, reliving last night's memory.

Picking up a square of bread I quickly realized what Sarvaan meant. It was a moist, almost sticky bread. When I bit into it, cherry oil gushed into my mouth.

Oh, this is great.

The syrup topping was rose flavored. Liquid sugar glazed my tongue with every bite. If this syrup and oil had been poured onto Sarvaan, I would have to eat my husband.

"So who are you facing today?"

"A competitor from Takshaka Kula."

I froze with bread stuffed in my mouth. I swallowed.

"Balnak?"

"I wish. I could go ahead and beat him into submission for you. Today I fight a warrior I've never had dealings with before."

"So what's the plan then?"

His eyes were cocky. He threw a piece of bread in his mouth and winked.

"Win."

***

As Sarvaan escorted me into the arena, I couldn't help but think back to Nishala's condition. She wanted me to enter the trial.

How would I ever be able to do combat against these warriors built like living mountains of muscle? And even if somehow she trains me to be the best warrior ever imaginable...How would Sarvaan react? Nishala didn't specify winning the trial, just entering it. I'm sure Sarvaan wouldn't be too angry as long as the end result wasn't facing him in combat and of course me getting a Nagini body. And anyway, how in the world was I supposed to compete in the trials with no way to hold myself on the pillars as Naga do?

My mind was in another world as the horns sounded for the match to begin. I hadn't even registered Sarvaan hugging and kissing me before he left to climb up his stone pillar. A tinge of his warmth and scent was left on me at least. It made me nuzzle my own shoulder to sniff the last of him as it faded. King Vasuki walked into the fighting area and began to announce the competitors.

"Today's match will be between Sarvaan of Karkota Kula..." I jumped up and down, screaming and hooting for my love when his name was called.

"Vrishal of Takshaka Kula..." Vrishal's kula made a chant out of slapping their chests with their swords.

"Take him down, Sarvaan. Show him what awaits Balnak."

I looked over Vrishal as he clung to his pillar. He had opted to wield a sword in each hand instead of a sword and a shield.

I hope Sarvaan can handle two swords.

King Vasuki gave the signal after introducing the warriors and the match began. Sarvaan leapt to the center pillar, but Vrishal was still on his starting pillar. He moved from one side of the pillar to another, and shook his tail at Sarvaan each time he changed sides. He held his twin swords across his chest in an 'X.' It was an interesting tactic. It forced Sarvaan to decide carefully which angle to strike from, risking a sword to his scales if he chose incorrectly.

Come on darling. Show him who the real king is.

My arms unconsciously shot out slightly to the left, imaging myself in the battle. Sarvaan struck to the right side of Vrishal's pillar. Vrishal feigned and shot around the side Sarvaan was vulnerable and caught him on the side with his swords. Scales fell and blood stained the stone of the pillar.

I would have hit him. I guessed correctly. Go me!

That's because you're stronger than Sarvaan.

I looked around and realized the voice wasn't someone around me. It was *her*.

You again. I'm trying to support Sarvaan, can we have this discussion another time?

Your soul companion is one of the strongest warriors in the kingdom. But you are stronger. Do you remember the cave with my image carved on its walls? Return there when you want to have an honest conversation.

I snapped back to reality as Sarvaan took another slash, this time to one of his arms. He'd had enough of Vrishal's games, I saw it in his eyes even from where I sat. Sarvaan unwrapped from the center pillar and leapt to his starting pillar. Vrishal leapt to the center pillar to chase. Sarvaan leapt back to the center pillar meeting Vrishal face-to-face. Sarvaan attacked one of Vrishal's sword arms, forcing his opponent to drop his sword to the ground below.

Yes, take him down.

Sarvaan attacked with a shield bash and then a sword strike, doing a two-strike combo over and over. His shoulder and back muscles rippled as he put all of his strength behind the strikes until finally, Vrishal's other sword went flying to the ground. With no weapons, Vrishal panted for a moment and then put his palms together and bowed to Sarvaan, expressing that he was yielding.

Fuck yeah! That's MY husband!

As Sarvaan and Vrishal embraced and the arena boomed out thunderous applause, I ran through the dirt to put my arms around my true love.

"That was amazing! That was fucking awesome!"

"Well I told you my plan was to win."

We kissed and squeezed each other and he twirled me around, lifting me up high again to show me off to the crowd. In the distance I spotted Vrishal getting scolded by Balnak. Balnak glared at me and his eyes felt like venom burning my skin. I made a gesture, pointing at him.

You're next, fucker.

The crowd caught sight of this. Some cheered. Some laughed. Some gasped. Balnak bared his fangs at me and walked away.

I can't wait to make you kneel to me, slime ball.

Chapter 15
Shadow ~ रक्षक

Charged by Sarvaan's second win of the trial, I decided to keep Nishala waiting no longer. That night, I snuck out after Sarvaan's breathing slowed to a sleeping pace. Nishala was sitting by her campfire in warrior's leather armor with two swords on the ground when I arrived. One was a training sword, made of wood, the other was her real one. It was the sword I'd pointed at Sarvaan the first time I met him.

"I was beginning to wonder if you weren't going to show."

"You'll have to excuse me, I'm newly married and my husband is competing to be the king. Lots to do." I made my voice sound prissy and dainty to mess with her. A sharp chuckle escaped her lips.

"How have his matches in the trial gone?"

"He's done amazingly. Two wins so far."

"You're going to do even better." She handed me a training sword and took her real one in her own hand.

Nishala must have been eating wild mushrooms to truly believe I would be better than Sarvaan. Sarvaan was a fighting machine. He had the strength of two tigers and the intellect of a military general. What did I have? I was a few inches over five feet tall and weighed a quarter or less of what Sarvaan and the other warriors did. Nishala hit my training sword with her own, I snapped back to the present.

"I apologize if I'm interrupting your fantasies. Shall we practice another time?"

"No, I'm sorry, I—"

"First thing to get out of the way: you are no ordinary human. No human has ever just fallen into Naga-Loka as you did. Your soul wanted to be here, even if your brain did not."

That sounds like the logic Prathavi has been trying to get me to believe. How the fuck does that work anyway? I want to be here even if it was by accident? I do love Sarvaan with all my heart. I couldn't imagine if I hadn't met him.

Nishala smacked my arm with the side of her blade this time.

"Ouch! Nishala, what was that for?" I rubbed the spot she smacked. She started circling me.

"Your body is here but your mind is not. I used to be a warrior, I've seen Naga die because their mind and body were not in the same place."

"Sorry, there's been a lot on my mind lately."

"Then allow me to ground you in the *here* and *now*."

Nishala lashed forward at lightning speed, putting a bleeding slash on my thigh. I knelt from the pain.

"Fuck! How am I supposed to explain this to my husband?"

"Why didn't you dodge, or parry?"

"Because you—"

"NO! Because YOU aren't fully here."

Nishala knelt by me, she was breathing like she had run a marathon. Her hot breath blew my hair back with each exhale.

"Do you want your Nagini form?"

"Yes."

"Louder!"

"Yes!"

Nishala grabbed the collar of my robe and pushed me to the ground. I was laying on my back looking up at her. She pointed her sword at my face.

"Say it like you mean it! Make me believe!"

"YES! I want to be Nagini. I will be Nagini!" I filled my lungs with air until I couldn't anymore as I screamed.

Nishala reached down and grabbed my collar again, yanking me to my feet without effort.

"Then attack me."

"What?"

"If you don't attack me I'll carve you up some more. There's plenty more of your pretty skin to slice."

I lunged forward and swung my blade with brute force. I'd seen Sarvaan do it plenty. Nishala parried my strike.

"Good, but you fight like a Naga man. Has your husband been teaching you?"

"He has, yes." My teeth were gritted, my heavy breathing forcing spit to fly to the ground.

"What has he been teaching you?"

"I see myself alive and succeeding in my mind, then staying alive and succeeding."

"That's a good foundation. But there's another layer you need to learn." She unleashed a series of strikes at a slow speed, allowing me to get my reflexes used to parrying and dodging.

Her movements weren't like the Nagas I'd seen in the trial. Their stances were more open, chest out. Nishala moved with her elbows close to her chest. Her arms were like a serpent moving through water. She was highly guarded until she needed to strike.

"You've got to go even further than that. Not only do you need to see yourself succeeding, you need to see your opponent not succeeding."

We practiced for the next hour or so. I felt like I was two warriors. I was Priya, the warrior Sarvaan was training for self-defense. Then, there was my shadow. The persona I took on at night when I snuck away from Sarvaan and our warm bed. When we ended our training session, Nishala applied a healing salve to the slash she had given me.

"This will ensure there is no scar here." Her fingers pressed the salve into the wound without delicacy.

"Th-ank you." I winced. The salve stung and Nishala's fingers pressing into the slash made it worse.

"Nishala."

"Yes Priya?"

"Be honest with me. Why do you want me to compete in the trial?"

"You want me to be honest?"

"I do."

"You haven't been honest, so why should I be?"

"What do you mean? How have I been dishonest?"

"Does your husband know you come here? Does he know why?" Her face touched the side of mine, her tongue flicking my ear and making my neck curl. "Does he know I almost gave you bliss?"

I moved my head away from hers.

"I'm being dishonest with Sarvaan. Not with you. There's a difference."

"We Naga are a communal people. If you lie to one of us, you lie to us all."

After she finished treating my wound I turned to face her.

"I haven't been lying. He doesn't even know I sneak out."

Nishala laughed, her breasts bouncing as she did.

"And you think that makes it any better?"

Fuck this. I've had enough of Nishala for the night.

I stood and walked toward the treeline in the distance to head home. I heard her cackle increase in intensity behind my back.

"Til next time, Priya, til next time!"

***

I made it through the forest with the river in sight. I was exhausted beyond belief and ready for my warm husband and warm sheets. As I neared the river, a large shape descended from the trees and landed in front of me. Balnak. I screamed from surprise and fell backwards.

"What business do you have with an exile, young consort?"

"None of your fucking business. Are you stalking me now?"

His long arms reached down and picked me up from the ground. I was directly in front of him now. I had my dagger on me. I could end this bullshit. Nishala said to visualize not only me succeeding, but my enemy not succeeding. In my mind I cut Balnak's head off in a slow, painful process. I held his head up like a trophy. A warning not to mess with me.

"Oh but it is my business little human. If I tell Sarvaan of this, he'll surely end his union with you. Once word spreads that you collude with exiles, no one in the kingdom will want you. You'll be begging for my cock when no one else will give you theirs."

My hand had been creeping to my thigh where I kept the dagger strapped. I gripped the hilt through my robe, ready to stab him wherever I could. A noise to my left distracted both of us. It was a twig breaking. When Balnak's head looked toward the noise, a Naga arm was around his chest and a sword was on his throat. Nishala.

"Step aside or I'll cut your throat." Nishala's teeth were pressed together, she hissed through them.

"Nishala...you would know of throat cutting, wouldn't you?"

She pressed her sword to his throat enough to draw blood. Balnak's hands raised.

"Alright then. I'll leave and let you women play together."

Nishala's sword moved to point at Balnak's face in a lightning swift movement. He slowly backed away and slithered into the darkness. When he reached the river he leapt into it and disappeared.

"Are you alright?" Nishala sheathed her sword.

"Yes. Thank you for doing that."

"Is he the one you spoke of the last time you visited?"

"Indeed, he's been a constant nuisance."

"Is he competing in the trial?"

I nodded.

"Well there you have it. That's why I want you to compete in the trial. So you can put that rat in his place."

She slithered back in the direction of her camp.

"What did he mean? When he said you knew of throat cutting?"

Nishala stopped. She didn't turn around.

"I competed in the last trial, one hundred years ago. I killed my opponent. I was exiled for it."

Ice shot through my veins as she slithered out of sight.

Settle down, Priya. If we want to kill Balnak, better if we're trained by a killer.

***

When I arrived back home, I slipped out of my damp robe and visited the hot spring in the basement. My muscles ached from Nishala's training. I didn't bother slowly dipping in, I dunked myself immediately. The salve on my slash wound had already hardened and there was barely anything visible there now. I submerged all of my body into the hot water. Only my nose and above weren't under the water. I closed my eyes, and deeply inhaled the steamy air. The warmth soothed my nostrils and lungs.

I hate that I'm practically lying to Sarvaan every time I sneak out. I'm afraid he wouldn't understand. What am I thinking? Of course he'd understand. He's amazing and he adores me and loves me with all his soul. The next time we talk I'm just going to tell him. He may be confused about me needing to enter the trial, but if it means me getting a Nagini body, he'll surely be on board.

My fingers ran over my lips and down my neck as I floated in the hot water tossing around my thoughts. I traced circles in the steam clouds. I ran my fingernails over the water's surface over and over.

Why did Nishala want me in the trial in the first place? Learning that she'd competed in the last trial and killed her opponent shined some light on the answer, but I still don't have the whole picture. Was she trying to live through me since she failed?

I thought of Prathavi's words at Sarvaan's match.

Then there's Prathavi. The ancient queen. The warrior Nani told me about. Somehow she's talking to me. Somehow her essence is bonded to mine. I caught a sword with my bare hand, and without injury. Am I a living incarnate of her essence? I have many questions for her when I speak with her at the cave. Why the cave though? It felt as though she was within me, why would I need to be in the cave to speak with her.

I dunked my head under the water out of frustration.

After drying myself off I crept back into bed with Sarvaan. My skin was still radiating warmth from the hot spring so his body latched onto mine and pulled me into him. I snuggled against him where his chest and neck met. He stirred into a half-awakened state.

"Priya...you're warm, are you feeling alright?"

Okay Priya, channel your queen energy and let's tell him. I need to tell him about Nishala to relieve this crushing feeling on my heart. He's a good man and I don't need to be lying to him.

"Yes. I couldn't sleep so I took a dip in the hot spring. Go back to sleep my love. I'll join you."

Fuck. I'm married to a monstrous man but I'm being the monster.

His hand found my ass cheek and pulled me into him. If I were pressed into him anymore I wouldn't be able to breathe. My breasts pressed tight against him with each breath as if I were in a corset. I was comfortable though. The last thing I remember before drifting off to sleep was Sarvaan's tail slowly slithering around my feet, my legs, and my torso.

I'm wrapped in a bundle of love, with a ribbon of lies tying it all together.

Chapter 16
Threads ~ समुदाय

T he next day, Sarvaan and I decided to do the bonding ritual again.

"Tell me a secret." I almost choked on my juulava wine.

"Ok, here it goes." He stared at me intently as I gathered my courage.

Stop being a coward. Just tell him already!

"I've been sneaking out to see Nishala the exile. She's teaching me combat as well. She knows how to make me a Nagini. Her condition is that I enter the trial."

Sarvaan's face twisted into anger almost immediately.

"What? Sneaking out? To see an exile? Priya, that's treason!"

He dropped his glass of wine, staining the couch.

"And she wants you to enter the trial? Does she think she can train you to beat me in combat?"

"No, Sarvaan! Please listen—"

His hand shot to my throat, he lifted me above the couch and slammed me against the wall. I heard a crushing sound as the impact produced spider web fractures in the wall.

"You've betrayed me!"

His fingers tightened around my throat. I couldn't breathe. I tried to take his hand off me but it was useless. He was five times my strength at least. I felt my eyes bulging because of the extreme pressure. I heard a crunch as my throat crumpled under his grip.

"NO!" I sat up in bed drenched in sweat. My hand went to my throat. It was fine. I was fine. The light from the jewels indicated it was morning.

"My love, my dear, my Priya." Sarvaan's words and sudden entrance into the bedroom made me jump. When he was close to the bed I leapt to his chest and hugged him tight.

He'd never hurt me. He'd never hurt me.

"Oh, hello. You're going to spoil me and make me expect a morning greeting like this every day."

I kissed his chest and forced a smile onto my face.

"You're well worth it."

He sat me on the bed and crawled beside me.

"I wanted to run an idea by you."

"Okay, Tell me."

"The other day you said you'd be interested in getting involved in the community. I could show you around Bhogavati, show you how our community is involved in the nurseries, making of clothes, getting food to the markets. Would you be interested in that?"

"Yes, I'd like that." My nose nuzzled his.

He'll never hurt me...he'll never hurt me.

The first place we visited that day was the nursery in the Karkota Kula neighborhood. We found a dai taking care of the eggs.

"Hello Sarvaan! Hello Priya! Good match yesterday...you're on your way to the crown." She mimicked a fighting stance. Sarvaan and I chuckled.

"Thank you, I do what I can. Priya would like to be part of the community. Is there anything we can do to help today?"

"Yes! Come with me." Her face glowed with delight at the mention of help.

The dai led us to a room with a coal fire roaring and eggs lined around it. Right as I entered, my skin felt the licks of heat radiating from the fire.

"This is where we bathe the eggs in the heat of coal-fire to awaken them. More coal needs to feed the fire and each egg needs rotating. Think you two can handle that for a few minutes?"

Damn that fire is hot, are they trying to saute the eggs? Nagas were beings of water, yet born of fire, interesting.

"Yes, we'll handle it." I answered, shielding my face from the heat.

"Okay then, I'll be back in a little while to check on you. Should you need anything just come find me."

The dai took her exit and Sarvaan to the fire and picked up a shovel laying on the floor.

"I can see the fire is roasting your face. I'll handle the coal shoveling." He slithered into a small room which held the coal stores and I heard the sound of metal scraping against rock.

"Let's flip some eggs."

I started at one end of the line of eggs around the fire and flipped them to the opposite side that had been exposed. Each egg was the size of a pomelo. I had to grab them with both hands to rotate them.

They're much larger than the eggs Sarvaan put inside me. Remembering him pumping his eggs in me made my legs tremble.

Sarvaan returned with a shovel of coal and placed it on the fire. The flames roared to life, sending a fresh wave of heat over the eggs and my face.

"Sarvaan, I noticed these eggs are larger than...yours."

"That's because these are fertilized and almost ready to hatch."

"So I'd be carrying ten of *these* in me when I'm a Nagini?"

"Your body will be changed to be able to handle them. That's of course, if you choose to bear our offspring."

"Of course I'd—"

The egg in my hands wiggled.

"Sarvaan! It moved!" He slithered quickly by my side.

"This is wonderful! You'll get to see a freshly hatched Naga youngling."

Two tiny Naga hands punched through the egg shell. A small head punched a third hole in the shell. Its small serpentine coils pulled the rest of the shell off of its body.

Holy shit...I'm holding a baby Naga. If only my university professors could see me now!

The Naga youngling looked at me with yearning eyes.

"Does it...need breastfeeding or something?"

Sarvaan's chest pulsed with a stifled laugh.

"No, Nagas aren't mammals."

"Then why do Nagini have breasts?" I looked at him sternly.

"A Nagini's breasts contain a milk of sorts, but it's what is used to fertilize her eggs."

I thought back to the nude Nagini breasts I've seen so far. They didn't have any nipples.

Huh. I was wondering why they didn't have any nipples.

The dai poked her head back in the room and leapt for joy upon seeing me holding a youngling.

"Oh! Good, he's been a stubborn one. He was supposed to have hatched yesterday. You must have a gifted touch, Priya."

Having hatched a Naga youngling in my hand made me think of mine and Sarvaan's future.

I would love to give him children if my new Nagini body allowed it. Nagas didn't raise their own children. Would I grow attached and want to go against tradition? Did Nagas meet their parents later in life and have any sort of relationship with them?

***

After the nursery, Sarvaan took me to one of the many gardeners who grew food for the city.

"I've told you before that there is no cost for goods because there is no currency. This is how the cycle gets completed. The community gets free food, but are expected to help deliver food from the gardeners and farms to the markets for distribution."

"Fascinating!"

More and more I realized that the communities of Bhogavati were the heart of its economy. The community produced and consumed as one connected circle. When we arrived at the garden, there was a wooden cart with two wheels and long handles. Sarvaan took the handles and wheeled the cart down a dirt path beside the garden which led into its heart. Flowers with fruity scents and grass with earthy fragrances lined the dirt path and hypnotized my mind.

"Ah Sarvaan, just the strong warrior I need! I've got almost two cartloads of yield needing to be moved to the temple market square."

The gardener slithered to me and shook my hand with a fervorous wobble.

"You must be Priya. I haven't had the pleasure of meeting you yet."

"The pleasure is all mine. Sarvaan is taking me on a tour of the city to demonstrate how community members help their neighborhoods."

"Sarvaan is a generous soul. Thank you both for helping me today."

Sarvaan and I got to work loading the gardener's vegetables and fungi yields into the wooden cart. Sarvaan did eighty percent of the work. He could lift half my weight in crops with one arm tied behind his back. When the cart was full with a mountain of carrots, tubers, and mushrooms, Sarvaan hoisted me to his chest, and then put me atop the mountain of crops.

Nagini princess to garden princess. Interesting.

The cart with its load was probably the weight of a car. Sarvaan pushed it like he was kicking a pebble down the street.

"Sarvaan, I wanted to talk with you more on the subject of children."

"What's on your mind my dearest?"

"Would you be proud of me having our children? Would you feel any attachment to them if they are raised away from us?"

"I'd be proud, but in a different way than you probably think."

"How so?"

"I'd be proud to have produced offspring with my soul companion, less than being proud of the offspring themselves."

"That is different from my world's view on making children for sure."

"There are two relationships that Naga value: our connection to our soul companion, and our connection to our community. If you look around you can see the community is made of Nagas Karkota Kula . These Nagas are my family. They could be my brothers, my sisters, my aunts or uncles, my parents or grandparents. Instead of celebrating immediate family as humans do, we celebrate family as an entire community."

"So if...when we choose to have children together, you'd be okay with never seeing them?"

"I would see them though. Just as I see the rest of the Nagas around the city."

That makes a lot of sense. The neighborhood literally is the entire family as one.

"I also don't want you to mix my words or feelings." He stopped the cart and leaned over, face-to-face with me. His hand stroked the side of my face.

"Having offspring together isn't just a sexual ritual. It is a sacred thing between soul companions. I love you, Priya. I'd be honored to make offspring with you."

Damn, he can really melt my heart. I'd be honored to make children with you as well Sarvaan.

After delivering the cart of crops to the temple market square, the final stop was the Vastrashala, where weavers and tailors crafted clothing and other textiles for the community. This was an area I already had some practice with. As a girl, Nani would show me how to create the handwoven skirts, shawls, wraps, and sashes the Naga tribespeople from her heritage wore.

After weaving for about an hour, I had an idea.

"Sarvaan, do you think I could ask the weavers to help me make something for myself? The only clothes I have were given to me when I arrived."

"You've done well today helping others, I'm sure they'd be glad to help make you something special."

I jumped up and down and clapped excitedly. I gathered the weavers and told them my idea. They exchanged glances. They were confused at first, then intrigued.

We started with a mekhala, the traditional wrap-around skirt of my Nani's people. The base fabric was deep black, but I had the weavers thread it with stripes of Karkota green and gold.

For my upper body, I chose a vatchi. It was a sleeveless bodice that left my arms free. Red fabric, the color of warrior's blood, with gold embroidery tracing patterns that mimicked both serpent scales and the geometric designs I remembered from Nani's old photographs.

Finally, a shawl. Black with borders of green, red, and gold woven together. I would drape it over one shoulder, leaving the other bare. The weaving had taken all day, even with several sets of hands. I put on the newly made garments and stood before a mirror. Before me was someone I didn't recognize.

Is that me? I look like Nani from her old photographs when she visited her ancestral homelands. I look like the Nagini princess I was promised to be as a child. I look like a member of Karkota Kula. I'm all of these. Combined into one essence.

"You look absolutely lovely, Priya." Sarvaan admired my new attire with his pupils wide.

"I'm no longer the human who fell into Bhogavati. I'm Priya of Karkota Kula. Moving forward to my destiny, while honoring my past."

"You're honoring the universe with your beauty." His hand found my face. I leaned into his hand.

***

I changed from my newly woven attire and back into my green and gold lehenga choli. I didn't want to get my new garments dirty on their first day in this world. The jewels around the city glowed a soft dusk-like light as we walked home. Sarvaan and I stopped at a park to sit and rest before heading home. His arm was draped over me and his tail was playing with my feet and I swung them back and forth.

"Thank you for showing me more of this world and how to contribute. I like being part of your world."

"You're my favorite part of my world, Priya."

He leaned over and kissed me. It was a single peck on the lips, but I didn't want it to end. My hands held his face to mine. Our lips exchanged slow, soft kisses. My breathing got heavier. Our kisses got deeper. Our mouths opened wider each time. Our tongues began to twist and flick inside each other's mouths.

I have to have him. Right now.

"Sarvaan. What would you say if I told you I was so fucking horny right now and I couldn't wait until we got home?"

I looked around. There weren't many people in the park, maybe ten or so, but people were around us. It made me a bit excited to think about, actually.

"I'd say you'd probably need to satisfy your urge. If not you'll go absolutely feral. Feral soul companions are bad luck." He grinned at his joke.

I was too horny for jokes. I climbed onto his lap and hiked my lehenga to allow me to straddle him on the bench we were sitting on. I kissed him like I'd spent hundreds of years in the desert and his mouth had water in it.

"Do you care if people are looking?" His cock was hard and pressed into my pussy lips.

"No. Let them look. I'm with my soul companion." I rubbed my hips back and forth getting him into me as quickly as I could.

Sarvaan kissed all over my chest and neck and I started bouncing on his erection. Each time I brought my weight down on his wide base a small half-moan half-squeal of pleasure escaped my lips. The rush of people being around me set my body on fire hotter than the coal fire from earlier. I bounced fast and hard, looking around me, seeing onlookers smiling and blushing at us.

They like it! Oh fuck this is hot!

Sarvaan's tongue entered my mouth and I felt his cock twitching. His fingers gripped me and dug into my back and shoulders.

"I'm there..." I felt the bulge starting at the base of his cock. His hot sex breath hissed into my mouth and I devoured it.

"Cum for me!" His grip intensified. He was climaxing.

His cock began to pump his hot fluid into my pussy. With each pump I clenched around him and bounced up and down. He let out a guttural grunt with each bounce. Fluid seeped out of me, covering my ass, his lap, and the bench with cum. It was over within minutes, but fuck it felt great.

I leaned forward against his chest. We just sat there breathing into one another.

"Did fucking...in public bother you...Sarvaan?" I asked between my panting.

"If you liked it, then I like it. For the record, I really liked it."

I know he'd never hurt me. He'd truly never hurt.

I sat up and kissed him some more. We sat and kissed under the trees and soft light with him still inside me, and our laps soaked in our fluids.

Chapter 17
Cave ~ बीज

As we ate breakfast the next morning, Sarvaan and I kept exchanging glances like we were criminals who got away with the perfect crime. Sex in the park with people watching kept playing in my head. The way Sarvaan smirked at me, it replayed in his head as well. A thought kept interrupting my bliss, however. Prathavi wanted to talk. She wanted me to meet her at the cave that Sarvaan took me to to train in darkness.

I wonder if there's a casual way of telling your spouse that an ancient queen's spirit talks to you.

"Sarvaan, there's something I need to talk to you about."

"You can tell me anything, Priya. What is it, my love?"

"Do you remember us discovering the image of queen Prathavi carved on the wall of the cave the other day?"

"I do."

I just stared at him. I couldn't bring myself to say it. I took his hands in mine and tried again.

"Look, what I'm about to tell you will make me sound like I'm out of my mind, but I swear to you it's true."

"Well let's hear it then. You have me intrigued."

"Since I arrived here, Prathavi has shown me visions and spoken to me in my mind. The last time she spoke to me was at your last match of the trial. She told me to speak further, I'd need to go to the cave again where her image was carved on the wall."

Sarvaan's eyes went to my hands holding his, then back to my face.

"You have an ancient warrior queen talking to you in your mind? The same one your nani told you stories about as a child?"

"Yes..."

Ok, he either runs away now or he's all in. There's no in-between.

"Priya...this sounds serious. We need to leave at once." He rose, warrior energy taking over his body.

"You don't think I'm mad?" He pulled me to my feet.

"All of this can't be a coincidence. Niyati is at work here. Destiny should not be postponed."

I have the most perfect fucking husband in the whole fucking world.

***

About an hour later we were hiking up the mountain again that held the cave where I'd first discovered Prathavi's image. Where I'd caught Sarvaan's sword in my hand with no injuries. The bridge below that stood over the crystal lake looked so serene from this altitude.

"What do you think she wants to talk about?"

"She keeps telling me I'm strong. Strong like she was."

"Maybe she's trying to help you become the fiercest human warrior ever seen. Or maybe she knows you've been seeking transformation into a Nagini and knows a way to help."

Shit. I really need to tell him. I want to so bad. I want to celebrate with him that I already have a way to be Nagini.

"Yes, perhaps she does."

The mouth of the cave was in sight now. We both sat to catch our breath. The chilling air of the mountain drove me into Sarvaan's body to stay warm. He wrapped my body with his. He was my personal Naga igloo.

"Would you wait just outside for me? She usually only speaks to me when I'm alone or alone with my thoughts."

"Of course. I'll be right here waiting."

I left Sarvaan's warmth, holding onto his fingers until distance made it impossible. I entered the cave, stumbling around in darkness. There were no torches here. No flashlights or lanterns. Every Naga had jewels that glowed growing directly on them. The earth and stone grew natural glowing jewels within it as well. The glowing jewels in the earth were too difficult to remove. I was stuck in the dark.

Alrighty Prathavi. I'm here. I feel the carving on the wall.

A soft light emitted from the jewels depicted on Prathavi's hood in the cave carving. The carving moved, taking stone from the cave wall to become three-dimensional. My feet carried me backwards, but my eyes couldn't look away. The carving had come to life. Queen Prathavi stood before me now. Earth and stone turned to green and gold scales.

Green and gold...Nani's colors...my colors.

"Hello Priya."

"You're here...but, I thought you were in my head?"

"I exist in small glimpses, wherever the memories of me are strongest."

"Nani's stories. They put your memories of you in my mind. That's why you can speak to me."

"She planted the seed, you nurtured it. I am a sliver of memory made manifest."

"How is that possible? How did my nani create a memory of you, and put it into my mind?"

"You're full of questions. You should worry about yourself, not me."

"Me? How do I fit into the equation? I didn't ask to fall into Bhogavati from my realm."

"Really? Remember Priya, I've been with you for a long time. I've seen through your eyes, hear through your consciousness." Her finger pointed at my head. "You've been clinging to your nani's words you entire life. You truly believed you were a Nagini princess. You became an archaeologist. Deep in your soul, you've been searching for Bhogavati. I know because I've heard your mind's whispers. I've sensed yearning to find evidence that Naga-Loka existed in the physical world and not just through divinity."

I fell to my knees.

"But I didn't ask to have to give up my world. My family. I didn't want to be trapped here."

"You're not trapped here." Prathavi bent her body to peer into my eyes. "I've seen what you've seen. I've heard what you've heard. Nishala will show you the way to become Nagini."

"That's a long shot. How do I even know she's telling the truth?"

"You've known in your heart, even before she revealed that she had the answer. You've been making conscious, calculated decisions this entire time."

I stood, kicking and slapping the cave wall in a tantrum.

"What kind of fucking logic is that?" Tears of frustration streamed down my face.

"You could have not trusted Nishala, but you chose to. You could have opted for exile instead of being a consort, but you chose to become a consort. You chose that path because the King said *humans* couldn't travel outside of this place. You've been setting your plan in motion since you arrived here."

An angry sob escaped my lips.

She doesn't know what she's fucking talking about.

"Don't I?"

"Get out of my head!"

"You're the one who put me there, Priya."

"You said Nani's stories put you there."

"No, I said she planted the seed. You're the one who grew the seed. You gave me a form."

"Could you just...tell me why you're here, and why I'm here, and cut the shit?"

Prathavi's hand shot forward, grabbed me by the fabric of my clothes, and pressed me against the cave wall. My feet dangled because of the height difference between us.

"I'm here because you grew the seed of a memory into reality! You're here because you decided that you didn't want to just be a Nagini princess in your head...you wanted to be a queen!"

Her grip softened, I slid down the wall and my feet touched the cave floor.

"You wanted this world. It's yours."

Ye sab Chutiyapa hai, *that makes no sense.*

"But it's not my world. It's your world." My hands touched my knees, I was breathing heavily with adrenaline in my system.

"This is our world."

"Is it? And after I complete whatever ritual Nishala has in store and I am Nagini, whose world will it be then? Yours or mine?"

Her finger lifted my chin. Her eyes locked into mine.

"When the ritual is complete, there will be no you and there will be no me. There will be us."

***

When I emerged from the cave I told Sarvaan of what transpired. He was more excited about Prathavi's words than I was. I had to omit the part where Prathavi confirmed Nishala's ritual would transform me, and instead told him she indicated that I'd find a way to become Nagini.

"Do you know what this means, Priya?" He picked me up, bring me to his shoulders. "It means there's an actual method out there somewhere that will transform you."

"I just don't know what to think of her telling me I chose this. I fell down a fucking hole. How is that choosing anything?"

Sarvaan laid back on the dirt and rocks, laying me across his chest. I was small enough to lay on his body without any of me falling off.

"This hole you fell down...did you seek it out?"

"Well no I..."

Shit. I did seek it out. Sunil told me to wait and I went anyway.

"I guess I did. We had just excavated a new cave. We were excited to see what discoveries could be found within it."

I gulped, replaying it all in my mind. Sarvaan's hands rubbed my chest and my hair.

"I was told to wait for someone else to arrive. My boss. I went anyway."

My face twisted and tears burst from my eyes.

"I did this all to myself. All of it! I took my world away from myself!"

Sarvaan's arms wrapped me and turned me to face him.

"Hey, Priya, that's not true..."

I buried my face in his chest scales, muffling more sobs.

"Think about what you've accomplished..." Sarvaan grabbed me and sat me up, lifting my chin with a finger.

"You gained a soul companion. You have access to the wisdom of an ancient warrior queen. You are literally living in a realm you've dreamt of your entire life. You'll be the first person ever to be transformed into a Naga. You'll be able to return to your world whenever you want and see your family. You have everything you've ever wanted right now."

I haven't thought of it that way. Everything I've wanted since I was a girl...it was within my grasp.

My frown morphed into a smile and I kissed my amazing husband.

"You really will never let me be unhappy with you?"

"No, never. I'll fight your unhappiness with every fiber of my being."

"And I'll love you with every fiber of my being."

I really will, Sarvaan. I promise. I'm not lying to you because I'm trying to hurt you. I'm really just unsure of how this will all unfold. Unsure about what Nishala has planned.

Sarvaan laid out a blanket to lay on in the grove next to the river. We decided to spend some more time out on the edge of the realm before going home. He'd brought a pouch of snacks, so we made an impromptu picnic. I really loved laying on Sarvaan's body and looking at the sparkling starry jewels in the trees and in the ceiling of Naga-Loka.

"Sarvaan, what's it like being a Naga?"

"Well, I've never been anything else in my life, so I wouldn't know what to compare it to."

My hand slapped his side playfully.

"I'm serious! I want to make sure I'm prepared." My hands took his and held them again my chest.

"Well let's see...we are able to shapeshift into human form. I feel more durable in my Naga form, almost invincible. Our scales are tough and insulating, so you won't be afraid of things like thorns on bushes or being too close to flames."

"What about slithering compared to walking on legs?"

"That one definitely took some getting used to. If I had to describe how slithering feels, imagine hundreds of toes on the bottom of your feet, working in tandem to move you."

"That sounds like it would tickle."

"Like this?"

Sarvaan's tail pearls brushed the bottom of my feet and my leg kicked out of reflex.

"Hey!"

I rolled over to face him. My mouth found his. The sounds of nature around us was soothing as our lips locked and tongues writhed together. Sarvaan's yearning fingers yanked my top over my head and sent it to the ground. His long, forked tongue stroked down the middle of my chest, pricking my nipples enough to make me gasp in pleasure. I was suddenly midair. He lifted me from him and placed me on the blanket on my hands and knees.

"Haan...do with me what you want."

"I plan to." Warm breath caressed my neck.

My pants were pulled off of me in a split second. Both forks of his tongue entered my pussy and started exploring. They flicked inside my walls making my legs shake and my hips bounce back and forth.

"Yes...fuck..."

One fork of his tongue slid out of my pussy and pressed against my asshole.

"Put it in. I need it in me, now." I moved my ass up and down on his tongue fork to get my ass lubed up with his tongue fluids.

The tongue fork poked it slowly, then slid in more and more until each of his tongue forks were all the way in each of my holes.

"That's it...that's great." I was having the time of my fucking life.

His tongue forks made a repetitive rhythm. They pulled all the way out, and then slid all the way back in, and made a flicking motion. One of Sarvaan's hand reached under me and started to play with my clit. His other hand covered both my tits at once, massaging them and plucking on my nipples each time his tongue forks made the flicking motion when they were all the way inside each of my holes. Each plucking motion sent shocks through my body.

"Sarvaan! Fucking...shit...I love you...I love you!" My pussy clenched, my asshole puckered, and my back arched.

I was breathing so hard I felt like I was going to have a heart attack. My body was covered in sweat but the air outside brushed over my skin, bringing a cooling sensation. Sarvaan's chest pressed against my back. His lips grazed my ear.

"My turn."

He flipped me on my back. His enormous cock was hard and ready. I expected him to drive it into my pussy, but instead he laid it between my tits.

Oh baby. Hell yes, let's get dirty.

When I knew what he had in mind, I held my tits together as tight as possible around his large cock. His cock pulsed and squirted some fluid on my tits to get things started. The feeling of warm, thick, oil covered my chest as Sarvaan started to pump his cock between them. He was so long that the tip was hitting my chin with each thrust. I opened my mouth to catch the tip each time.

"I love when you let me fuck you in dirty ways." He grunted above me.

"You can fuck me in any dirty way you want, husband."

Damn my tits look so nice being perked up right now. I'd want to fuck them if I had a dick too.

Sarvaan's hands grabbed my hips and he pulled me forward and back to match his thrusts. He was using me as a fuck toy and I loved it. I saw his cock bulge at the base and then the bulging moved toward the tip. I felt him try to pull away, to cum off to the side. I squeezed my tits together hard to hold his dick in place.

"No, cum on me. I want every drop."

Sarvaan's face howled in pleasure as his cock exploded a stream of warm cum all over my tits, chest, belly, neck, and face. I held my mouth open and managed to catch a couple mouthfuls that I swallowed. Sarvaan fell to my side and draped his arm over me. His cum covering my body looked like something poured an entire bucket of milk on me. I used a corner of the blanket and wiped what I could from me and rolled over snuggling to Sarvaan's body.

"I really enjoy fucking you in every way possible...I love you so much." He was breathing hard, but it was calming.

"It's a good thing I love being fucked in every way possible by my one true love then."

We spent the night on the edge of the realm, too tired to clean up and go home. I was wrapped in a blanket and Sarvaan's body, and my entire front was sticky with his cum.

Chapter 18
Palace ~ राजनीति

When I awoke the next day, I had an overwhelming sense of duty overtake me. I had nurtured the memory of an ancient warrior queen within me my entire life. It seemed that all of the decisions in my life had led me to this realm. A yearning took over my mind, a yearning to be involved in the kingdom's affairs beyond just helping my local community. Sarvaan would surely win the crown in the trial, and I would be a queen.

After I finished munching on a piece of spiced cheese for breakfast, I brought it up to Sarvaan.

"Sarvaan, if you complete the trial undefeated, you'll be King, correct?"

"Yes, that's true. Usually there's a week between the end of the trial and the coronation of the new ruler of Naga-Loka."

"What would that make me, if you are crowned king?"

"If I am crowned king, then you'd be my queen of course."

He said it so matter-of-factly. I would just...*be the queen.*

"If there's a chance of me being a queen to a kingdom, I'd like to see how our kingdom interacts with other kingdoms. I'd like to see how diplomatic affairs are handled."

The wine he was drinking sloshed over his face as his face lit up with excitement. The drops ran down his chin and over his beautiful chest scales.

"That's great to hear! I love that you want to be so involved. Karkota Kula are Nagas who specialize in trade and diplomatic relations. There is a meeting each day at the palace to discuss such affairs. Would you like to attend?"

"Yes, but, would we be allowed to just walk in and sit in on these meetings?"

"Not anyone from the public is allowed. But you are my soul companion. You are Karkota."

Sarvaan's arms went around me and hugged me tight. He almost squeezed the cheese back out of me. He released me and his eyes went wide.

"I'll have to find my diplomatic attire. I forgot where I put it."

He slithered off to our bedroom to find his attire, and my mind was in a similar place. I went to the bedroom I had claimed when I first arrived. The mekhala, vatchi, and shawl made with Nani's colors and Karkota Kula colors lay on the bed.

If I'm going to be in the presence of government officials, I want them to know who I truly am. I shed my robe to the floor and reached for the mekhala, wrapping it around my hips. It was mostly black fabric with strips of green and gold. It represented me as a girl, being a blank canvas that Nani decorated with green and gold jewels.

I am my past.

Next I donned the vatchi. Its threads felt silky on my chest. My fingers grazed over the gold embroidery, tracing the serpentine patterns. It represented where I am now. Between two warriors, Sarvaan, and Prathavi.

I am my present.

Lastly, I draped the shawl over my right shoulder. It held all of the colors from my past and present. It represented where I wanted to be.

I am my future.

"Wow..."

Sarvaan was standing in the doorway. His voice made me flinch. I turned to face him, smiling with my past, present, and future covering me.

"You think so?"

"Very much so. I could never tire of seeing you wear it. You're splendid. You're captivating. You'll definitely make the droning meetings more exciting."

Sarvaan's diplomatic attire was dynamite. It was comprised of a green, decorative scarf and a blue sash across his body diagonally. The tail of the scarf was hanging down the middle of his chest drawing my eyes to his muscles even more than usual.

"I mean, they won't be looking at me when they have you to admire." I walked to him and ran my hands up and down his chest, playing with the scarf tail along the way.

"Good fortune on both accounts then. If eyes are upon us then they'll have to listen to what we are saying."

I slapped his arm playfully as I smirked at his joke.

I'd always had eyes on me throughout my life. Ears listening to my words would be something new.

***

As Sarvaan and I headed to the palace, my new attire certainly caught more eyes than usual. I tried to act as regal as possible. When I caught someone staring, I flipped my hair at them and smiled. If they wanted to look I'd let them know who I was.

"Oh Sarvaan, Priya is so gorgeous!" A Nagini woman said in passing. She touched the fabric of my regalia and jittered with energy.

"She truly is." He was smiling and wore a face of pride.

Ultimately, I wanted Bhogavati to know there was Naga in me one way or another. Naga heritage, and Naga future. Two cultures, merged into one queen...me. We entered the palace and when it looked like someone was going to say something about me being there, their eyes would shoot to Sarvaan and they'd just let us pass.

Hmm, having a massive warrior husband is good for more than just looks and sex.

Sarvaan led me to a large room with a high ceiling and long table with seating for several dozen. The chairs had an ergonomic wave pattern to them.

Serpent bodies demand serpent chairs. Makes sense.

There were already six or so Naga sitting in the room. Again their gaze shot to me and when they looked as if they were about to say something, their eyes caught sight of Sarvaan. Sarvaan was easily the most massive Naga in the room.

"Sarvaan, we haven't seen you stop by in some time. How are you?"

"It's a good day to conduct business. I've been busy with the trial, but I look forward to getting back to my trade and diplomacy duties."

The Naga turned to me, searching for something to say.

"Priya, your attire...it's very unique."

I put on my best pompous expression and waited a few seconds to respond, as if I hadn't heard him speak.

"Priy—" When he was about to open his mouth to repeat his words I spoke.

"Yes. A unique attire is demanded for a future queen. Wouldn't you agree?"

On the inside I laughed until I cried. The Naga was lost for words. He raised his hand as if to attempt to speak and then other members of the meeting started filing in and he chose to keep his mouth shut. Black scales caught my eyes. Balnak walked in and took the seat at the head of the table. He hadn't yet noticed me or Sarvaan.

"Why is Balnak here?" My whisper was sharp in Sarvaan's ear.

"He is the minister of trade, unfortunately."

Fuck. Why him? Why now?

"Alright everyone. Thank you for attending today. It looks like concerns for today are vaults two, nine, and thirteen, as well as Lanka's demand to increase our tribute of gold to them." He spoke with a toxic charisma. He could fool those who hadn't seen his true nature, but I saw the venom spraying from his mouth.

Lanka...the Rakshasa kingdom? Why would Bhogavati need to tribute gold to them?

A Naga with gold scales, from Vasuki Kula raised his hand. Balnak nodded to him.

"Yes, Chitrak, what is your business?"

"I'd like to discuss the vaults first. They are short of gold and gemstones. Are we sure the contents are being catalogued accurately?"

"Tell you what, I'll personally see to it that all of the contents are taken into account by my own staff. The records and actual contents will be equal when I am finished looking into the matter."

There was something about Balnak's answer that didn't sit well with me. I hated Balnak beyond reality, but there was something else to his words. I'd been lied to a great deal in my life and his words were definitely lies.

"Does that satisfy you Chitrak?"

"Yes Minister, my business is now finished."

"Excellent, let's move on to Lanka."

The Naga at the table suddenly erupted in a chaotic amalgamation of heated words and shouting. Balnak slapped his tail pearls against the table to quiet them.

"I know this is a heated subject, but my instinct tells me to increase our tribute to them. We don't want war to spark on our borders just because of a squabble over gold."

"I think that would show weakness."

Everyone's heads and eyes turned to me, Balnak's included. His eyes registered Sarvaan, then back to me. Sarvaan gave him a look that seemed to say, *if you even look at her wrong I'll rip your tongue out and feed it to you.*

"Excuse me?"

"It sounds like Lanka is trying to bully Bhogavati. If we show weakness and give in, then we show them we can be walked upon."

A whole room of Naga heads and eyes shifted again back to Balnak.

"My my, Priya those colors are excellent at *distracting*. Try to wear the colors of your kula when representing yourself in an official capacity."

I didn't respond immediately. I waited until he was going to speak again.

"Now, back to the matter at han—"

"My kula is my past, my present, and my future. This meeting isn't regarding fashion, it's regarding trade." All the heads and eyes were back on me.

"She makes a good point. Let Lanka whine all they want to. We give them enough tribute as it is." One of the Naga spoke up and raised their hand in agreement.

"Agreed!" Sarvaan's hand raised immediately as the first Naga finished speaking.

Slowly, everyone's hand was raised. My eyes never left Balnak's.

Your move, ass face.

"Ve-ry well..." He finally spoke after an uncomfortable few seconds and scribbled on a parchment in front of him.

What are you up to, Balnak? I'll find out...whatever it is. I'll show the kingdom who you truly are.

***

The trade meeting concluded and Balnak was the first to leave. He slithered with a frustrated winding motion.

Good, be frustrated. I exist now to frustrate you.

Sarvaan's hand gripped my shoulder.

"That was mesmerizing Priya! You were amazing. You're such a natural." He leaned in and gave me a quick kiss on the lips.

"Thank you, my darling. It was fun watching him squirm."

As we were leaving the room, King Vasuki entered the doorway. Sarvaan quickly bowed and I curtsied.

"Ah, I thought I heard your voice Priya. Would you and Sarvaan care to accompany me in meeting with the diplomat from Lanka?"

Before I could answer, Sarvaan poked me in the back.

"We'd be honored, your highness!"

"King Vasuki, may I ask why you thought of us for this occasion?" I rubbed my back where Sarvaan had poked me.

"I heard your riveting speech on the subject of tribute to Lanka. We could use fierce advocates for Bhogavati like you." He led us out into the hall and along his side as we migrated to a different meeting room.

This room was almost identical to the one we had come from, but there was just one person sitting at the massive table. He looked like a human man, but his body was as large as a Naga's. His skin was blue, and his fingernails were in the shape of sharp claws. He was handsome, almost magically so, as if a jinn had granted his looks to him. When King Vasuki entered the room he stood and bowed.

"Ah, King Vasuki, it's a pleasure to meet with you again."

Vasuki made a cordial gesture.

"Keshvaan, I'm always fond of our meetings. This is Priya and Sarvaan of Karkota Kula. They'll be sitting in today."

Keshvaan's eyes were glued to me. I found them to be predatory, but curious, and hiding immense intellect. Sarvaan kept near me more than usual, he sensed it too.

"It's nice to meet you both. Vasuki didn't tell me his citizens were so beautiful." His eyes moved between my face and Sarvaan's with the same admiration.

Is he…flirting with both of us?

"King Vasuki, I'll get straight to the point. King Ravana has asked that your tribute to Lanka be increased by a further five percent."

King Ravana…as in…THE King Ravana? In my world he was ancient history. Down here, it seemed history was still alive.

"I see. I've spoken with my associates here and they disagree."

My neck and face ran hot. He was putting me on the spot. Keshvaan's eyes swayed over to me and Sarvaan.

"Oh? May I ask why…you disagree?"

What do I say? What the fuck do I say?

"Because we feel Bhogavati pays enough tribute. What is the reason for the increase in the first place?" Sarvaan to my rescue.

Keshvaan's claws tapped on the table one at a time.

"King Ravana has discovered some discrepancies in our shared borders. Our border should extend further according to ancient texts."

"When can we see these ancient texts to verify their legitimacy?" I didn't need Sarvaan to rescue me this time.

Keshvaan paused. I could see the wheels turning in his mind.

"I will add this to my next meeting's agenda, I do not have them on my person. Apologies."

King Vasuki stood, then Sarvaan. I embarrassingly hesitated but stood a moment later.

"Well then Keshvaan, it seems our next meeting will be a busy one. I'll be sure to bring my best scribes."

A flash of annoyance burned on Keshvaan's face for a split second. He stood and bowed to the King.

"Excellent, your highness, King Vasuki. Until next time…"

With a saluting gesture on his head he left the room.

"Sarvaan, your soul companion is better at politics than I ever imagined."

My cheeks grew hot.

"She is amazing at everything, actually."

Oh you amazing, beautiful man.

"I wasn't impressed by Keshvaan. He seems like he's hiding something."

"I concur." Sarvaan agreeing with me made my chest rise with pride.

"I'm sorry to hear. Maybe one day you'll all be fond of each other, who knows?"

Balnak wanted Bhogavati to pay more tribute, and Keshvaan couldn't even produce the text that would justify the increase. I smell a pile of shit.

***

The final meeting at the palace was regarding which crops to harvest and which to trade to other kingdoms in exchange for exotic imports like foreign foods and spirits. I didn't have much to say in this meeting, so my mind wandered.

If I can expose Balnak in whatever he and Lanka are wrapped up in, his shot at the crown will be destroyed and Sarvaan will have one less warrior to compete against in the trial. Balnak's sorry ass can be arrested and thrown in some Naga dungeon somewhere.

I was brought back to the present by Sarvaan's hand moving to my thigh. I looked at him and smiled. My mind was about to wander off again when I felt Sarvaan move his chair closer to mine. His fingers crept under my skirt. My eyes went wide with adrenaline and lust at the same time.

Really Sarvaan? Are you that horny?

The look in his eyes confirmed that he was indeed.

I'm game, husband. Show me what you have in mind.

I parted my legs for his fingers. Under garments weren't really a thing in this realm, so his fingers touched my labia soon after going under my skirt. A moan was swallowed as a gulp. The fact that there were twenty or more people in the room and they had no idea what freaky shit Sarvaan was doing to me under the table made my nipples hard. My clit throbbed to life between my legs. Sarvaan slid a finger in my pussy. My lips stretched around his finger, it was so large it felt like a dick was in me.

Hai...

If people wouldn't have been talking in the meeting, my breathing getting heavy would have definitely been heard. My gaze found Sarvaan's face and he was doing his best to conceal a grin, but I saw what he was hiding.

Yeah I see that grin, Sarvaan. You cocky, handsome fucker.

A second finger pressed against my pussy. My hips moved as subtlety as I could move them indicating that I wanted it in me. His second finger sliding into me made me gasp, loudly. A few people looked. My pussy gushed with juices when their eyes were on me. There were the equivalent of two cocks in me and they didn't know it. I played the noise off as a burp and the eyes turned away. In the park I wanted them to see. Here I had to hide it. Both made me dripping wet.

Sarvaan...you are...in trouble...when we get home...I am going to make you scream my name.

I was wishing that I could scream Sarvaan's name. I was wishing he'd throw me on top of the table and plow me with all his might right in front of everyone. I wondered how many of the people in the current meeting would stay and watch. A third finger pressed into my pussy entrance. My eyes snapped to Sarvaan.

Oh really? Oh fucking really? Well I'm not backing down now. If I can handle that beastly cock of yours I can take anything.

Three cock-like fingers were pumping in and out of me now. My legs shook and my clit felt like it was on fire. Sarvaan's thumb pressed into it and rolled it around like a joystick. In my mind I wanted to screech my pleasure out loud. I wanted to rock my hips into his hand like I was fucking an invisible man. My pussy clenched, butterflies fluttered in my stomach, and there was a small puddle on the chair I was seated in. I couldn't control myself. I stood, everyone looked at me. I was breathing like I'd seen a phantom and my skin was hot like lava.

"I feel strongly that we could divert ten percent more tubers and we'd still have enough food for the third district!"

Good thing I didn't say what I wanted to say. Oh fuck, oh shit, fuck my pussy harder, and I love you Sarvaan could have gotten me some strange looks.

Chapter 19
Secrets ~ चुम्बन

"I have to ask, Sarvaan, what do Nagas use these for?"

After the meetings, Sarvaan and I returned home and were lounging in the den. I was running my hands over the hood on his head and he was using the scales on his fingers to comb my hair. I'd noticed his tail pearls and grabbed them, holding them up.

"I think you already know, my love." He gave me a wink.

I did indeed remember how I'd used them so far. They were pristinely smooth. I shivered remembering how they felt on my skin. How they felt inside me.

"Give me a serious answer, you brute of a man!" I slapped his chest in protest.

"You strike me for no reason my dear. I am telling the truth."

"Really? An entire part of anatomy just for pleasure?"

"I think it's more common than you think." His finger felt between my thighs until it brushed the top of my clit.

My mind remembered the events of the day, Sarvaan being naughty with me in the last meeting of the day. I hopped onto his lap and threw my arms around his head.

"I liked what you did today. I REALLY liked it." My fingers gripped the back of his neck with more pressure.

"I liked it as well. I liked watching you squirm in pleasure under my touch."

My clit sprang to life thinking back to the squirming I did earlier.

I'm squirming right now, husband.

I'd changed from my meeting attire into a simple gown. I lifted it over my head and let it fall to the floor. Sarvaan's arms brought me towards him, pressing my tits to his chest. His mouth found mine and our lips fought to see which of us was dominant. Sarvaan towered over me even with me on his lap, so his lips won. I felt his cock get hard. The shaft pressed against my pussy. The tip rubbed between my labia, getting my juices on it.

Good, get that dick wet. I've got a surprise for you.

Pulling back, I turned around placing my hands on the table in front of the couch, offering my rear to Sarvaan. His excited fingers grabbed my hips.

"This seems familiar..." His deep voice echoed down my spine.

When I felt the tip of his cock press into my pussy, I pulled forward, looking back at Sarvaan with a sly smile.

"Not there." I pushed my ass back and rubbed the tip of his cock between my cheeks, letting it caress my asshole. "Here."

Sarvaan's eyes widened.

"Are you sure?" He looked down at his seven inch dick with its four inch base.

"Not all of it will fit, but you can put in what you can..."

"You spoil me, Priya..."

I turned back around and braced myself. The excitement of trying anal with Sarvaan made my clit throb.

"I'm going to put some of my fluid on you to provide lubrication."

Before I could try to understand what he meant, I felt a squirt of hot, oil-like fluid on my asshole. The warmth of it was soothing. I raised my ass letting it run down my pussy lips and onto my clit.

"You never told me you could do that on command!"

"There are many things for you to discover about Naga anatomy..."

His hands pulled my hips back gently, easing the tip of his cock into my well-lubed ass. My fingers raced to my clit and started rubbing the fluid I'd caught running down my ass and used it to slip my clit between my fingers and trace circles around it. The one inch tip of Sarvaan's cock was thrusting in and out of me now, then he started with the two inch part of his shaft. I positioned my legs further apart and relaxed my rear.

"Bahut tight..." My eyes turned to Sarvaan's face. His eyes were rolling in the back of his head with pleasure as my ass wrapped his cocked in tightness. The fluid he squirted initially was doing wonders. I barely felt as half his cock was pumping in and out of me. My fingers were using his excess fluid to flick my clit and then run all my fingers over it in a row.

"I'm okay, Sarvaan, you can fuck harder if you want..."

Sarvaan's pace picked up and so did my fingers. The yearning to go deeper into my ass radiated from his cock, but I knew the three and four inch parts of his shaft would do damage. Sarvaan's thrusts were so rigorous that I felt the three inch shaft of his cock trying to stretch my ass and get in me. He was controlling his urge the best he could.

"Sarvaan, you be a good warrior and a good husband and cum on your wife's asshole, alright?"

He responded with a series of grunts. Even though only half of his was inside of me I knew he was about to burst. My hand was playing tennis with my clit between my legs and I felt my body's core heating up to its pinnacle. I braced my legs in place, trying to imagine what his load would feel like in my ass. I was surprised when I felt Sarvaan slip out of me and unleash a river of hot fluid between my ass cheeks.

"Priya! My amazing soul companion...I love you!"

The waterfall of warm fluid cascaded down my ass cheeks and legs, my hand playing with my clit caught a handful and slathered it on my clit and pussy lips sending me over the edge as well.

"Hai! Sarvaan! Fuck I love you so much!"

Sarvaan had fallen to the couch and I followed suit, snuggling on top of his heaving chest.

"Priya...you make my heart beat...so fast. More than any...combat match."

"I feel the same way." My hand grabbed his and placed it over my left breast. My heart was pounding as hard as he'd just pounded me.

Okay Priya, you just gave him bliss, now would be a fantastic time to tell him about Nishala.

My eyes were staring into Sarvaan's as my thoughts raced.

"What are you thinking about, Priya?" Both of my hands cupped his hand on my chest.

"I'm so glad it was you that King Vasuki chose."

He chuckled.

"About that...after I escorted you to your chamber, I briefed the King on us finding you. I told him you were the most beautiful foreign being I'd ever seen."

My heart was swollen with pressure. It ascended into my throat and demanded my eyes tear up.

"You really said that?"

"Yes, and I still say it in my mind every time I look at you."

My lips pressed to his for a few quick kisses.

"Well, I remember thinking you were superbly handsome when I first saw you."

"You must have poor eyesight, should we get your eyes looked at?"

My leg raised and I used my heel to hit Sarvaan's side playfully.

"Ok, I changed my mind. You're only mildly handsome."

"Is that so?"

His tail pearls brushed the bottom of my foot. My leg jerked to the tickling feeling.

"Hey! None of that!"

"I insist you elevate my status back to superbly handsome, or I'll tickle your feet all night."

"Fine. You're superbly handsome."

"Could I pass for impossibly handsome?"

"I'd say impossibly full of yourself."

"Close enough."

***

It didn't take long for Sarvaan to fall asleep after our exercise that day. I slipped out of the house as his breathing slowed to that of a deep slumber. Nishala was waiting for me at her camp as if she'd been following my trail ever since I emerged from the river in the forest.

"I'm disappointed to hear that you still haven't entered the trial yet."

What? How did she know?

My face must have betrayed me. Nishala saw the surprise.

"I may be an exile, but I still have ways of getting information when I need it."

My hand went to my hip.

"It's complicated Nishala, my husband is competing in the trial. This could cause a lot of tension between us."

"You can deal with the tension in your union when you're queen of Bhogavati." She turned to retrieve her sword.

My training sword was on the ground in front of me. Anger boiled to my head and I picked it up, slashing at her back. She reacted the moment I picked up the sword and dodged out of the way. Her surprise turned into admiration. I didn't back down or step back. The essence of Prathavi held my legs in place.

"Weeeeeell then, look at you Priya. You push back on entering the trial, but you have the heart of a warrior after all. Something has changed since you were last here."

"Yeah, it has. I found out that I'm right where I want to be."

Nishala's earlier comment finally registered in my mind. Queen of Bhogavati.

"I hope this means you've decided to enter the trial. Remember, the knowledge I have to transform you into a Nagini will only be revealed when my condition is met."

She slithered forward with a series of slashes. My body moved like air, dodging the first two, I brought my sword up to parry the next two.

"About that knowledge...what does it entail? I assume it's some spell or ritual?"

Another series of slashes, seven this time. I dodged and parried them all.

"I can tell you that it will be very difficult...and very painful."

"Your words being cryptic causes me more pain than any ritual."

Nishala spun around, and slashed me on the knee and forearm. The pain made me kneel to the ground.

"Aahh! Fuck!"

"I am a protector of secrets. Just because you feel entitled to the knowledge I possess, doesn't mean I have to give it to you freely. Protecting knowledge is a sacred duty."

Prathavi's unseen hand gripped me and pulled me to my feet in a lunge towards Nishala. I screamed with the ferocity of the ancient warrior within me and unleashed a barrage of strikes and slashes at Nishala. She sent a counter slash my way. I ducked to the ground, kicked her hand, and shot my legs forward and down to send me to my feet again. My kick weakened Nishala's grasp on her weapon and I was able to yank it from her fingers.

"Your sacred duty is interfering with my life." I stood in a fighting stance with both weapons now.

Nishala began to clap.

"Good to meet you, Queen Priya."

A smile carved its way onto my face.

"It's called *the kiss of scales*." We'd trained for an hour and sat down around Nishala's campfire to rest. She had packed my slash wounds with her healing salve again so I could return home without marks to show.

"Why are you the only one who knows of it?"

"I wasn't supposed to know of it." She threw a tree branch into the flames and watched the embers flurry into the air around us.

"I saw the ritual in a dream. A human woman in red, black, and white taught it to me."

My throat clenched.

Red, black, and white...the colors of the Naga human tribe.

"She said I was destined to pass it down to another human." A brief glimpse of sorrow washed over Nishala's face. "When the Trial of The Crown commenced years later, I entered with the hope of becoming Queen. In my first match I killed my opponent, leading to my exile. As my opponent lay dead in front of me, I thought back to that human woman. I wondered if I wasn't meant to pass along the ritual after all."

Her beautiful purple eyes turned to me.

"And then you came along." Her eyes turned back to the fire.

"Why did you kill your opponent? Was it an accident?"

"No. I killed him on purpose."

But why, though, Nishala?

The question hung in the air until Nishala finally took a long breath.

"Remember how I told you some men hear *yes* when you say *no*? " She didn't need to say anymore, My face fell to the ground. "As he died in front of me, I wrapped my arms around him and brought his ear to my lips. The last words he heard were: *I told you I'd kill you. Look what you've made me do.*"

My mind instantly pictured Balnak. Beaten and bloody in front of me.

I know exactly what you mean, Nishala.

***

I snuck back through the front door and quietly closed it. My body was damp from river travel and sweating.

"Where have you been?"

I squealed as Sarvaan rose from the couch.

"Shit, Sarvaan you scared me."

His face was stern. It didn't soften when his eyes met mine as usual.

"You've scared me tonight as well Priya." He slithered closer and put his hands on my shoulders. His head cocked to the side.

"Your clothes are damp. What happened? Why were you gone?"

Shit. Fuck. Fuck. Shit. Fuck.

I hugged him tight and put my face into his body.

Okay, Priya, this is a major fuck up, time to turn on the charm.

"I'm so sorry, my love. I couldn't sleep and went out for a walk around the city so I wouldn't wake you. My walk turned into a run to get my energy out and I must have sweated a lake into my clothes."

My face nuzzled into his scales to really get him to relax. He once again proved to be the perfect soul companion when his posture softened and his arms wrapped and squeezed me.

"You worried me, Priya. Next time leave a note, alright?"

My head pulled back and met his eyes.

"Of course, my love, I'm so sorry for worrying you."

"I'm fine now that I know you're safe. Do you feel ready for sleep?"

"I do, I tired myself out. I'll be there in just a moment, let me slip out of these sweaty clothes."

I took off my clothes and put them in the laundry area to be washed. As I walked to join Sarvaan in bed I caught sight of myself in a mirror on the wall. The Priya in the reflection seemed to have a life of its own. She was judging me.

You don't deserve such a good man. Why have a soul companion if you're going to lie to them? You're supposed to bare your soul to him, not hide it.

Fuck you, don't rub it in. I'm trying to figure a way out of this. I'm sure he wouldn't be my biggest fan knowing that I'm colluding with an exile. An exile I almost fucked.

Chapter 20

Arena ~ युद्ध

A soft smoothness caressing my face woke me the next morning. My eyes opened to see Sarvaan's tail pearls stroking my cheek. When my eyes opened the pearls rolled down my neck and breasts, and danced down my belly.

"I have a surprise for you today, Priya."

Oh wow, horny man. I mean, with a face and body like yours I could fuck anytime.

He leaned over, pressing his body to mine into the bed sheets. His tongue found mine and our lips smacked. My legs spread instinctively but he rose from the bed

"Get dressed, breakfast is waiting in the den."

Oh, different surprise.

A dress found my body and I joined Sarvaan in the den.

"So what's the surprise you seem so excited about my dear?" I sat beside Sarvaan on the couch and put my legs over his body.

"I just received word this morning that my third match is this evening. If I win—"

"*When* you win." I corrected, shoving some herb-covered cheese into my mouth.

"*When* I win, I'll advance to the final match. My opponent is Balnak."

My body shuddered with disgust for even the mention of Balnak's name.

"Priya, I'm going to beat him to a pulp. I'm going to humiliate him in front of everyone...for you."

"You really know the way to my heart. Sarvaan. I love you."

"And that's only part of the surprise." His hands gripped and rubbed my legs.

"Are you trying to spoil me rotten?"

"Only on a constant basis."

"Alright then, when do I get to know what the next part is?"

"When you've finished eating, I'm going to take you there. But first, you'll have to change into something more fitting."

Sarvaan led me through the streets of Bhogavati to show me the next part of this morning's surprise. He had me put on some padded leather armor. Luckily, since Nagas are shapeshifters, they make armor a human form can fit into as well. Sarvaan mentioning Balnak earlier had me thinking of the strange events at the palace the day before.

"Sarvaan, do you find it weird that Balnak advocated to increase tribute to Lanka, and that the diplomat from Lanka couldn't produce the evidence that would justify the tribute increase?"

"I did, yes. But the treasury has people who handle and look into those matters. I'm sure it will get taken care of."

I'm not so sure, my lovely husband. Balnak and Keshvaan had the faces of schemers. There may be collusion at play.

"Well to be sure, you should torture Balnak when you're the king."

"Oh? Shall I hang him by his tail for the whole kingdom to see?"

"That would be grand, actually." I bumped Sarvaan playfully with my butt. His serpent body bumped me back.

The arena that the trial matches were held came into view. My eyebrows furrowed.

"Are we going to the arena?"

Sarvaan smiled back.

"We are. Why should we have to go practice in the wilds when there's a perfectly good arena here?"

"Are we allowed to do that?"

"I'm *almost* the king of Bhogavati. Who would argue with me?"

"You're sexy when you're cocky, Sarvaan."

"I thought I was sexy all the time, Priya?"

"You are."

Sarvaan grabbed me, lifting me to his chest.

"Does that mean I'm cocky all the time?"

He kissed me.

"Yes, and I love it."

***

As we entered the arena I noticed how the silence was so different than the roaring cheers and applause.

"It's so quiet. So different than when a match is going on."

"Yes, too quiet. Silence makes my body want to move."

"When did you first start to feel that way?"

"As a juvenile. I was scrappy, always getting into fights. When the Dhayas recognized this they put me through warrior training. The training helped me learn to channel the restlessness into action. Into sacred duty."

"I understand that. More than you. In my realm women aren't supposed to be adventurers or explorers. But I always had the urge to dig into mountains and find the places that didn't want to be found. To crush rocks and find their secrets."

"It sounds like you and I were meant to be, Priya, despite being separated by entire realms."

I smiled at Sarvaan, tucking my chin close to my neck.

"I agree, meri jaan."

Sarvaan led me to the center of the arena, to the fighting area where the three pillars stood. My head tilted back looking to the very top of the pillar.

"And just how do you think I'm going to climb that?"

"You don't seem to have trouble climbing on me, what's a few more feet?"

He handed me a practice sword.

I slapped his body with the side of the sword.

"Watch your mouth, that's no way to speak to a lady."

"Apologies, my lady. Are you ready?"

"What's today's lesson, exactly?"

"No lesson, we're just going to have some fun."

My body moved on its own, charging at Sarvaan. Surprise filled my eyes and his. I leapt into the air when I was close enough, I jumped higher than I'd ever jumped before and slashed at his head. Sarvaan ducked, my feet landed in the dirt behind him.

Prathavi, is that you? Did you do that?

Sarvaan's body twisted around and came after me, his sword swinging so fast it was a blur of grey and silver. My sword parried one of his strikes. My hand felt the sting behind the sheer force he swung with. It felt like I'd struck the side of a boulder. My sword remained in my hand, I didn't let go. A vision clouded my mind.

I saw Balnak in the dirt in front of me.

"Kneel." He resisted, tried to stand. I lashed out with my sword. "I said Kneel!"

Back in the present Sarvaan slashed left and then right, followed by a leg sweep with his tail. My sword clanged against his, parrying the two slashes, making my hand shiver with numbness. The tail sweep sent me to the ground. Another vision came.

I saw myself laying on the ground, Sarvaan on one side of me, Nishala on the other. The earth tried to consume me. Sarvaan and Nishala grabbed my hands and held on as I was covered in earth.

Sarvaan's next slash came down at me while I was on the ground. Everything slowed down in my eyes. He looked as though he was going to pull back at the last moment, taking it easy on me since he'd swept me to the ground.

I'll not take any handouts, husband.

My body rolled to the side. His sword cut into the dirt. I jumped to my feet and slashed, cutting into his arm. Blood splattered onto the ground. My hands covered my mouth.

Oh no! I cut him for real!

He inspected his arm as if it were a bug bite. Blood trickled down his elbow. He laughed.

"Priya, you got me good! You're becoming fierce with a blade."

"Are you okay? I'm sorry I didn't mean to actually cut you."

"It's fine, meri rani, my everything."

His body assumed a fighting stance again.

"Shall we continue?"

I grinned, changing stances. I tucked my elbows close to my body as Nishala taught me.

"Have you been practicing on your own? You're doing well with adopting several fighting styles I haven't taught you."

Oh shit. Come on Priya, think!

We started to circle each other.

"I pay attention when you have your matches."

He dashed to me, putting steel in my face. My head ducked and I stepped back.

"Hopefully paying attention to me more, right?"

"Sarvaan, are you jealous?"

His tail swept me again. My back hit the dirt and air rushed out of my lungs. The dirt was soft enough that it didn't hurt falling into it.

I'd never been with a man who literally swept me off my feet before.

Sarvaan dropped his sword and crawled over me. His eyes met mine and he kissed me. His hands were all over me, fueled by the energy of our combat. My legs wrapped around his body above me and my lips moved over his with energy to match his.

I love when you go crazy for me.

His long, fast breaths sounded like a beast in the rut. He kissed my neck and I felt his breath like hot streams of fluid hitting my skin to contrast the cold dirt my back was against. My hips moved against his body, dry humping my clit against his body through my armor. Sarvaan's hands gripped the armor and literally tore it open revealing my nude skin underneath. My pussy got so fucking wet feeling him literally rip armor from my body.

I'm going to have to cool this brute down or he'll kill me with sex with this amount of energy.

My hands grabbed his face and forced his eyes to mine.

"Sarvaan...Sarvaan my husband...a good warrior kneels first." A grin curled on my lips.

"I'll gladly kneel for you, Priya." His hands shot to my ass and lifted my hips off the ground to his face.

His tongue extended and slapped my pussy lips and clit.

"Haan..." My arms strained to maintain my hips in his face.

Each fork of his tongue went in different directions. One curled around my clit, and the other slid into my pussy.

"I fucking love you, you beautiful brute." His hands were pulling my hips into his mouth, I moved my pussy up and down, letting his tongue hit the spots I liked.

Sarvaan still exuded aggression from our combat and his lust combined. His fingers squeezed my ass cheeks like they were stress balls, pumping my cheeks with each lick his tongue sent over my clit and into my pussy. His tongue forks writhed in a wavy motion in my pussy and on my clit that made my hips twirl and shudder. My left leg twitched from the feeling. He was making my body malfunction.

"Lick me like you mean it, husband!" My legs shook and clenched around Sarvaan's face. His tongue in my pussy pumped in and out faster and the one on my clit was pricking my bud with the end of the fork. My back arched each time his tongue pumped or pricked me. My breathing slowed as I reveled in the aftershocks of my orgasm. It quickened again when Sarvaan wrapped my body in his coils and brought my hips to where his rock hard cock was.

"Okay, my fierce warrior. Time to claim the spoils of war." His body wrapped around me spread my legs as I lay in midair.

A gasp for breath sucked air into my lungs when he plunged his dick into me. He used his coils to pull and push my body with each thrust. His pace was rushed, like he had to fuck me or he'd die. It felt great. I relaxed in his coils as he used me like a fuck toy. Each time he'd finish a thrust, a loud, screeching moan would come out of me and echo around the stone walls of the arena. One of his hands caressed my face and ran down my chest, the other grabbed my tits.

"Priya...you do things...to me...that no one else...does..."

His thrusts were long, fast, and yearning now. Something felt very different, and very good suddenly. The four inch base of Sarvaan's cock felt as though it extended some, and more of it was trying to enter me. His cock was plunging into my soul, it felt like. My moans at the end of the last thrust turned into something more.

"I'm going to die! It feels so fucking good!"

With a final, strained thrust, Sarvaan exploded into me. His load was always big, but it squirted out the sides of my pussy lips as I clenched around his dick to send his body into ecstatic convulsions. Sarvaan brought my body to his chest which I instantly snuggled into. He laid down on the ground and put me on his chest so I wouldn't have to lay in the dirt.

Even after fucking my soul into another realm, he's a gentleman.

Something was different about this time making love with Sarvaan. He was breathing like a race horse and just holding me close, shuddering. My hand stroked his chest and I cooed at him soothingly.

"I love you, Sarvaan. I love you. You're mine and I'm yours." He squeezed me.

"You're perfect Priya. I hope you know that."

His words were caught somewhere between bloodlust, actual lust, and his love for me. As I laid there against his body, one thought kept poking into my thoughts.

I want him to fuck me like that when I have my Nagini body.

Chapter 21
Mob ~ मुकुट

Sarvaan's third match in the trial was against a white and silver scaled Naga named Ravanak from the Shesha kula. As the warriors fought, clinging to their stone pillars, my eyes wandered to the spot just below where Sarvaan plowed me into the dirt. A loud gasp from the crowd brought my attention back to the fight. Ravanak had slashed Sarvaan across the chest in a wide arc. Blood covered the pillar Sarvaan was on.

Shit! Come on Sarvaan, kick his ass!

Ravanak was crafty. He hung upside down on his pillar to confuse Sarvaan. It worked the first time, leading to the wound on his chest, but he was getting wise to the gimmick now. Sarvaan was in the arena, but in my mind I was fighting Ravanak. I saw myself clinging to the stone pillar, dodging his slashes and counter attacking with my own as he hung upside down. The fight in my mind took a turn when I discovered Ravanak's attack pattern and started striking him when I saw openings.

I've got you figured out, Ravanak.

Sarvaan took a different approach. He leapt to the same pillar Ravanak was clinging to and started to unleash a brutal series of strikes. Sarvaan took more slashes to the body and arms, but his sheer brute force led to even more wounds on Ravanak.

Stop it, Sarvaan! You're trading blows. You're not being smart!

Despite my internal protests, Sarvaan's assault weakened Ravanak. Ravanak didn't have any more energy and fell to the ground to concede the match. Cheers and applause erupted once more throughout the arena. The Karkota Naga sitting near me shook my shoulders with their hands and embraced me as if I were a natural born Naga. I was about to join Sarvaan in the fighting area as I'd done after his other victories, but the audience fell silent. Gasps ran rampant through the crowd and they pointed to the far end entrance to the building.

"Who are they?" A group of twenty black scaled Naga were slithering towards Sarvaan.

Takshaka Kula.

A Naga behind me shouted in my ear over the noise.

"Takshaka Kula hasn't taken kindly to Sarvaan advancing so far in the trial. You're about to witness a kula war. Come! Let's defend our kula's honor!"

A kula war? Sarvaan couldn't fight off twenty Naga.

My legs carried me with the other Karkota Naga onto the arena grounds. When the Takshaka Naga saw us running into the arena, they picked up their pace. I made it to Sarvaan before the Takshaka mob did.

"Priya, you need to go, now!"

"I'll do no such thing! Hand me a sword."

Sarvaan stood in front of me as the Takshaka Naga group encountered the Karkota entourage that accompanied me. Primal hisses and the clanging of steel filled the air.

"Priya, please get to safety."

I spotted Ravanak's sword he dropped when he fell and dove to the ground to pick it up.

"Safety is for housewives. I'm the wife of the future king."

Sarvaan smirked, he knew I wasn't submissive and wouldn't listen anyway. He probably gave in because there was no more time to talk. Two Takshaka warriors pushed through the Karkota entourage and engaged him. Sarvaan tackled one to the ground immediately, stole his sword, and attacked the second with a flurry of dual swords.

"Takshaka blood is the blood of warriors! No other kula shall claim the crown!"

The Takshaka warriors were chanting as they fought. My sword readied to help Sarvaan with the warrior he was engaged with, but one of the Naga slithered behind me and hissed at my back.

"What do you plan to do with that weapon, human? Trim your fingernails?"

His voice made my body spin to face him.

"Come here and find out."

My body assumed the graceful fighting stance as Nishala had taught me. My mind raced with visions of me triumphing over my enemy as Sarvaan taught me. The Naga charged forward at me. His stance was sloppy, he obviously wasn't a warrior, and if he was, he wasn't a very good one. My feet launched me an impossible distance into the air. I flew over this seven foot warrior, slashing at his hood as I went. My feet planted into the dirt where he had charged me from.

"Ah! Filthy surface dweller! I'll skewer you for that!" His hands touched his hood where I'd slashed him. Blood covered his fingers and ran down the back of his neck.

Holy shit! Did I just jump like ten feet in the air?

My mind was still paralyzed from how high I jumped. The Naga readied another charge my way. Green and blue scaled hands grabbed him on either side of his body, lifted him into the air, and slammed him to the ground in a crumpled heap. Sarvaan had lifted and body slammed another Naga warrior with the ease of lifting a chair.

"Priya, are you hurt?"

I threw my sword in the air spinning, and caught it, almost dropping it. My body struck a pose as if I were a performing act.

"Not a scratch husband, not a scratch."

Three more Takshaka warriors charged at us from behind Sarvaan. He spun to face them, using his body to block them from me. As we braced for more fighting a sharp, ringing hiss echoed in our ears. The Takshaka warriors heard it too. The dirt between us and the Takshaka mob erupted like a volcano, sending dirt clumps flying through the air. Standing between us and the Takshaka warriors was a giant, golden scaled snake with five heads. It was more like a dragon, as wide as a car and as long as a bus.

"You dare defile the sacred ceremony of the trial?" The colossal snake snapped all five jaws at the Takshaka mob. They stopped running and knelt before it. "I'll have no more of this!"

Wait, gold scales, and they knelt to it...is that King Vasuki?

Royal guards swarming the arena answered my question. Vasuki assumed his half humanoid and half serpent form.

"Jail them all for the night." He said simply to his guards. The guards started shackling the Takshaka warriors and hauled them out of the arena.

Vasuki turned to Sarvaan and me.

"Sarvaan of Karkota Kula. Congratulations on your victory today. As is tradition when a warrior has only the final match left in the trial, I'd like you to join me at the palace for a crown fitting."

Sarvaan bowed low to the ground. I knelt with my knees in the dirt.

"It would be an honor, your highness. Thank you."

The king's eyes fixed to me now.

"We've got to stop running into each other like this, Priya. Sarvaan will be jealous."

I coughed out a chuckle at his joke. King Vasuki and his guards left and the crowd in the arena murmured and gasped among themselves at the action the day had brought. Sarvaan pulled me to him, almost crushing the breath from my lungs.

"I'm glad you're not hurt, Priya. I don't know what I'd do if you had been hurt."

"I'm alright...Sarvaan...really..."

He pulled me from his body and our faces met.

"You're my world, Priya."

"And you're mine, Sarvaan."

We kissed. Our tongues twirled with hot passion. The crowd clapped and cheered at us as our mouths moved over each other's lips.

So this is what it feels like to be a queen.

***

"Hold still."

"I am holding still."

"Be even more still."

Apparently, being fitted for a crown required even more precise measurements than being fitted for a custom dress. Sarvaan stood in the center of the room as King Vasuki's attendants measured his head. They had iron replicas of different sized crowns to test on his head.

"Hmm. Your head is larger than usual. We'll have to make a custom iron crown to test on you."

A human would have been insulted at the prospect of having a larger than normal head. Sarvaan's chest puffed out with pride and a smirk came across his face as the attendant informed him of his large head. Vasuki slithered over to my side.

"This is probably going to take some more time. Would you like any refreshments while you wait, Priya?"

"No, thank you, your majesty."

I remembered the conversation with Sarvaan earlier about Balnak and his possible misdeeds. Sarvaan was convinced the treasury would take care of it.

Hey...we're in the palace right now. I wonder where they keep their records.

My head leaned close to Vasuki's ear to whisper.

"Actually, I'm curious, where are the records kept regarding the storage and allocation of gold?"

"The records archive is in this very building. They are marvelous, troves of secrets kept record of. I could arrange my royal guard to escort you. I imagine as a human you've never seen a Naga records archive?"

It was almost too easy. As if he knew what I wanted. I'll take it though.

"I haven't, and that would be lovely." Sarvaan was looking at me, confused over what I must be whispering to the king about. "I'm going to get a tour of the records archive, I'll be back in a bit. If you finish up early come find me."

"I'm sure you'll have more fun than I will, my darling."

"I'm sure you'll look kingly, my darling." My mouth blew Sarvaan a kiss as Vasuki's royal guard led me out of the room.

I was led to the top floor of the palace. Along the way the walls were decorated in tapestry and abstract artwork featuring color combinations of the five kulas. Every now and then a painting of a past Naga ruler appeared. We eventually reached a red wooden door. A guard unlocked it and Vasuki ushered me inside.

"I have other matters to attend to, I hope you find our archives to your interest."

"Thank you, King Vasuki. You've been so kind to me."

"We should all be kind to each other. Unkindness is a filthy way to live."

I curtsied to King Vasuki and he and his guard took their leave. I opened the red door that had been unlocked for me and was greeted by a long corridor of more red doors. Each door had a symbol on it made of simple black lines. Some lines were curved, and others were straight.

It looks like some kind of language script. Oh I relish the mysteries that must lie in this place.

Opening the first door I came to, I walked into a room filled with still air and dust. Ten wooden tables with several wooden trunks atop them were scattered around the room. I moved to one of the trunks and opened it. Stacks of parchment paper sat inside the trunk. Each stack was wrapped in a gold ribbon and sealed with a wax stamp.

It'll take forever to go through all these documents! I'll have to return with Sarvaan later—

My ears twitched as the sound of the red exterior door opening caught my attention. I closed the trunk I'd opened and listened.

"In here? Seriously Balnak?"

Balnak? Fuck! The universe really likes to watch me squirm!

In the corner of the room, there were five trunks piled on top of one another. I quickly dove behind them to hide.

Balnak entered the room followed by...Keshvaan. The diplomat from Lanka.

"I can never be too careful these days." Balnak closed the door to the room.

"Why are you here Keshvaan?"

"This is where you wanted to talk, isn't it?" Keshvaan brought his blue-skinned arms to his chest and leaned against one of the tables.

"I mean here in Naga-Loka. Don't play games with me!"

"I had to return with a forged document because you failed to keep things tight on your end."

I knew there was no ancient text! But what does Balnak have to do with all of this?

"My end has been perfect. What do you speak of?" Balnak produced a sword to Keshvaan's neck. Keshvaan smirked at this gesture.

"We both know killing me would incite ten different wars." Keshvaan's finger lowered Balnak's sword for him. Balnak sheathed the weapon.

"And what I speak of is the special advisors King Vasuki pulled into his meeting with me."

"Special advisors?"

"Yes. Priya and Sarvaan are who the king introduced them as. Though delicious, Priya immediately demanded I produce the ancient text responsible for the increase in gold tribute."

Balnak flinched when my name was mentioned. A grin forced its way on my face being called delicious.

What's delicious is watching Balnak's dirty plan be unmade.

The dust in the room swirled around in the air as I breathed. A speck of it caught in my throat and I felt my throat clenching to produce a cough.

No. No! Don't betray me like this. They'll kill me if they find me hiding here!

I held my breath and gripped my throat tight with my hand.

"Priya...that meddling alien."

"Because I've had to procure forged documentation, my fee has increased, by the way."

"Don't talk to me of fee increases! I'm paying you to start a war so I can look like the hero king of this realm! You'll get your gold when you deliver me a war."

Balnak's fangs were in Keshvaan's face now. The blue-skinned Rakshasa fully stood, no longer leaning on the table. My face started to go numb. I really needed them to wrap this meeting up. Me holding my breath and gripping my throat was stalling the cough, but wasn't going to stop it. My throat was swollen and my mouth was filling with spit.

"I'll deliver a war like no one else. Trust me." Keshvaan's charisma oozed from his body and voice. He winked at Balnak like he was trying to take him home and fuck him.

Balnak opened the door with an angry huff and slithered out. Keshvaan followed. Shutting the door.

Almost there throat...almost there...just a second longer.

When I finally heard the red exterior door close I bent over to my hands and knees coughing spit on the floor.

So Balnak's trying to start a fake war with Lanka so he can swoop in and stop the war to look good? What a fucking psychopath.

Chapter 22
Forum ~ षड्यंत्र

S arvaan and I enjoyed some wine and lounging to decompress from the day's events when we got home. Balnak's plan I'd learned of earlier swelled in my chest. I needed it out of me. I needed more wine in me first. I took a sip letting the cherry flavor rinse my mouth.

I have to tell him, he should know.

"Sarvaan, I have to tell you something."

He put his glass down and leaned towards me. The soft glow of the jewels in the walls reflected in his scales. They reflected in his purple eyes as well.

"What is it you have to tell me, my love?"

"Today when King Vasuki showed me the records archive, Balnak and the Lanka diplomat, Keshvaan, entered the archives to speak freely. I heard them talking of a scheme involving what I'm sure to be treason."

His hands took mine and squeezed them. I took a deep breath. The incense burning in the room and the cherry flavor of the wine mixed in my lungs, calming me.

"Treason? How do you mean? Did they see you?"

"No, I hid. Balnak said he was paying Keshvaan to help start a war between Bhogavati and Lanka. He plans to start the war, become king, and look like a hero when he puts the war to rest."

"What?! Priya, we should go to his majesty with this information immediately."

"I agree. There's one problem though. I don't have any actual records of this. There's mountains of records in those archives."

"I'll help you then."

"I'm not sure that would do any good either. There's an entire corridor of rooms full of mountains of records. If someone knows we are looking, Balnak could send someone after us, or send someone to destroy the records altogether."

Sarvaan's arms draped over me and pulled me into his lap.

"Then what do you propose we do?"

I honestly had no clue. But what I did know is that Sarvaan needed to become king.

"You need to win your match against Balnak. When you're king you can order an investigation into the matter and issue official punishment."

Sarvaan threw his head back and laughed. His deep voice made my breasts jiggle.

"Is that it? I plan on doing that anyway."

My hand found his sternum.

"I know. I believe in you."

My body fell to Sarvaan's chest and my eyes closed. Exhaustion washed over me like a warm bath. It had been a hell of a day.

Fuck. The trial. I need to enter it somehow so Nishala will teach me the ritual to turn me into a Nagini.

My body lifted into the air as Sarvaan carried me to our bedroom and laid down snuggling me on top of his chest. Warm sheets and smooth scales caressed my skin.

Maybe I'll tell Sarvaan the truth after he wins against Balnak, and I'll just concede the match immediately. That way I satisfy Nishala and Sarvaan gets to become king.

My body rose and fell with each deep breath Sarvaan took.

What am I actually afraid of here? He adores me. I'll just tell him.

"Sarvaan, what would you say if I wanted to enter the Trial of The Crown?"

My words murmured into his chest scales. He said nothing.

"Sarvaan?"

My eyes rose to his face. He was asleep.

Why does this keep happening to me?

***

With the final match of the trial in two days, Bhogavati hosted a grand ceremony in the center of the city to have the public meet with the remaining two competitors, and get to know their stances of political policy. I wore my green and gold lehenga choli with a blue, jeweled belt around my waist. My golden serpent earrings hung from my ears. Sarvaan wore a blue sash going diagonal over his chest.

"Priya..."

Sarvaan's voice pulled me from my own mind. My thoughts were racing with Nishala, Balnak, and the possibility of being the queen of Bhogavati in just a few days. Sarvaan's final match against Balnak to determine who would wear the crown was in two days.

"You look so wonderful. I just want to put you on my shoulder and show you off to everyone."

"And you look like a handsome king. So what exactly is tonight supposed to accomplish?"

"Tonight the citizens of Bhogavati get to know me and my stances on certain political issues. More than that though, they want to know their ruler intimately."

Sarvaan leaned over and kissed me. I held his face on mine with my hand on the back of his neck. The smell of jasmine and sandalwood incense in the air put me in an especially sensual mood.

"I like getting to know you intimately."

Someone tapped me on my shoulder. It was King Vasuki. Sarvaan bowed immediately. Vasuki locked arms with the both of us and pulled us up before any further formalities could be issued.

"I am only king for a few short days now. Come, it's almost time to commence the forum."

"The forum?" My head tilted slightly with the question.

"Yes. Sarvaan and Balnak will sit before the crowd and address them directly." My head turned to Sarvaan.

"Did you prepare a speech or something?"

"No. True character comes from the heart. The heart doesn't need a page to read from."

He's a Naga poet and doesn't even know it!

Vasuki led us to the center of the city square. There was a stage setup with a long table and chairs on top. He led us to one side and stayed until we were sat.

"I know you'll sway their hearts. Good luck."

And with that, Vasuki disappeared into the crowd. He was the king of Bhogavati, surrounded by royal guards, golden scales all over his body, but he could disappear like a magician. After we were seated, Balnak and some trade representatives from Takshaka Kula stepped to the stage and sat at the opposite end of the table. Sarvaan was Balnak's opponent, but his venomous eyes stung me instead. King Vasuki cleared his throat, silencing the crowd.

"Citizens of Bhogavati. These two astounding competitors are the final two left in the Trial of The Crown. In two days time, they will battle in the final match of the trial. The victor of that match will be the ruler of this realm for the next one hundred years."

Murmurs washed over the crowd like a tidal wave.

"With both competitors present and seated, I declare the forum in session."

Vasuki sat in the back of the stage with his guards and the crowd came to life with discussion. I wasn't sure how it was supposed to work with so many voices crying out for attention. It looked as though the competitors were in charge of picking citizens in the crowd to speak with. The whole process reminded me of a political debate. Sarvaan was the first to pick someone to hear their concerns.

"Yes, you there." Sarvaan's finger landed on a Naga from Shesha Kula.

"In recent decades, animosity between kulas has become a problem. Fights and squabbles break out more these days than they used to. How would you calm the waters between the bloodlines?"

Sarvaan stood to address the crowd.

"I agree that troubles between the kulas shouldn't exist. I think more multi-cultural events to encourage kula mingling and friendship would help to ease these troubles. There could be events where each kula teaches about their traditions and values."

Cheerful chatter cascaded across the crowd as Sarvaan sat. Balnak was next to choose someone. He pointed without saying anything.

"Minister Balnak, what makes you more fit to rule than your opponents?"

Balnak rose from his chair and gestured to the crowd.

"As you know my citizens, Bhogavati is being threatened with war from the kingdom of Lanka. I am of akshaka Kula. War and strength is in our blood. I will die to protect this kingdom from any bloodshed, but if blood must be shed, then I will shed the blood of our enemies first."

Applause and cheers from the crowd followed.

"Must there be bloodshed at all?" I didn't mean for the words to come out of my mouth, they were meant for my thoughts.

The crowd fell silent and Balnak glared at me, burning a hole into my soul.

"What was that, consort?"

"You speak of drawing the blood of other kingdoms. What about a future without war entirely?"

Sarvaan leaned into my ear.

"Have I told you how much I love when you humiliate Balnak in front of crowds?" His breath tickled my neck.

"Of course, I will avoid war at any cost, but Lanka isn't a kingdom to be negotiated with. If they want war, then war will come."

Balnak sat and the crowd talked among themselves with the weight of that prospect hanging in the air like the smoke from the burning incense in the city square. It was time to pick another citizen and address them, Sarvaan looked left and right, and spotted someone. He pointed.

"You, let's hear your concerns."

"Sarvaan, your consort, Priya, is a human. How does this affect your ability to rule?"

Heckles and gasps filled the air suddenly. Balnak's face morphed to smugness in physical form.

"While her beauty is unmatched in this realm, my soul companion being human will have no harmful effects on my ability to be king of Bhogavati. If anything, being with Priya has opened my eyes to a world beyond her own, and given me wisdom to ensure everyone in this kingdom is treated fairly, and with compassion."

A lump formed in my throat. I wanted to cry but not in front of all these people. Sarvaan sat as I swallowed my tears and stared into his eyes calm and composed. The crowd was feral now as it was Balnak's turn to choose a citizen to speak with. He pointed to a Nagini woman in the back. She slithered forward so her voice was heard.

"Minister Balnak, as Minister of Coin, how do you explain the treasury's failure to renegotiate the gold tribute to Lanka? You spoke earlier of war, but surely as the Minister of Coin, a war can be easily avoided?"

The crowd's chatter was made of shouts and screams now. Conversation was getting heated. Balnak rose, putting his hands up to ask for silence.

"There has been...no failure on the treasury's behalf. Lanka asked for an increase in their tribute of gold, and produced documentation that legitimizes these claims—"

"But have these documents themselves been legitimized?"

Balnak's expression said he would have sunk his fangs into my neck if no one was watching.

"Sarvaan, are you going to speak for yourself or are you going to keep allowing your consort to speak for you?"

Sarvaan was about to speak. I stood and got there first.

"I'm not being allowed to speak. I AM speaking. I am a citizen of this realm now. I'll speak just as anyone in the crowd would be able to speak."

I walked out to the edge of the stage and addressed the crowd directly.

"Would you have a ruler on the throne who bowed to bullying because a document was waved in their face? If you give in to bullying, it only continues."

Balnak pushed back his chair and slithered to face me.

"Listen here, human…"

Sarvaan got to me first and put himself between us.

"Oh that's charming, Sarvaan, your consort acts like a queen but she can't face me without you. Is that the way it is?"

Sarvaan's hand gripped Balnak's bicep. Balnak's hand returned the grip in kind. My chest heaved, I was hyperventilating. My eyes remained focused and my posture was calm despite my heavy breathing. Sarvaan's body tensed. I'd seen him do that when he was about to strike his opponents in his matches.

"Citizens of Bhogavati…"

King Vasuki approached Sarvaan and Balnak, placing his own hand on the both of theirs, lifting them from their grip on each other. He did it as effortlessly as a mother settling a quarrel between children.

"What you have here are two very passionate candidates. Give them a round of applause won't you?"

The crowd was wired with energy, expecting a fight. They started clapping slowly as the energy in the air died down to a civil level.

"In two days, these two fine competitors will engage in combat in the final match of the trial, and you can see them in all their athletic glory. Until then, I hope you stay to enjoy the festivities."

Vasuki snapped his fingers and two sets of his royal guard took Sarvaan and Balnak, separating them. My hand rubbed Sarvaan's abdomen to bring him back from the brink of bloodlust.

"Hey, it's over, you're here with me."

His eyes looked down at mine.

"I wish we could just have the match here and now. He disgusts me."

"I'd pay to see that. Take me home husband. I'm growing tired."

Sarvaan's fingers interlaced with mine and he escorted me away from the city square. A thought crossed my mind. It made my shiver from disgust.

What if Balnak cheated in his match with Sarvaan? Nishala had killed her opponent in the trial. What if Balnak did the same? I'm going to need a backup plan in case Balnak cheated his way to the crown. I needed to revisit the records archive and find some concrete evidence of Balnak's corruption.

"Actually, let me catch the King one last time and thank him for being a good host."

"Alrighty, I'll wait for you here."

I raced into the crowd looking for King Vasuki. My head turned left and right, frantically trying to locate his majesty. In my haste I bumped into the back of someone and fell to my butt. Gold scales turned to face me.

Oh no, I bumped into the King!

Vasuki smiled, offering me a hand to lift me. His guard swarmed to his side.

"Priya, what a lovely surprise. Are you enjoying tonight's festivities?"

As I was lifted to my feet I brushed dirt from my dress.

"Yes, I am, thank you. I was looking for you actually."

With a flick of his wrist his guards dispersed, but kept in a subtle circle around him.

"Seek and you shall find, as they say."

"Well, I was hoping to get another tour of the records archive."

"You really are a glutton for information, aren't you?"

"I am. Information was my entire life in my realm. The archive is so big, I wasn't able to fully take in the experience."

I've been lying to my husband. Now I'm scheming with the king. You're in deep girl.

King Vasuki put something cold in my hand. I looked down, opening my hand to reveal a small key in my palm.

"Here, it will open the archive door. You can return it to me another day. Enjoy the rest of the evening."

He turned to join with his guard again. My fingers felt the cold metal of the key. It slowly warmed from my touch. Vasuki turned back to me one last time before vanishing in the crowd.

"Oh, and Priya..."

My eyes met his.

"There can be vermin lurking in the records archive. Do be careful."

Before I could respond, Vasuki's face became everyone else's face as it melded into a sea of scales.

He knows something...I can feel it. But what does he know exactly?

Chapter 23
Vermin ~ छुरी

"**Y**ou were amazing with the crowd, Sarvaan...absolutely...amazing."

I was pacing in the den, talking with my hands. Sarvaan was sitting on the couch, watching me with a chuckle.

"Me? No, you were the amazing one, Priya."

My eyes stared at him and just blinked.

It did feel great to address the crowd. To feel their energy.

Sarvaan's tail wrapped my legs and brought me to him.

"Excuse me? Can't a lady walk on her own?" My hands landed on his chest as he brought me to his lap.

"You can, but you weren't, I was growing impatient." We both smiled and brought our lips together, smacking through the wide grin on our faces.

I love this man. I love him so much. My courage allowed me to talk to an entire kingdom today. To embarrass a candidate for king of Bhogavati. But it wouldn't allow me to tell Sarvaan that I needed to enter the trial in order to become Nagini.

As our kiss deepened, my mind was racing.

I'll need to sneak into the palace tonight and find evidence of Balnak's corruption. I can't take Sarvaan. If we're both caught there could be consequences for both of us. If I'm caught alone I could still be pardoned when Sarvaan is crowned king.

I would need a way to ensure Sarvaan wouldn't wake early and catch me sneaking around. There were so many documents in the archive that I'd need to be gone almost all night looking through them. A note saying I went for a walk wouldn't cut it. My face pulled off of Sarvaan's.

"Let's get drunk to celebrate being amazing today."

"Fine idea, my lovely." Sarvaan rose from the couch to fetch us some alcohol.

I'm getting my husband drunk so he'll stay sleeping while I sneak around like a spy or a thief. This is a new low.

One thought kept stabbing at my mind. Balnak knew of my dealings with Nishala.

The faster I get dirt on him, the faster I ensure he doesn't unleash my secrets.

***

My legs carried me into the streets of Bhogavati after Sarvaan slipped into a drunken slumber. I picked out the most basic looking dress from my closet, and made sure it didn't have any bright colors or fancy designs. Naga were shapeshifters and had human forms they sometimes walked around in, so I wasn't the only human form on the streets. Getting into the palace would be the difficult part.

I'll tell them I'm Priya of Karkota Kula. Sarvaan is almost king, they'd let me in for sure, right? No that's stupid, why would the consort to the future king have business at this hour in the palace.

My hands nervously gripped the key Vasuki had given me.

Wait. That's it. The key is the answer.

As I approached the royal guard in front of the palace, I held my head high, not wavering or flinching. My body held the stance of someone who was supposed to be there. Someone regal. My legs didn't even stop walking when I went between the guards. Their hands gripped my shoulders and stopped me. My eyes gave them a look that said: *what is the meaning of this?*

"Halt. The general public isn't allowed in the palace at this time."

"I'm not the general public. His majesty has allowed me access to the records archive so that I may audit its contents. It's a special project he's working on."

"Do you have a writ of passage from high majesty?"

My hand produced the key King Vasuki had given me. The key had Vasuki's unmistakable seal on it. My face wanted to be smug, but I showed some appreciation to win them over.

"He gave me this and told me I could access the archive whenever I needed to. Could I also trouble one of you to escort me? I've only been there once."

They exchanged glances. One of them peeled off of his station and took me by the arm.

"It would be my honor, Lady Priya."

My lips curled into a hidden grin as the guard escorted me into the palace.

The guard walked with me until we stood in front of the red exterior door of the records archive.

"Thank you. I appreciate the escort."

"Anything for his majesty." His arm unlocked from mine and he slithered away.

"I'll be sure to tell him you helped in this endeavor."

My eyes turned to the red door. I unlocked it with the key and went inside the main corridor.

Ok, let's see how fast I can go through millions of documents.

At work I had always been the 'paper girl'. I was a specialist archaeologist, but the men didn't see it that way. When there was paperwork to be filed or organized, I was the one doing it. Because of this, I had a special system for thumbing through endless stacks of paper.

I've been focusing on finding this evidence and not on what I'd do with it. Would I find King Vasuki tomorrow and hand it to him? Or is there a special process for treasure fraud?

An hour passed. I'd found nothing but legitimate receipts.

Where the fuck is he keeping the records. There must be records, even if they're fake.

Another hour passed. I'd been through every paper in every trunk of the first room.

It's going to take multiple nights to go through these. There's at least fifteen rooms just like this with as many or more trunks of documents.

I closed the last trunk. My hands were on the trunk and my body leaning forward. My breathing was fast from my search.

"Imagine my surprise..."

My legs twitched into a jumping motion. I spun around to see Balnak standing in the doorway. He didn't make any noise opening the door.

"...when I told the palace guards I needed access to the archives, and being told that you were already here."

King Vasuki had warned me of vermin in the archives, and I'd found it. Balnak closed the door behind him and threw a heavy trunk in front of it.

Fuck. Fan-fucking-shit-tastic. How the shitting hell am I supposed to get out of this?

"I told the guards we'd be working for hours and needed to not be disturbed."

"I've only looked through this one room. There are plenty of others." My eyes never left his.

"Do you think I would keep evidence of my dealings in the archive?" His eyes never left mine. We were two predators, sizing up which of us was the apex predator.

"I don't think that highly of you Balnak, so yes I was hoping you'd be foolish enough to keep it here." He visibly hissed and spat a steaming glob of venom to the floor.

The slit containing his genitals opened. His cock and scrotum fell out, dangling in the air.

"I'll forgive you and forget all about this misunderstanding if you just hop up on this table and spread those pretty brown legs of yours. Sarvaan has kept you around so I assume you have something sweeter than honey between them."

What if I just kill him now? Then I can 'enter' the trial, collude with Sarvaan to lose on purpose. I get to be transformed into a Nagini, he gets to be king, and Balnak gets to be dead.

"I'll pass. I doubt you can please any woman, let alone me."

He slithered forward with feral speed. My hand went to my thigh to grab the dagger but he was too fast. My back slammed against the stone wall behind me. I coughed as breath was punched from my lungs. Balnak's four hundred pounds of body was pressed into me. I couldn't move an inch. He brought his lips to my ear, flicking his tongue on it.

"You'll just have to be my human fucktoy until you realize that you're meant to be unioned to me…"

His hand grabbed between my legs.

No. No! NO! Fuck that! This isn't going to happen—

His fingers lifted my dress.

"Balnak! Get the fuck off of me or I'll bleed you dry and watch you die a slow death!"

Two giant fingers spread my labia.

"I mean it, you piece of shit!" My head moved so he had to stare into my eyes and see the rage in them. I wasn't going to look away like a scared little girl. He's going to have to look at me, dammit.

His finger entered me. My body jolted up to recoil against the touch. His mouth widened and his face pressed on mine, shoving his tongue into my mouth.

Nishala's words floated through my mind. For stabbing men who hear yes when you say no.

When my body jolted my hand slipped free from being pressed against the wall with the rest of me. It grabbed the dagger at my thigh. I acted like I was going to suck on his tongue and bit down on it hard instead. My hand stabbed him in the hip with my dagger at the same time. The copper taste of blood filled my mouth as Balnak hissed sharply and backed away.

"Leave or you'll be full of holes during your next match." The dagger was meant for Naga, so it was almost the size of a small sword in my hands. I held the dagger in a warrior's stance that Nishala taught me.

Balnak spat blood onto the floor and rubbed the wound on his hip. He knew even a small wound could mean he would feel it during his match in the trial. He slowly slithered backwards to the door, moving the trunk he'd placed there.

"Just remember that I know your secrets. Dealing with exiles is punishable by death. If my secrets come to light, so do yours."

When he was gone and the door closed, I moved the heavy trunk back in front of the door and clutched my chest. My heart was racing. It felt like I wasn't getting enough air. My vision was blurry around the edges. I spat Naga blood from my mouth until it was gone. Then, I collapsed to the floor.

I didn't stand or even move when I woke up. My cheek was to the floor. My eyes just stared forward. Tears filled them.

No no, don't you fucking cry. You're a warrior. You're a queen. Queens don't cry!

It didn't matter how much I told myself not to cry. I cried. There were no sobs, just tears streaming from my eyes and onto the floor.

He has to pay for this. He has to be held accountable. Sarvaan must know what happened here. If I can't kill Balnak, I know Sarvaan can, and will, after knowing what happened.

My arms raised and pressed my hands to the floor, pushing me to my feet. My hands brushed dust from my dress and wiped my eyes and cheek. I was going to walk away from this situation with my head high. No one brings down a warrior queen.

The moment I was home and the door closed, a tearful sob escaped my lips.

"Sarvaan! I need you! Sarvaan!" My words cracked between sobs.

Thuds sounding like a bull running through an enclosed space echoed through the walls as Sarvaan made his way to the den. When he saw me his hands grabbed my shoulders.

"Priya? Priya! You're crying...why are you crying?"

"I went to the palace...to try and find...evidence against Balnak..." I could barely speak as my words and my sobs competed over the breath in my lungs.

Sarvaan's eyes widened. His mind seemed to arrive at what I was about to say before it escaped my lips.

"Balnak...found me...snooping."

"No...Priya, no..."

"He violated me, Sarvaan...he...put his..." The word wouldn't come out. A choking sound came instead. Sarvaan's grip on my shoulder strengthened.

"...inside me...I stabbed him...with a dagger...to get away." My body fell to the floor. My arms hugged Sarvaan's lower body, hot tears smearing on his scales. "I'm so sorry Sarvaan! This is...all my...fault."

Sarvaan grabbed me and pulled me to my feet.

"NO! You have nothing to apologize for! This isn't your fault."

My tears turned to anger. My bloodshot eyes stared at Sarvaan.

"I want him dead."

Sarvaan let out a hissing roar and grabbed the table in front of the couch. He ripped the table in half with his bare hands. Splinters of wood floated through the air in the aftermath.

Yes. Get angry. Balnak needs to feel pain like he's never felt before.

"And dead he shall be!" Sarvaan's voice had never been so loud or deep before. It sounded like there was a monster hidden in his throat.

Sarvaan grabbed one of his swords lying against the wall and stormed out the door of the house.

Chapter 24
Rage ~ सच

My legs were running from pure adrenaline as I tried to keep up with Sarvaan slithering through the streets looking like a sword-wielding madman. My thighs stung as the air rushed past them. My feet ached and asked for relief. My brain didn't register their complaints. At one point I lost sight of Sarvaan because of how much faster he was than me. I started to follow the strange looks and screams instead. Sarvaan was shouting from the top of his lungs, asking anyone he encountered where Balnak lived.

"Sarvaan!" My voice echoed into the night air.

My legs couldn't move another step without rest. My hands grabbed my knees and I bent over. My chest heaving from panting.

I have to find him. I want to watch Balnak suffer.

I took off running again. Naga scales turned black as I entered the Takshaka neighborhood of Bhogavati. Naga were in the street talking and whispering to one another. I knew I was on the right track when they pointed as they whispered. My legs followed their fingers, as if they were there to guide me to Sarvaan. My ears caught the sound of a door being broken off of its hinges. My legs carried me towards the sound. I ended up on a small side street. The sounds of furniture breaking, hissing, and angry words came from one house in particular.

"Out in the street, Neech harami!" Balnak's crumpled body was thrown from the open doorway. He rolled into the street and Sarvaan leapt from within the house and got on top of him.

Sarvaan's hands were around Balnak's throat, crushing it under his weight. I walked closer, staring into Balnak's eyes as he choked. He caught sight of me, reaching a hand out to me.

It doesn't feel very good to be crushed, does it?

Balnak flipped Sarvaan over and his fists and tail flailed, trying to get the upper hand. Sarvaan's rage was insatiable. He was back on top of Balnak within seconds. Sarvaan's fists pounded into Balnak's face one after another. Sarvaan's stamina seemed to have no end.

"You dare violate my soul companion! My wife!" Sarvaan's voice was a demon roaring to life.

Balnak would never hurt me, or anyone else again. Sarvaan would have no one to compete against in the trial. Killing Balnak was the bow that tied everything together.

Scales scraping over the tiled marble in the streets caught my ears. The city guards were starting to arrive.

No. Kill him, my love! He can't be allowed to live!

My thoughts were not brought into realization. Seven guards pried Sarvaan and Balnak around. Sarvaan had some marks, but Balnak was bruised and bloodied all over. A guard's spear was thrust into Sarvaan's face as he tried to claw his way back to fighting Balnak.

"Save the aggression for your match in the trial! If there's anymore fighting between you two between now and then...you'll both be disqualified."

A smug grin shot over Balnak's face.

"You've got bigger things to worry about than me Sarvaan...your consort colludes with Nishala the exile. I've seen her sneaking out to meet her. I wonder what they talk about?"

Sarvaan's face was still filled with rage, as if he didn't register what Balnak said. His expression softened. He was thinking. His eyes glued themselves to me. Confusion washed over him. I almost started to cry again. My tears were held back by rage. Rage that Balnak was allowed to breathe still.

For the entire walk home, Sarvaan was quiet. I didn't talk either. I knew there'd be plenty of talking when we were in private. When we arrived home Sarvaan held the door for me, glaring. I walked in and heard the door slam shut.

"Please tell me...that he's lying. I'll believe you over him. I won't even need convincing. Whatever you utter, I hold as true, just as I hold my love for you as the truest thing I know."

More of my tears fell to the floor, making tiny thuds in the silence. I turned to face Sarvaan, expecting rage. His face was sunken, defeated. I saw sadness. Pain.

"She's been teaching me combat, to defend myself."

"So have I. Have I been a bad teacher?"

"No! You've been amazing. But I'm a human. Balnak is thrice my weight and stands two feet over my head. I needed all the training I could get."

"Priya...I'm not hurt because you've been training in combat. I'm hurt because you've been lying to me. The other night when you came home damp and sweating...you lied to my face, didn't you?"

He slithered past me, not looking at me or touching me as he usually did when he walked by me.

No. Fuck that. My story doesn't end this way.

My hand grabbed his and yanked, spinning him to face me. I stood body to body with him, my neck shooting straight up to look him in the eyes.

"I'm sorry I lied to you. I love you with all of my heart, but still land is strange to me. I've given my heart to men before and they still hurt me."

My fist slammed against his chest. Tears filled my eyes again.

"I didn't know how you would react to me visiting an exile. I was fearful you'd turn me in, or react with rage."

"You think that little of me?"

He turned to move away from me. I yanked his arm back to me.

"Where are you going? You're mine, don't you remember? There's nowhere you can go where I won't follow."

"Priya, I understand you were scared—"

My finger pointed into his scales, tapping with each point I made.

"I made a mistake. I'm not perfect. I'm sorry for lying to you. I'll never lie to you again. My world is your world. When I first arrived here I didn't know who I could trust. I know I can trust you. Please trust me."

A sob slipped out of me when Sarvaan's warm hands grabbed my waist and lifted me to him.

"You just lied again."

"What do you mean—" His finger pressed to my lips.

"You are perfect." My hand yanked his finger from my lips and I kissed him.

"You handsome, dumb brute. I love you. I live for you. I'd die for you."

My feet felt the floor.

"Come, let's soak in the hot spring, my muscles ache and I bet yours do as well." His hand tried to pull me but I resisted. He looked back at me confused.

"Actually, I had something else in mind."

"Oh?"

"I know I'm in no place to be asking for a favor. But after what happened with Balnak tonight, there's something I need to ask you. A piece of me was taken away tonight. There's something I need from you so I can be whole again. Something I *need* you to say yes to, no questions asked."

"I'd give you the universe if you asked for it."

My arms wrapped his midsection and I pressed my face into his scales, nuzzling against their smoothness.

"I've already got the universe. You *are* my universe."

He leaned down and kissed me. My hands held on to his face when he tried to rise back up. When I finally let him pull away, he turned to slither off to the hot spring. I grabbed his hand and gave it a tug telling him I wanted his attention. He turned back to meet my gaze. My feet paced backwards, pulling Sarvaan with me until my back was against the wall.

"If I'm going to have a memory of being fucked against a wall...I want that memory to be with you."

I peeled my dress from my body and let it fall to the floor. My hands pulled at Sarvaan's waist, showing him I wanted his body pressed to mine.

"And you're sure you want this?"

"I need this, and I need you."

Sarvaan's fingers took my wrists, wrapping them both easily. He lifted me into the air. My feet dangled below. He pressed his body against mine, gently holding it against the wall. His fingers clasped mine and pressed my arms to the wall along with my body.

"Put your hand between my legs. Make me squirm."

Sarvaan did as I told him. The warmth of his palm greeted my crotch. His thumb massaged my clit slowly. His fingers traced around my labia.

"Rough. I want it rough. I trust you." I needed his touch to be forceful, to erase the memory of Balnak from my mind.

Sarvaan's thumb mashed into my clit. Air inhaled into my mouth sharply. My toes started to curl and wiggle. His mouth met my neck and kissed it, dragging his fangs along my skin. My hips moved forward into his hand as much as I could in this position.

"Tell me how much you love me, Sarvaan…"

"I love you, Priya…"

"It doesn't sound like you love me enough. Tell me again."

Sarvaan jammed a finger into my pussy as he pressed into my clit still with his thumb.

"I love you more than anything, Priya…"

"I don't believe you. Tell me again!"

Another finger plunged into me. Sarvaan raised me by my arms and then let me down, dropping my body onto his fingers.

"You're my one and only love, Priya!" His lips sucked up and down my neck and shoulders now.

"Liar! I still don't believe you. Make me believe you…leave your marks on me. Show everyone I'm yours."

At my command he sucked on my neck harder. Heat rushed to my skin as he brought portions of my neck into his mouth with the suction. When he let go I felt my skin go back into place. I looked at the area he sucked and it was reddened.

"Yes! Mark me as yours. Now fuck me like the warrior you are."

Sarvaan's fingers left my pussy and were replaced by his cock. It had been against my legs the entire time and I yearned for it. Each time Sarvaan pumped into me, my ass cheeks squished against the wall and our teeth clattered as we kissed. My hips bucked into his, gathering all of him into me at the end of each thrust.

"Priya! You're my destiny! Tell me you believe I love you now."

"I believe you! Fuck me like the king you are!"

Sarvaan's pace picked up to speeds he'd never shown me before. Everything around me became blissful as my pussy clenched on his pumping wet cock in me. My vision was filled with swirling colors. My ears heard faint ringing sounds. My skin was on fire. Sarvaan must have felt it. His cock started to pulse. He was close. One of my hands wrestled free from Sarvaan's grasp and I gripped his chin, staring into his eyes.

"Would you do anything for your queen?"

"Would...tell me..." The strain in his voice as he held back his load made my pussy gush more than it already had.

"Go all the way. Give me your eggs. I want to feel them in me again."

Sarvaan let out a victorious roar of compliance and his thrusts slowed to deliberate, forceful pumps. The first pump produced one of his baseball sized eggs.

"Argh! Priya, take my eggs."

"Mmmmm, Haan..." My legs widened to be parallel with my hips, to allow room for his eggs.

The second pump made my hips feel like they were being ripped apart. Three eggs were pumped into my pussy at once. A feral roar came out of me as the eggs went into me. My arms and legs went limp from the pleasure. The third pump deposited another batch of three eggs. My back arched and my head went back. My eyes were on the ceiling and my soul was in paradise.

"You're my beginning and end, Sarvaan..." Was all I remembered saying.

"You make me and unmake me, Priya!" He let loose another straining howl.

The last pump slid the final three eggs into me. My entire body felt like it was on fire and being electrocuted at the same time. I didn't feel my body fall into his. I didn't feel him carry me to the couch and wrap my body with his. I didn't feel his eggs slip out of me because of the pressure.

All I feel is him. And me. That's all I need.

***

As we laid together in the hot water of the spring, I traced shapes on Sarvaan's chest using the water droplets accumulating on him from the steam. My chest was on his. My head was resting in my folded arm. Sarvaan's fingers ran through my wet hair. My cooing sounds echoed off the rocks in the basement. Sarvaan didn't know it, but I was gathering courage to tie up one last loose end. Balnak had revealed my dealings with Nishala, but Sarvaan didn't know exactly what our dealings were. It was time to be honest. No more secrets would be kept.

"Sarvaan, my darling, there's one more thing regarding my dealings with Nishala you need to know."

"Go on." There was patience in his voice. He sounded as if he was too tired to fight or squabble.

My head raised. I swam to be face-to-face with him.

"Promise me that you trust me. This is going to sound bad but I swear it's not what it sounds like."

Sarvaan's hand found mine and squeezed it.

"I trust you completely, Priya. You're my soul companion for life. Whatever you're a part of, I am too."

A deep inhale filled my lungs. As I exhaled, steam blew in a stream away from my face.

"Nishala knows of a ritual to transform me and give me a Nagini body."

Sarvaan's eyes widened. His grip on my hands tightened with excitement.

"Really? That's incredible. What does the ritual entail?"

"I don't know. She hasn't told me yet."

His eyes furrowed.

"Is she keeping it from you? Did she demand payment of gold?"

"No..." My fingers rubbed his. "She has a condition to be met before she'll perform the ritual..." My voice trailed off. This was the difficult part to explain.

"What's her condition?"

"She wants me to enter the Trial of The Crown."

Sarvaan's jaw slowly dropped. His grip on my hand loosened, but my grip on him tightened. I wasn't letting him take his hand away from me.

"She won't relent on her condition. And she won't tell me why."

His lowered jaw formed into a laugh. His laugh turned into a laughing fit. He brought me close, squeezing the breath from me. My hands clawed at his face, pushing my body so I could see his face.

"What are you laughing at Sarvaan?"

"Priya! Don't you see? Nishala wants to be pardoned from exile."

My face lost all expression.

How hadn't I seen this? Of course!

"Only the sitting ruler of Bhogavati can pardon exiles." Sarvaan rose triumphantly from the water, bringing me with him on his shoulders. "Tomorrow we visit Nishala and I'll give her assurances that I will pardon her if she performs this ritual."

"Really? Really?! Fuck I love you so damn much!" My thighs squeezed the shoulder I was perched on.

Hell yes! Fuck yes! I'll get to see my family...I'll have my happy ending with Sarvaan...I'll have everything.

Chapter 25

Pardon ~ स्वप्न

"So she killed her opponent because he violated her?"

"Yes, that's what she told me. I believe her."

It was the next day. Sarvaan and I had just exited the river near Nishala's camp.

"Who was ruler back then?" My hand squeezed Sarvaan's as we moved through the forest towards the camp. Wood smoke in the air told us we were going in the right direction.

"I'm not sure. I've only been alive for seventy-seven years. I've only ever been a citizen while King Vasuki has been our ruler."

"Seventy-seven. You're an old man, Sarvaan." His giant hand smacked my butt. I let out a tiny squeal.

"Not in Naga years. I'm in my prime."

"That's right, you said Naga live for about three-hundred years."

"What about you? I don't think you've told me your age. I'm not as familiar with human aging."

"I'm twenty-eight. I'm in my prime as well."

He looked down at me smiling. My eyes met his and matched his smile. Soon the trees cleared and we were in the grassy grove where I first met Sarvaan and Nishala. I had grown so much since then. In body, mind, and spirit. Nishala noticed Sarvaan before she noticed me. I was partially hidden from the grass in the grove, but Sarvaan towered a couple feet above me.

"What do I owe the pleasure, warrior—" Then I came into her view. "Well then. Now we have a party."

"Sarvaan knows about the ritual and your condition."

Her eyes flicked to Sarvaan and then back to me.

"Good for you. Nice to see you again Sarvaan. It's been too long."

"Likewise. We have a proposition for you."

Nishala sat on the log next to her campfire that she used as a bench.

"Oh, I love being proposed to. Do tell..."

"Tomorrow I have my final match in the Trial of The Crown. My opponent is a fool and is a warrior unbecoming. When I defeat him, I'll be crowned the new king of Bhogavati."

Nishala clapped slowly.

"Congratulations are in order then. They should be giving you the crown already with that confidence. Although, this seems to contradict the condition I gave to Priya."

Come on Nishala, don't be so stubborn. You'll get a pardon either way.

"A condition you gave to her because you want her to pardon you from exile. Am I correct?"

Nishala's posture shifted at the question.

"My reasons are my reasons."

"Priya told me of the events that led to your exile. I see no reason you should be exiled. I will pardon you and welcome you back to Bhogavati if you perform the ritual to transform Priya into one of us."

Nishala's eyes shot to me. She was glaring, as if I'd insulted her. A grin on her face said she was considering it.

"I accept these new terms."

My body jumped against Sarvaan's with excitement.

"But..." My body became still again, waiting to hear what she said next. "I'll have my pardon first. Then, when I'm officially a citizen of this realm again, I'll perform the kiss of scales."

Sarvaan smiled. My hands rubbed and squeezed the scales on his back. I could barely contain my joy.

"Thank you, Nishala. Really. Thank you."

My legs took me to her and my arms went around her neck.

"You're making a mistake. You're supposed to rule this realm. Not Sarvaan." She whispered it in my ear so softly that I doubt an insect could have heard it.

She held my arm tight as I embraced her. My smile faded hearing her words. I had to put the smile back on my face as I released her from my embrace and walked back to Sarvaan's side.

"Well then, I guess I've got a crown to go win, and a pardon to issue. We'll be seeing you very soon, Nishala."

"Oh yes, I don't doubt it."

As Sarvaan and I turned to leave, my eyes lingered on Nishala's face. It held so much disappointment. Sarvaan's hand tugging at mine peeled my eyes from Nishala's.

We just guaranteed your freedom, why can't you be happy for me?

***

Sarvaan and I were so excited and giddy it took us twice as long to get back to Bhogavati. We kissed and laughed and just held each other. Our energies were feeding into each other in a never-ending loop. When we arrived back home, Sarvaan took me down a hallway I'd never been down, or even knew existed.

"Where does this go?"

"You'll see...you'll love it, I'm sure." His hand squeezed mine as he led me.

The hallway gave way to stairs that led upwards.

We have stairs? We have a second floor?

A wooden door awaited us at the top of the stairs. Sarvaan opened it and gestured me through. Once through the door, my breath was taken from me. I was standing on a balcony, looking out over the cityscape of Bhogavati. The thousands of jewels embedded in the streets and buildings looked like a galaxy of stars from this view. My hands leaned forward on the balcony railing. A cooing sigh breathed from my lips as I took in the beauty of the city.

"This is so gorgeous, Sarvaan. I didn't even know we had a balcony!" Sarvaan's body pressed against my back and his arms went around my neck, his hands clasped together on the top of my chest.

"That's probably because we spend so much time in the bedroom..." His chest convulsed with a small chuckle. I slapped his arm.

"I treasure our time in the bedroom!"

We stood there for a few minutes, looking out across the swarms of lights in the background. My ears caught music down at the street level. It was slow and sensual. I turned and put my hand on Sarvaan's shoulder, assuming a stance for slow dancing. We swayed to the music, smiling and staring into each other's eyes.

"If someone had told me two weeks ago that I would soon be in Bhogavati...married to a devilishly handsome Naga warrior who would soon be king...and I was beloved by the denizens of the realm...and that I'd get to be a Nagini myself...I'd tell that person they were crazy."

"But you have been wanting all of this since you were a child, correct?"

"I have. But it was more wishful thinking. Wanting to believe in stories where I had a fairy tale happy ending."

Sarvaan spun me slowly and dipped me, kissing up my chest.

"All of the crazy events and situations that have happened since you arrived...were they worth it?"

"Yes. I'd do everything all over if I had the choice."

"Didn't queen Prathavi's spirit indicate that your choices throughout your life led you here?"

"I'm not all the way certain of her insinuations. What I am certain of is that I've always wanted to be here. And I'm certain that I want to be here with you."

Sarvaan's hand on my lower back pressed me to him. Feeling his warmth made the smile that was already on my face bigger.

"Even so, I've sensed a bit of angst about you."

"I just can't wait to see my family again. I want you to meet them. I want them to see how happy you make me and show them I'm safe and provided for."

"Your family, what are they like?"

"My brother, Vikram, always daydreams. He's always looking to the stars the same way I look at the rocks and stones of the earth. When I became an adult and moved away for university we got along better. Whenever we live in the same house we butt heads, we're too competitive."

"What does competitiveness with siblings feel like? I've never known any of my siblings intimately."

"It's not unlike you and other warriors. You all train to be the best and strongest and bravest, that leads naturally to challenges and trials of combat."

"And how about your mother and father, what are they like?"

"My mother feeds me too many sweets and hugs me too tight. She loves to bake, likes taking long walks around the neighborhood, and she's a better swimmer than the best Naga."

Sarvaan spun me around again, this time two spins, his eyes admiring all of me as I spun.

"My father is a person who recognized that I was easier to get along with when I'm encouraged than when I'm controlled."

"Yes, I see that too. He's a smart man."

"Just before I fell into this realm, he told me to follow my destiny and fulfill my dharma, no matter where it took me. It was like he was giving me permission to come here and get lost in another world."

The music on the street ceased, Sarvaan stopped swaying and just held me against him. On the balcony the scents of the city were stronger. The air smelled of heavy guggul resin incense, bathing our skin and scales in its smoky vanilla scent. A sharp and earthy marigold fragrance perfumed the breeze.

"Just before you fell into this realm I was simply focused on training for the trials. I thought the prospect of being king of Bhogavati was the best thing that could ever happen to me. I was wrong. You are the best thing that's ever happened to me."

Sarvaan must have read my mind. I wanted to kiss his stupid, handsome face for making my heart melt. His back on my lower back pressed up, lifting me to his chest. We kissed slowly. Our lips moved at a snail's pace as every inch of our lips moved across the other's mouth.

"Are you nervous about tomorrow?" I knew he wasn't, but I asked anyway.

"Of course not. That foul beast will have lost before he even realizes it. I nearly won already when I threw him into the street like the vermin he is."

"That's what I like to hear. My strong warrior king being confident." My legs curled around Sarvaan's body the best I could manage. We kissed slowly again. We both had everything we wanted. There was no reason to rush.

***

"You're making a mistake. You're supposed to rule this realm. Not Sarvaan."

Nishala's last words to me rang out loudly instead of the whisper it was before.

You're beginning to lose sight of the goal.

What goal? What are you talking about?

My dream had me standing in the middle of the arena. My bare feet crunched the cool dirt below. The arena seats were all filled, but the audience made no sounds or motions. Looking at where the three stone pillars stood, I witnessed a scene of horror. Balnak was lying in the dirt, bloodied and motionless, Sarvaan was laying on top of him in the same condition.

"NO!" My legs tried to run but it was as if I was trying to run through water. An unseen force slowed my movements.

My words didn't come out as sound either. I felt my breath exit my body, but no sound. My knees fell into the dirt and I pulled Sarvaan's lifeless head into my lap.

"Someone, please help him!"

A shape manifested in front of me. It was Queen Prathavi. She was wearing the mekhala, vatchi, and shawl I'd made to honor my past, present, and future.

"I did this for you...for us."

"What? Why? I love him! He's my everything!"

"I killed them, so that only you would remain." She slithered to me, picking me up by my collar. My body was midair, looking down at her. "You can't run from me. I'm part of you, and you can never run from yourself."

Prathavi drew a sword and thrust her arm forward as if to impale me. I held my hand up to stop the blade. My hand caught it as I'd caught Sarvaan's blade in the cave. Suddenly, the hand she was holding me in the air with started to meld into my body. Skin and scales bonded together. Both bodies seemed to become viscous and melt together. My bones bent and broke and contorted to merge with hers. I screamed but no sound came. Piss and blood fell to the dirt as both of our bodies writhed in unimaginable pain.

You think you have it all, Priya. You can have even more. You're meant for more.

Chapter 26

Fall ~ नियति

Prathavi's words rippled around in my mind as I was getting dressed for Sarvaan's final match. My mekhala, vatchi, and shawl went on my body instead of Prathavi's like in my dream last night.

What had the dream meant? What more was I meant to have? What more was I meant for?

I put on my golden serpent earrings and added a sword to my hip. The attire was complete now. I looked like a warrior queen.

Yes...

My hair flipped as my head spun around trying to see where the voice had come from. Realization dawned on me.

"Oh, it's you again."

Silence filled the room.

"Nothing more to say? How convenient."

As I turned my back to the mirror and went to leave the room, I felt a hand grip my shoulder. There was no one else in the room with me. My body slowly turned back to the mirror. Queen Prathavi's reflection was showing instead of mine. Her hand stretched out of the mirror and to my body. She wore green and gold regalia and jewelry, as if her colors were a union of Karkota Kula and Vasuki Kula.

"What do you want from me?" I removed her hand from my shoulder. It fell back into the reflection with the rest of her.

"Nothing. I'm one of the few who truly wants nothing from you, Priya."

"Then why are you here? Why do you haunt my dreams?"

"I'm here because I wanted to see how beautiful...and how vicious you look. You've made me proud, Priya. As for your dreams...to find the culprit you need only to look in the mirror..."

As I stared at her reflection, it started to melt away and fade back into my own reflection. Before I could process her words, Sarvaan was standing in the doorway, admiring me.

"You look divine, my love. I'm not worthy."

My body was against his in an instant, my head back as far as I could get it looking up at him.

"You're the *only* one worthy of me."

"I'm glad I managed to fool you into thinking that." His smile hid a laugh. My hand smacked his side.

"I'm the one who's fooled you into loving and pampering a human woman."

"What? You're a human woman? Off with you at once!" His belly shook with laughter. I clung tighter to his body.

"Sorry, no giving me back now. You're stuck with me."

"I'd rather be stuck with you than anyone else."

I love this man. Bahut zada

***

When we stepped out of our door and into the streets to head to the arena, we were greeted with at least ten Karkota Nagas. They cheered and clapped for us when they saw us. Sarvaan posed for them and waved at them. As we went along our way, they followed us. With each street we passed, more Nagas followed and our small group turned into an entire procession.

"This is amazing, Sarvaan! Look how many follow us." My neck turned back to count, but there was an endless sea of faces.

"Yes, kulas like to show their devotion to prominent members during important events. The thinking is, the more people you have devoted to a cause, the stronger the conviction is to that cause."

"So they're channeling their essence into you?"

"Exactly."

If that was true then Balnak would be a mass of bloody pulp today. The crowd swelled beyond a hundred bodies now as we all moved through the streets. As we got closer to the arena, clouds of smoke from incense and ritual fire burning to celebrate the occasion engulfed us. The curls of heavy smoke caressed my body. They smelled of pure cream due to the sandalwood being burned. Mogra flower petals flew through the air like flocks of birds. They were intensely sweet, almost stinging my nostrils with their fragrance.

So this is what it's like to be celebrated. To be honored. Nani, I hope somehow you can see me. What I've gone through...what I've become.

As if the thick fog of smoke in the air was acting as a hallucinogenic chemical, a vision came to my mind. There was nothing but white all around me. No walls, floor, or ceiling. Nani manifested in front of me.

"Nani! It's you!" My arms were around her in an instant.

"Bitiya...My little princess has grown into a queen!" The lump in my throat made me cry like a baby as I hugged her.

I didn't want to let go. I knew this wasn't real but I wanted to hold her a little longer.

"The stories you told me...they were true..."

Her hands pulled me from her to look me in the eyes.

"I simply guided you. *You* made them true." Her hands shook me slightly as she talked.

"However I arrived here, I'm going to be a Queen today, Nani." My hands both went to my face to wipe my tears.

"Just make sure you become the queen you always wanted to be." Her mouth slowly turned into a smile. Then, Nani's form dispersed into a whirlwind of crows and parijat petals.

The vision came to a stop when Sarvaan's hand gripped my shoulder.

"Today will be a good day, Priya. It will live on in our memory and in history for ages to come."

I gulped down the urge to cry some more. We were in front of the arena. Droves and droves of people formed endless lines to gain entry. Royal guards found us in the crowd and ushered us in so Sarvaan could take his starting position and I could be seated.

I will be, Nani. I will be the queen I always wanted to be.

***

Every seat was filled in the arena. Some Naga had climbed the stone walls and sat upon it. Others were crowded along the sidelines in the dirt. Sarvaan walked me to dedicated seating area for the competitors' loved ones as usual. Even it was almost over flowing. The Nagas gathered in the seating area moved to the side for me so I could have a front seat. As I passed by them, their hands touched my shoulder briefly. A show of affection and community. The time came for Sarvaan to part with me and assume his starting position.

"Kick his ass. Make him bleed." Sarvaan's fingers rubbed my neck.

"I could just hug him and forgive him instead." He couldn't hide his smile.

"Do that and I'll kick your ass."

"I have no doubt." His fingers released their hold on me and he slithered to his starting pillar.

King Vasuki made his way to the middle of the arena. Somehow an already cacophonous crowd grew louder.

"Citizens of Bhogavati...the time has come to witness the final match of the Trial of The Crown..."

My eyes shifted to Balnak's pillar, he was already coiled around it. His eyes stared straight ahead in a meditative trance. A smug grin was on his face.

What are you up to? I know you're scheming to try and cheat your way out of this.

"At the end of this match, Bhogavati will surely know who is to be its ruler for the next one hundred years..."

Sarvaan's body heaved and twitched with restless energy.

Center yourself, husband, concentrate and put an end to this once and for all.

"Let's get down to it then. Competitors, when you hear the sound of the horns, you may begin."

The Karkota Nagas among the crowd tapped their tail pearls against stone and delivered a melodic chant. The Takshaka Naga pounded their chest like gorillas, roaring and hissing into the air.

Okay...here we go.

When the horns sounded, Balnak's first maneuver sent him to the very tip of his stone pillar, coiled as high as he could bring his body to go. Sarvaan spun on his own pillar to face Balnak. His head tilted in confusion.

What the fuck is this bastard trying to pull...

"Balnak! What is the meaning of this? Get down here and fight me like a warrior!"

"I'm doing what I'm meant to do, Sarvaan, I'm looking down on you like the lowly sap that you are..." Balnak took his sword and shield and tossed them to the ground below. The entire crowd gasped sharply, me included. A screech erupted from my throat.

"Don't fall for it, Sarvaan! He's unarmed! Your victory is assured!"

My screeches were drowned out by the roars of the crowd.

"Fight me with just your hands, Sarvaan, lest you want Priya to think you are a coward? Then she would surely want to union with me instead."

No! Dammit no! Sarvaan, don't you dare fall for this shit!

Sweat started to pour from my forehead and chest. It felt as if a hot coal was stuck in my body.

"I've beat you with my hands before. I can do it again!"

"You surprised me while I was in my bed. Do you think you can win when I'm not in a helpless state?"

Sarvaan tossed his sword and shield to the ground as Balnak did. My heart fell somewhere into my body.

"NOOOOOO!" I tried to leap over the railing and into the arena but the Naga near me grabbed me and held me from doing it.

"This is his match, interference would disqualify him!"

My hands shoved their fingers off of me. My hands covered my mouth and I bit into my skin.

Fuck, fuck, fuck, fuck, FUCK!

Nishala's voice taunted me in my head.

You're supposed to rule this realm. Not Sarvaan.

Prathavi's voice was next.

You've been setting your plan in motion since you arrived here.

You're here because you decided that you didn't want to just be a Nagini princess in your head...you wanted to be a queen!

You wanted this world. It's yours.

You think you have it all, Priya. You can have even more. You're meant for more.

Tears flooded my eyes so much, I had to wipe them every few seconds. Sarvaan leapt to the middle pillar and then flung himself at Balnak, roaring along the way. Balnak jumped as Sarvaan was in midair and they collided, wrapping around the center pillar with fists and claws flying. The roar of the crowd had gotten too loud and I couldn't hear. I had to be closer to Sarvaan. My legs carried me from the seating platform. The Naga around me were too preoccupied to stop me this time. When my feet crunched into the dirt I sprinted as fast as I could. An arm of gold scales caught me when I was halfway between the seating platform and the fighting area. It was King Vasuki.

"Apologies, Priya, I can't allow you to go any further."

I barely acknowledged the king. Sarvaan and Balnak's words came to my ears now.

"Why don't you just give up, Sarvaan? I'll treat Priya nicely, I promise!"

Blood splattered the stone pillars and scales flew like grenade fragments.

"You'll do no such thing, pile of slime!"

"Are you afraid she'll take to me more than you? Are you afraid she'll like my cock more than yours?"

Balnak was putting Sarvaan on tilt, letting his emotions get the better of him. Sarvaan started to get sloppy. More punches and claw rakes from Balnak landed on his scales.

"Shut your trap! Your words are foolish!"

Balnak's arm wrapped around Sarvaan's neck and put him in a neck hold.

"I'm going to fuck her until my seed leaks from her eyes…"

Sarvaan struggled but Balnak punched his ribs each time he did.

"Not…going…to….happen!" Sarvaan freed himself from Balnak's hold and his hands went around Balnak's neck.

My body felt feverish now. Each blow that struck Sarvaan struck me, too. I flinched with each drop of blood spilled. My hands clenched with each fist that pounded into his scales. Balnak put his thumbs between Sarvaan's hands and his own throat. Sarvaan's strength began to wane and Balnak pried Sarvaan's fingers from his throat. Balnak's hands found Sarvaan's wrists and held him in place.

"I haven't even told you the best part…I'm going to fill Priya full of my eggs until she can't even walk."

Get him out of your head! You're letting him have the crown!

Salty tears washed over my lips. My vision was blurry from the tears and anxiety. Sarvaan screamed and strained against Balnak's grip. It was no use. Balnak thrust down with his arms, throwing Sarvaan from the pillar. Sarvaan's body landed with a thud that I didn't hear. Chunks of dirt flew into the air when he landed. If the crowd made any sounds, they didn't make it to my ears. My mouth was moving but I didn't hear the words I shouted.

"I'll challenge that vile piece of shit! I challenge you Balnak!"

My words didn't change what had already happened. King Vasuki moved his arm and released me from my position.

"The sting of destiny is the sting we least expect." My face shot to his. My lip quivered.

"Do you know something I don't?"

His hand grabbed my shoulder and gently moved me towards the fighting area.

"I know many things. I know you should be with your soul companion. Go. Be with him."

Balnak was escorted away by the royal guards as I ran to the heap in the dirt that was Sarvaan. I cradled his head in my lap as I did in my dream. His eyes were open. A frown covered his face.

"Sarvaan! Sarvaan!" My hands shook his head.

"I failed..."

My hands brought his head into my chest and I cried onto his neck. Everything I thought I had came crashing down in just a few short minutes. A vile criminal of a man would be king. Sarvaan wouldn't be able to pardon Nishala. I wouldn't be transformed and get to see my family. The love of my life was a broken shell of his former self. It was over. Sarvaan had lost.

Chapter 27

Challenge ~ रानी

The crowd's murmurs and chatter was nothing compared to my wails. My arms held Sarvaan's head in my lap as tears flowed like a waterfall onto his scales. Finally, I felt Sarvaan's body move. He curled closer to me, holding me with his arms.

"Sarvaan...you're still with me..."

"I'd never leave you...soul companion...is forever."

My mind raced trying to decide what to do next. We'd need to get as far away from Bhogavati as possible when Balnak was crowned king. He'd surely have us hunted down and killed.

We could hide in the mountains on the edge of the realms. We've already been there and know the terrain.

So, you're choosing to be defeated, then? The mighty Priya, defeated by indecision.

Prathavi's voice dispersed all other sounds from my mind.

I haven't chosen defeat. Sarvaan was actually defeated! We have no choice but to hide now.

Only cowards who accept their fate think they don't have a choice. Those who make their own fate choose to do so, they don't wait for destiny to change their fate for them.

"I'm not a coward." The words came out as I held Sarvaan's head. His eyes slowly moved to my face.

"I know that. Why would you think that you are?"

Prathavi's words whispered into my mind again.

What separates those who get what they want and those that do not, is the willingness to fight for it. The crown, the promise of your transformation, your life...they are only lost if you give them up willingly.

I was on my feet before my brain registered the decision.

"I'm not a coward! I won't accept this! Balnak has to pay!"

Sarvaan rose with a concerned look on his face.

"Priya, what are you talking about? He's won, nothing can be done."

My hand grabbed my sword from its sheath. My body trembled with rage and purpose. The cold metal burned against my hot skin.

"Priya, my love—" Sarvaan's hand grabbed my shoulder.

"I'm willing to fight..." I sprinted towards the exit of the arena, ripping my shoulder from Sarvaan's grasp.

Sarvaan was faster than me, so he followed by my side.

"Priya, whatever you're thinking of doing...it's not worth it. If you harm him now you'll be exiled!"

I'm not going to harm him. I'm going to unmake him.

***

My body pushed through the immense crowd exiting the arena. Large Naga bodies were pushed aside by my petite human body like bowling pins. My eyes spotted a crowd gathering outside of the arena. Balnak was being congratulated. He shook hands with the crowd as they left the arena. King Vasuki stood by his side. When the king's eyes spotted me, they never left me. He spotted me at a distance most eyes wouldn't have. Sarvaan's fingers kept trying to grab my clothing, but I kept slipping from his grasp.

"Priya! Please stop!"

"I can't! I won't!"

I was just a few rows of Naga bodies from Balnak now. Feral screeches exited my lips as I shoved my way to the front.

"Move! Out of the way! Move!" Their smooth scales brushed against my skin as I squeezed through any opening I could find.

My hand clutched my sword hard. When the last line of Naga bodies disappeared and I stood before Balnak, I pointed my sword at him. His hand was being taken by King Vasuki's at the time. An awkward silence ran through the crowd.

"I challenge you in the Trial of The Crown, you corrupt sack of dung!"

King Vasuki released Balnak's hand. Balnak's face formed a smug grin.

"You just can't accept defeat can you, human? I'll be your king and that's final."

My arm thrust the tip of my sword toward Balnak, the blade trembling along with my hand. Sarvaan's tail slowly wrapped my waist to keep me from moving.

"You're corrupt! You're deceiving this kingdom! The crown isn't yours until you've answered my challenge!"

My feet pushed forward. I wanted to be in his face. I wanted to feel the fear in his breath. My muscles strained against Sarvaan's tail and his body moved an inch. The crowd gasped as I inched forward. Sarvaan's hands went to my shoulders now to anchor me. King Vasuki glanced at Balnak.

"Balnak, Is there any basis to these accusations? Is there something to be said?"

"All there is to be said is that Priya of Karkota Kula has poor sportsmanship. You'll notice she brings no proof of her accusations..." His back turned to me and royal guards escorted him away.

My heart was pumping so hard I saw my pulse in my vision. Vasuki walked to me and placed a hand on my head. My pulse and breathing calmed immediately.

"I'm afraid divine law says that only Naga may compete in the trial and issue challenges."

What?

My eyes met the king's. His comment took me out of my state of rage.

"If anything changes in the next eight days before Balnak's official corona-tion, I'd be honored to witness the challenge formally."

Did...did he just... What the fuck is going on...

Sarvaan's hand clutched mine as the king walked away, keeping his eyes on mine.

"Come, Priya, let's get home. We've much to prepare for."

"Sarvaan did you just...hear him?" His hand squeezed my fingers tight.

"Not now. Not here."

***

The moment we got home and Sarvaan shut the door his face sunk. I'd never seen such a look of disappointment directed towards me in my life. My heart felt a stabbing from the look.

"Why did you do that, Priya? Why did you challenge him?" His hands stroked my face.

"Because he can't get away with what he's done. I won't let him." My hands went on top of Sarvaan's, squeezing them.

"I lost, Priya, it's over. It's done. We should pack our things and flee." He released his hands from my face and slithered towards the hallway that led to the bedroom.

"And do what? Hide for the next one hundred years? I'm a human, Sarvaan, I don't want to spend my entire life running and hiding." My face was hot. My lungs were tired. My eyes burned from strain and tears.

Sarvaan stopped moving. His back was still to me.

"You didn't lose because of inability, you lost because Balnak is a pile of dirty slime and he was vile and made you go into a rage over thoughts of what he'd do to me."

Sarvaan slithered to the couch and sat, putting his face in his hands.

"Do you think I'm a weak warrior? Is that why you think you can beat Balnak?"

I walked to stand in front of him. My hands pried his off of his face. I kissed him.

"You're the strongest warrior I know. But, it's not going to take a warrior to beat Balnak. It's going to take a queen."

I stood and tugged on Sarvaan's arm as hard as I could, straining groans escaped my mouth as I did.

"Now pick yourself up...and let's go see Nishala. I've issued my challenge...and I need to be a Nagini...to enter the trial against Balnak...before his coronation."

Sarvaan rose quickly, glaring at me.

"Nishala? We promised her a pardon first. She's not going to give up her leverage before she's pardoned!"

Sarvaan's shouting reverberated through my small, human body. He squeezed my hands. My hands pulled from his and punched his giant chest muscles over and over.

"Shut up! Just shut up!"

"Priya! Stop!"

He picked me up by my waist and brought me to his chest. My hands gripped his neck, squeezing his scales.

"You gave me happiness, Sarvaan, true happiness! I won't give that up! I didn't issue the challenge to hurt you or prove anything. I issued the challenge so I can keep and cherish the happiness you've given me."

My forehead pressed to his.

"Your warrior queen needs you by her side. You're done brooding. You're done sulking. Be the mighty warrior and loving soul companion that I need you to be. You're why I look forward to waking up each day. I need you."

A moan of relief expelled from my lungs when his arms wrapped and squeezed my body to his. We kissed again. We kissed slowly as we'd done on the balcony. My feet touched the ground as he lowered me.

"You've got a mighty way with words Priya. Has anyone told you that you should be queen?"

My hands slapped his chest with excitement.

We're back in business. We're so back.

Chapter 28

Kiss ~ परिवर्तन

My legs sprinted through the grassy grove leading to Nishala's camp so fast my skin stung from the grass whipping it. I even beat Sarvaan to the camp. He slithered next to me a moment later.

"Nishala! Where are you! Nishala!"

A rustling sound came from her tent. She slithered from it and rose, her eyes flicking back and forth between me and Sarvaan.

"My word, Priya! Are you trying to wake Yama himself?"

Her expression changed from surprise to concern, seeing the way Sarvaan and I were breathing and the urgency on our faces.

"What is it? What's happened?"

Sarvaan's face lowered, he gritted his teeth.

"Balnak defeated me in combat. He used my love for Priya to destroy my mind. With my mind destroyed, my body was defeated."

Nishala's eyes kept flicking back and forth between Sarvaan and I. She took in a deep breath.

"So why come here—" I stepped forward, interrupting her.

"I issued a challenge to Balnak for the crown."

A smile crept over Nishala's face.

"The king will bear witness to the challenge if I am Nagini."

Nishala's smile exploded into laughter. She laughed so hard she fell to the ground and pounded it with her hand.

"See, I told you she'd shun us. Let us go."

Sarvaan turned to leave, his hand on my shoulder to usher me his way. Nishala held up a hand signaling us to wait.

"Wait...aha...I apologize. I don't get much entertainment in exile. You two have proven to be well worth my time."

My foot stepped towards her. Sarvaan turned back.

"Would you be willing to transform me so I can enter the trial and defeat Balnak for the crown? Our agreement still stands. Once I'm queen I will pardon you."

Nishala slithered to be face to face with me.

"Tell me why you want it so bad."

"The crown or to be Nagini?"

"Either. Both. What's compelling you?" Her forceful breath blew my hair from my neck.

"I realized if I want my happiness I have to fight for it. I realized I'd have to twist fate to my liking to claim my destiny."

Nishala turned and went back to her tent.

"Does that mean she won't help?" Sarvaan asked, rubbing my neck with his fingers. His touch felt of desperation.

Nishala returned with a bowl of purple, fine dust.

"I can sense it now..."

She poured the dust onto her hand and kissed her fingers. She touched her fingers to my face, leaving trails of the purple dust on my skin.

"...you're ready for the kiss..."

She did the same to my other cheek.

"...of scales..."

THE END

Epilogue

My chest heaved, glistening with oil I rubbed on my skin as I stood at the wooden door.

I have to do this...I need to do this...

My shaking hand opened the door and I walked in. My walk changed to a swaying strut. Three Naga men sat on the large bed in the chamber. One had white and silver scales, the second was black all over, and the third covered in shining golden scales. They all licked their lips and changed positions in anxious anticipation. Three sets of Naga eyes widened at the sight of my nude body. My skin flushed with anticipation of my own as I bent down, letting my fingers caress my silky oiled skin from my belly to my feet, showing my toned legs and shapely ass to them. One of them moved.

"No no...not part of the deal. You stay right there...for now." My finger wagged side to side, scolding him.

He sat back down on the bed with a hiss. The other two Nagas snickered. My hips moved side to side now, as if I was dancing slowly for them to an imaginary, slow, and rhythmic song. My legs carried me in front of the middle Naga. My hands dragged on his scales near his vertical pouch to help produce his cock and scrotum. My legs slowly rose and I straddled the Naga's lap. I grabbed his warm cock as I sat down, putting it between my labia and his body. My arms wrapped around his smooth neck and I moved back and forth, rubbing my wet pussy on his shaft. The air filled with echoes of scales slithering over skin in wet sloshing motions.

"Come here, you're missing the fun..." I looked left and right to the other two Naga men, beckoning them closer with a gesture of my finger.

My mouth gaped wide as the Naga I was straddling entered me. My hands reached for the cocks of the other two Naga and ran my fingers up and down their lengths, using the cum on their tips as lubrication. The Naga to my left raised up, placing his dick between my tits. His dick landed with a warm, heavy thud. His hands pushed my tits together around his cock and he started to pump, sliding between them. My head turned to the Naga on my right to see another cock, hard and in my face. My mouth opened wide and fleshy warmth filled my throat. The room was suddenly a cacophony of moans, slick pumping sounds, and the hum from my throat with a Naga cock inside it.

You didn't think it would be that easy, did you? *Blood on My Crown* — Coming May 2026

I hope you've enjoyed your tour of Bhogavati

Did Sarvaan coil around your heart?

If this book made you feel something (whether you're fanning yourself, crying, or screaming into a pillow), I'd be honored if you left a review.

Reviews are how indie authors like me survive. They help other readers find their next obsession. Even a sentence or two makes a difference.

Want to know the moment Book 2 drops?

Below are the social platforms you can find me on for release dates, cover reveals, exclusive teasers, and the occasional unhinged update about what I'm writing next.

TikTok: @KellyMorgan_author

Instagram & Threads: @Kelly_Morgan_Author

BlueSky: @KellyMorganAuthor

Acknowledgements

Acknowledgments

First, to you, the reader — thank you for taking a chance on Priya and Sarvaan. Thank you for diving into Bhogavati with an open heart. You're why I write.

To my sensitivity readers, Ritika and Ayushi — thank you for your time, your insight, and your honesty. You helped me honor a culture with the care it deserves. Ayushi can be contacted at the following email if you too are in need of a sensitivity reader/beta reader: blessedwithpages@gmail.com

To my cover artist, OCD Vampire — you made Priya divine and sexy as hell, and you made Sarvaan into the monstrous heartthrob he was always meant to be. Gallery link: https://www.deviantart.com/ocdvampire

To my editor Tara, from Storyteller Supply LLC — thank you for catching what I couldn't see and pushing me to make this story stronger.

To my wife Dianne — thank you for believing in this weird, spicy dream of mine. Thank you for listening to me ramble about Naga cosmology at dinner.

To the monster romance community — you showed me there's a place for the weird, the passionate, and the unapologetically filthy. I wrote this book for you.

And finally, to the secret princesses still waiting to find their kingdom — keep looking. It's out there.

About the author

About the Author

This book started as "Indiana Jones, but spicy, and she falls in love with a snake man?"

That's how my brain works. A strange idea takes root and I follow it wherever it leads — through mythology, through monsoons, through scenes that made me fan myself while writing them.

I live to write the weird and the unapologetic. The stories that make you ask "who wrote this?" and then immediately look for more.

At the heart of everything I write is one question: can love and lust truly transcend physicality? What happens when the person who ignites your soul doesn't even share your species? Can desire bridge the impossible?

I think it can. I write to prove it.